DOROTHY MUST DIE

STORIES
VOL. 2

HEART OF TIN
THE STRAW KING
RULER OF BEASTS

DOROTHY MUST DIE

STORIES
VOL. 2

D A N I E L L E P A I G E

HARPER
An Imprint of HarperCollinsPublishers

CONTENTS

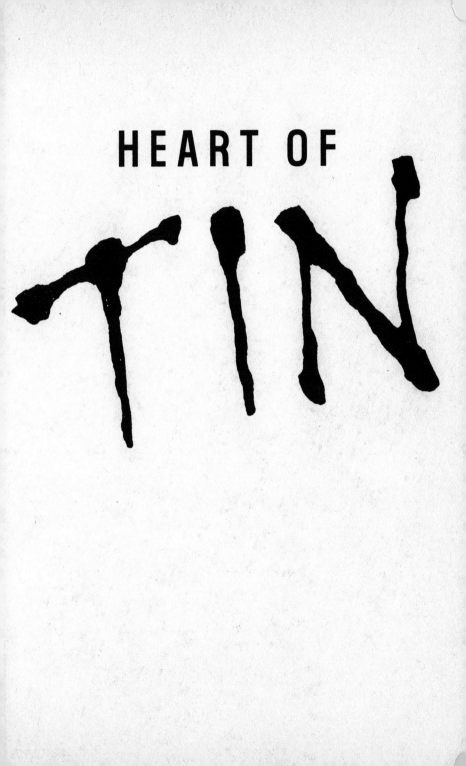

HEART OF
TIN

ONE

People say I'm heartless—pretty ironic, when you think about it. I've heard the rumors, the back talk. I know what goes on behind closed doors, and not just because I have spies everywhere in Oz. But that's not the whole story, not by a long shot. My problem, when you get right down to it, was that all I ever wanted was love.

Think about the first time you really fell in love. No, I mean, really think about it. How it was like your whole life before that moment was a black-and-white movie, and suddenly you stepped into Technicolor. (We don't have that stuff in Oz, but Dorothy's told me about it.) Now imagine the moment you fell in love was also the moment you got a heart—I mean, literally.

I'd had a heart back in the day, and thought I was in love, too. And then I'd lost both heart and girlfriend, thanks to one hell of a wicked witch, and I assumed I'd never have the chance to love again. Before Dorothy won me a new heart I could only listen to people talk about what it was like, while knowing I'd never again feel the same way, cry the same tears, experience the same joy. I thought I'd have to spend my whole life that way, in an empty colorless world, only able to imagine the kinds of experiences everyone else took for granted. Not just falling in love, but the whole package. The giddy first moments, the blowout fights—because you can only get *really* mad if you *really* care—getting to a place with someone where you can't imagine your life anymore without them.

That was never going to be for me.

And then Dorothy got here, and everything changed. Not just for all of Oz. For me. Everything I thought I knew about love—well, Dorothy rewrote the book. I thought I had been in love before her, but I didn't even know what the word meant. Dorothy didn't just give me a new heart. She gave me a new life.

So you can say what you want about the decisions I've made and the things I've done. Sure, there are some things I'm not proud of. It's possible I've even made a few mistakes. Even when I didn't have a heart, I was always a compassionate person. I don't like to see others suffer, even when it's necessary. I'm not like Scare; I don't thrive on the pain of others. And now that I have my heart—the heart that belongs to Dorothy—I know my own worth. I don't need to make other people feel small in order to boost my own ego. I do important things every day. I'm in charge of the safety of Oz, and I take my job seriously. It's actually pretty fulfilling, if you want to know the truth. I think I have a real gift. But the important thing, the thing you have to remember, is that everything I did—the good stuff, the bad stuff, and the stuff in between—was out of love. Judge all you want, but I bet you'd have trouble saying the same thing about your own life. I want that down on the record. All of it, everything, the whole shebang: it was for her.

It all started the moment Dorothy returned to Oz. She wasn't from our world, and we—the Scarecrow, the Lion, and I—knew that she'd want to go home. After she went back to Kansas, the three of us went our separate ways. The Lion, off to rule as the King of Beasts in the forest. The Scarecrow back to the Emerald City, of course, to take the Wizard's place as ruler of Oz. And for me it was back to the land of the furry little Winkies, where Glinda sent me to replace the Wicked Witch of the West as their ruler. The Winkies were a peaceful, dull people, and I had a lot of time to spend thinking about how much I missed Dorothy. About the last time I'd seen her, her face wet with tears as she kissed me good-bye. She'd hugged the Scarecrow, patted the Lion on the head—but *me*, she had kissed, sobbing all the while, and even though my cheeks rusted a little where her tears had stained them I left the marks to remind me of her.

Dorothy, goodness incarnate, with her sweet face and her little checked dress and her cute dog and her picnic basket. Dorothy saw the best in all of us from the start. Each of the three of us was missing some crucial piece of ourselves, and she never cared. She loved us for what we were. And once the Wizard placed that tiny new piece of magic in the empty space inside my chest, and

I could feel its power fill me with a love even stronger than the kind I'd known when I was an ordinary man, I knew that there was only one woman for me: Dorothy Gale, the savior of Oz.

So when I heard she was back, I just about lost it. I was staring out the window of my throne room in the Winkies' palace when one of the house Winkies knocked at the door. "Your Majesty," he said politely, adjusting his suspenders, "a messenger from the Emerald City has arrived." The messenger was a Munchkin, on the tall and skinny side for one of his people. His ink-black hair fell into his eyes, and he kept pushing it out of the way awkwardly.

"Your esteemed, uh, Highness?" the Munchkin began, stumbling over the title.

"That's right," I said. The Winkies might not be much, but I was still their king. And a pretty good one, too. Those people loved me. Just ask them. Well, maybe don't ask them *now*. But if you'd asked them then, I'm sure they'd have said I was a vast improvement over the Wicked Witch.

The Munchkin bowed sloppily, cleared his throat, inhaled deeply, and recited his entire message in one breath. "HergloriousnessthealmightyOzmarequestsyourpresenceatacelebrationhonoringthereturnofourbelovedliberatorDorothywhohascomeback—" My heart, silk pillow though it may have been, skipped a beat in my chest.

"Wait," I interrupted, and the Munchkin used the opportunity to take another huge breath. I kept talking before he could recite his stream of babble again. "Did you say—did you just say that Dorothy is *back*?" He looked confused for a moment. Obviously independent thought was not part of the job description.

"Er, yes," he said finally.

"Dorothy is *here*? In *Oz*?" My heart was racing. All this time I'd spent, daydreaming of just such an occasion, never daring to hope my desperate wish would actually come true, and now everything I'd ever wanted was finally within reach? "Where is she?"

"She's, uh, at the Emerald Palace," the Munchkin said, tacking on a hasty "sir" when I frowned. The tin plates of my face squeak when I smile or scowl, and sometimes it unnerves people. I used to feel bad about it. These days, it comes in handy. "That was the rest of the message," he added, looking sulky. "But you cut me off."

I ignored him. "But I must leave at once," I said, thinking out loud. "I must—I must—WINKIES!" I bellowed, and a flood of my subjects scrambled into the room, tumbling over themselves in their haste to answer my call. "Prepare my things! Bring my finest oilcan and dress my joints! Ready my carriage! I will be leaving for the Emerald City on the hour!"

"The party's tomorrow," the Munchkin mumbled. With an imperious wave, I dismissed him. I was so excited I didn't even care that he forgot to bow when he left my throne room. Dorothy—my Dorothy, the most beautiful girl in this world or any other, the kindest and the most good, she of the magical slippers and perfect pout, was back. Was it possible—could it be—that she'd come back for *me*? Did she remember the kiss she'd given me when we both thought we'd never see each other again? Was there a chance that I could finally have the happiness I'd longed for all those days in my palace—that I could finally have her?

TWO

I was so distracted that I barely even noticed the journey to the Emerald City. I hadn't left my palace in months, but I didn't even see the scenery of Oz as it flashed by. I couldn't stop thinking about seeing her again. When we drove through the jewel-encrusted gates of the Emerald City, I thought my heart would stop beating altogether. I couldn't stop thinking about Dorothy. What would I say to her? How could I possible tell her the depth of my feelings? "You are my sun, my moon, my starlit sky," I said aloud, trying it out.

"Pardon, sir? Are you asking about the weather?" called the Winkie coachman.

"Mind your own business!" I snapped. "Your lips are like a rose," I muttered under my breath. "Your breath like tulips—oh no, that's awful." Overcome by despair, I got out of the carriage the moment we pulled up in front of the palace, accidentally slamming the door in the coachman's face in my haste.

The palace was a hive of activity—Munchkins bustling back and forth, visiting dignitaries who'd arrived ahead of me thronging the halls in their finest dress, Nomes and Pixies gibbering delightedly in the corners. Tiny, buzzing globes of light swirled through the hallways, occasionally crashing into a wall and exploding into a shower of daisy petals. A plate of pastries sailed down one hall, floating on a current of chocolate-scented air as passersby snatched snacks. The last member of a small parade of Munchkins carrying a bundle of streamers down the hall tripped over a trailing bit of crepe paper and tumbled to the ground, sending the rest of the Munchkins falling like a line of dominoes. The bundle of streamers gathered itself into the shape of a giant bird and flapped toward the ceiling, cackling hysterically, as cursing Munchkins chased after it. I even caught the briefest glimpse of Ozma herself, drifting down a hallway in a wispy black dress with a long, lacy train, but Dorothy herself was nowhere to be seen, and when I moved to run after Ozma a Munchkin servant stopped me. "Welcome to the palace, sir," he said gravely. "I shall show you to your chambers."

"I want to see Dorothy," I snarled, and the intensity of my voice was such that it startled both of us. "I *must* see Dorothy."

"I'm sorry, sir," he said, sounding a little less certain. "Dorothy's guests must wait until the banquet tomorrow night."

"I'm not her guest," I said. "I'm her dearest friend. Don't you know who I am?"

"Of course, Sir Woodman," he replied. "But I'm afraid there are no exceptions. Even the palace staff don't know where

Dorothy is right now. She's asked not to be disturbed while she prepares for the celebration." I realized that badgering him wouldn't get me anywhere.

"Very well," I said. "You may show me to my rooms."

The last time I'd been in the palace it had been under the Wizard's control. The guest rooms then had been nice enough, but Ozma had clearly had them all redone. The ceiling of my room was high, the bed enormous. The windows were paned with green-tinted glass—an homage, most likely, to her predecessor. In the bathroom, fluffy green towels unfolded and floated in the air, singing a soothing lullaby when I entered, and the bath began to fill itself with sweet-scented water foaming with green bubbles. A green rubber duck popped into existence, sending green droplets flying into the air.

"I won't be needing that, but thank you," I told it, and obediently the water drained out of the tub and the duck vanished. I sat cautiously on the bed, hoping the oil from my joints wouldn't stain the soft coverlet. I wanted to make the best possible impression. At home, I preferred to sleep upright in a wooden cabinet.

Dorothy would want to see me right away, of course. Why else had she invited me? It would only be a matter of moments before she'd come to my chambers herself.

But she didn't. The only possible explanation was that she didn't know I was in the palace, and so the next morning I oiled my joints quickly and made sure the tin of my face and chest was brightly polished before I set out in search of her. I cornered the first Munchkin I saw—this one cleaning an already-sparkling window with a bucket of water in which several small, brightly colored fish swam about cheerfully. "I must get a message to Dorothy at once," I burst out. She turned around in surprise.

"Who—" she began, and then she recognized me and her irritated expression changed to a smile. She gave a little curtsy. "Oh, hello, sir. I wish I could help you, but—"

"You have to understand how important this is. Dorothy has to be informed that I'm here! I must see her!"

Now she just looked confused. "But sir," she said politely, "Dorothy *does* know you're here. She's aware of all the guests that have arrived. Would you like to see the Scarecrow or the Lion while you wait for the banquet tonight? They got to the palace just yesterday as well." I gaped at her. Dorothy knew I was here? But why hadn't she sent for me? The servant looked at me almost pityingly. "I know Dorothy and Her Majesty, Ozma, have been very busy preparing for the banquet," she added. "I'm afraid I can't help you, sir." She turned back to her window.

What could Dorothy possibly be doing to prepare for a banquet that was so important that she couldn't see me? I thought about looking for the Scarecrow or the Lion, but it was Dorothy I was desperate to see and I didn't want to share my disappointment with anyone. How could she possibly have failed to summon me if she already knew I was at the palace? Was there a chance she *didn't* want to see me as badly as I wanted to see her? Surely not—but nevertheless, doubt began to creep in at the corners of my mind. In dismay, I returned to my chambers, where I summoned the Winkie coachman and spent the afternoon with him playing chess. I was so distracted I kept thinking we were playing checkers instead, and the pieces obligingly transformed from rooks and pawns to checkers counters. The coachman let me win anyway.

Finally, it was time to get ready for the banquet. I carefully re-oiled my joints and summoned a maid to polish me to a blinding glow. When she could see her own reflection in my patchworked tin chest, she curtsied and began to leave, but I stopped her. "You are my sun, my moon, my starlit sky!" I proclaimed, testing the words' effect.

"I beg your pardon, sir?" the maid asked politely.

"Oh, it's hopeless," I said miserably, sinking into a chair and burying my face in my tin palms. "Absolutely hopeless. I don't know how to tell her. I don't know the right thing to say."

"To whom, sir?"

"To Dorothy," I mumbled into my fingers. "It has to be exactly right, so that she knows how I feel, but it can't sound desperate—she has to see me as dashing, and I want to remind her of everything we shared, and tell her how beautiful she is, and how special, and how noble and generous and sweet and good and—"

The maid pulled up another chair. "If you don't mind some advice, sir," she said, "that's an awful lot to try to fit into one hello. Why don't you just be yourself?"

I lifted my head and stared at her. "What do you mean, be myself?"

"Well," she said reasonably, "you had all sorts of travels

together, didn't you? It's the stuff of legend, sir. Everyone in Oz knows about how you and Miss Dorothy and the Scarecrow and the Lion defeated the Wizard and sent him away, and liberated the Winkies, and how honorably Dorothy behaved to the winged monkeys, and all of that. You're a noble figure, sir. You're a king and a soldier and I think Dorothy would have to be an awfully silly girl not to be impressed by all of that. So just be yourself. If it's meant to be, it'll be."

"But what if it's not meant to be?" I asked her. "How do I convince her?"

"That's just not how it works, sir. You can't convince people of feelings they don't have. But you'll know, I'm sure you will. From the way she looks at you. She's a smart girl, that Dorothy; she couldn't have saved Oz otherwise. She won't beat around the bush if she has feelings for you, too. Anyway, you look very handsome."

This little maid was the most sensible person I had talked to in months. "That's very good advice," I said. "Thank you, you've been a big help. What's your name?"

"Jellia, sir."

"Well, Jellia, perhaps you'll keep this conversation to yourself." She winked at me and made a zippering motion over her lips.

"What conversation, sir?" she asked.

The ballroom was packed. All of Oz, it seemed, had turned out to witness our savior's return. A huge orchestra, set up at the far end of the enormous hall, played cheery waltzes.

Rainbow-colored butterflies fluttered gaily over the instruments, sending showers of confetti swirling through the air. My old friends the Scarecrow and the Lion were there, of course. The Scarecrow was dressed in a new suit chosen for the occasion, and the Lion's fur had been brushed to a burnished golden glow. The Scarecrow caught sight of me first, and waved merrily. I crossed the crowded room, making my way through throngs of Ozians decked out in their finest clothes, to greet my old friend. "You made it!" he shouted over the noise, clapping me on the back and shaking my hand. The Lion roared his approval, sending a brief tremor of fear through the nearest partygoers before they realized who was doing the roaring. I wondered briefly if the Scarecrow was resentful—after all, not too long ago, this palace had been his. But if he was upset to have been deposed by Ozma, he didn't show it. Of course, his face was painted on, so his expressions were sometimes hard to read. Anyway, as happy as I was to see them, I had larger matters on my mind than catching up. "Have you seen her?" I asked the Scarecrow frantically. "Where is she? Is she here?" He gave me a long, strange, startled look.

"It's good to see you, too," he said, laughing. "Tin, what on earth? We haven't seen each other in ages, and—" A hush fell over the throng, and I knew at once that she had arrived. My stuffed heart in my throat, I turned to face the ballroom's grand entrance.

The sweet-faced girl I remembered was gone, replaced by a woman so beautiful that I nearly wept. Her dress was of the same blue gingham that she'd worn during her last sojourn in Oz, but it was cut to flatter her figure, and ended inches above her knees. It was stitched with gold thread that sent dazzling rays of light across the room and left bare her long, pale legs. Instead of the silver slippers she'd left Oz in, she wore a towering pair of glittering red heels that shone so brightly that they drowned out all the other light sources in the room, pulsing slightly as if in time to the pattern of her breath.

After a moment I noticed the people at her side: a frumpy old couple, looking lost and out of place, who could only be the Aunt Em and Uncle Henry she'd spoken of so fondly when she was last in Oz. But these humble people could hardly be related to the glorious creature whose radiant smile dominated the whole room. Dear little Toto yapped happily at Dorothy's heels, oblivious to the power radiating from her shoes. And of course, Ozma stood behind Dorothy with an expression that looked almost . . . disapproving. Like all of us, she must have realized that tired old Aunt Em and Uncle Henry had no place here. But if they were with Dorothy, did that mean she had returned for good?

Dorothy moved through the joyous crowd, greeting old friends and new ones with the same grace. She was as regal as a queen. I waited for her to catch sight of me, preparing myself to hold her in my arms at last. But as she approached, the Scarecrow ran to Dorothy and swept her up in his arms, tossing her into the air as she shrieked with joy. The band struck up a waltz and they whirled together across the purple-lit dance floor. I knew he had no idea of the depth of my feelings for Dorothy, but I couldn't help staring after them in a frenzy of jealousy nonetheless.

At last, as if he could feel the force of my gaze burning a hole through his head, he danced Dorothy back to me. I had been waiting for this moment for so long, but all the flowery words I'd prepared vanished. I remembered what the maid had told me— *just be yourself.* But now that I was actually holding Dorothy in my arms, I could barely even manage to stutter a hello. Up close, her beauty was even more stunning, more astonishing. There was a new light in her eyes and her cheeks were flushed. The air around her crackled with magic. There was no mistaking this Dorothy for the child who had left me when she went back to the Other Place. This Dorothy was like a brand-new person.

"Tin Woodman!" she shrieked in my ear, her voice even more musical than the notes the orchestra played. At last, I remembered myself, and twirled her around before dipping her so low her long ringlets nearly brushed the ground. She laughed gaily. I pulled her close to my chest, and the orchestra slowed the tempo to something more romantic. The people around us cleared a space, surrounding us in a transfixed circle as I moved with her in tighter and tighter circles. The whole world fell away—it was just me and her, the strawberry-sweet smell of her hair, the softness of her skin a perfect contrast to the hard metal of my arms and torso. I was so overcome I would have swooned, but I couldn't allow the moment to end. "It's so good to see you again," she murmured in my ear, her gentle voice sending a shiver through me. "I've missed you so much." Was there a knowing sparkle in her eyes, a special look that was just for me? Did she know how I felt without my even having to say it out loud? I took a deep breath.

"Dorothy, you are my moonlit star—" I began, but her gaze suddenly focused on something over my shoulder.

"Oh my goodness, Tin, look! It's Polychrome! How wonderful! Simply *everyone* has come to my ball!"

"Dorothy, my starlit moon—" I tried again, but she released me, sending me stumbling backward into the waiting crowd. "I'll see you again soon, darling Tin!" she trilled, clicking away briskly on her red heels. When I caught my balance again, she was already chattering away with Polychrome. I would have kicked myself if my joints were flexible enough. My *starlit moon?* The first time I'd seen the love of my life in years, and I'd called her a starlit moon? I cursed aloud, earning a surprised look from a Munchkin passing by with a tray of canapés.

"Penny for your thoughts, old tin can!" bellowed a familiar voice. I tried to control my emotions as the Lion slapped my back with one enormous paw, nearly knocking me over. "Where have you *been*, old sport? Heard you were in the palace yesterday, but haven't seen a peep of you until now. Hiding from your old mates, are you?"

"Not at all," I said, gathering the ruins of my dignity. "It's wonderful to see you. I wasn't feeling well, is all."

"Not feeling well?" the Lion asked. "Man, you're made of

tin! Don't tell me you're coming down with a cold."

"Nothing like that," I said. "Just tired from the journey. I trust you've been well?" The Lion brightened and launched into an enthusiastic history of his most recent triumph, the successful management of some arcane dispute between a badger and a dormouse who lived in his forest. I couldn't help but notice that his breath was rather rank. "And you?" he asked, finally bringing his ramble to a close. "How's life with the Winkies? Have you tried eating one? They look awful tough."

"Very good, very good," I said, only half paying attention. Across the room, Dorothy had rejoined Ozma. I tried to catch her eye to no avail. Should I go to her, or let her come to me? I'd ruined our reunion—completely ruined it. I didn't think I could take the Lion—predictable and good-natured as ever—for another moment. A wave of misery overcame me. "Excuse me," I said faintly, "but I'm still ill. I think—I think I have to go back to my room now."

Overcome with emotion, I broke into a half run and staggered out of the ballroom. The Wizard had given me my heart, but he'd never told me how to manage it. I'd gone so much of my life without one that I was out of practice. She'd told me that she'd missed me. I could have sworn that her look had been something special just for me. I'd flubbed my pretty speech, failed completely to tell her how I felt—but surely I still had a chance? I had no idea how to control the confusing passions that surged through my metal chest. I raced away from the ballroom and back toward my rooms. She had said we would be together. She had promised me it would be soon. I would let her accept the praise that was her due, enjoy her moment in the spotlight. I'd waited for so long. I could wait just a little longer, until I held her in my arms once more.

THREE

The next morning, I met the Scarecrow and the Lion for breakfast in the Lion's chambers. Like my own rooms, they were lushly appointed, but where my bed was a giant four-poster, the Lion's was something like an enormous dog bed. Special attention had been given to the walls, which were painted with shimmering murals of antelope fleeing in terror from some unknown foe—presumably the Lion. Even the magic of the palace couldn't cover up the Lion's distinctive perfume, and the servants had yet to clear away a pile of gnawed bones in one corner. The Lion was the only one of us who actually ate. He was working away at an enormous raw steak when we arrived. "Being the King of Beasts really activates the appetite," he mumbled through a mouthful of meat. The Scarecrow and I exchanged a glance. I was fond of the Lion, but couldn't help wishing becoming royalty had improved his table manners.

Dorothy was nowhere to be seen; probably she'd already

been witness to one of the Lion's breakfasts, and had wisely decided to pass on a second opportunity. I tried not to let my frantic anticipation show. Where was she? Why, after summoning me all the way to the palace, was she being so elusive? Was she just shy? Could it be that *she* was wondering if *I* cared about her in the same way she cared about me?

My mind was awhirl, but I made polite conversation with the Lion and the Scarecrow. We caught up on our respective comings and goings since Dorothy left Oz. The Lion was enjoying his new role as the King of Beasts, although he confessed to periodically snacking on one of his subjects. "Not the best for morale," he admitted, "but it does wonders for discipline."

After his brief stint as ruler of Oz, the Scarecrow had retired to a corncob mansion in the country. I wondered if he had any bad feelings toward Ozma. After all, the Wizard had appointed *him* the ruler of Oz, not that upstart fairy. But he was vague about what he'd been doing all this time. "Of course, it was such a wonderful surprise when Dorothy turned up on my doorstep with that funny old pair Em and Henry," he said, after he'd talked for quite some time about the technical difficulties of corncob architecture. I must admit I wasn't quite following his monologue, but I snapped to attention at that.

"You mean at the ball," I said.

"Oh no," the Scarecrow said serenely. "She came to my mansion, of course. Practically the moment she got back to Oz. Threw a little party for her. The Munchkins were over the moon. Don't think Em and Henry enjoyed it much, though. They kept talking about how much they missed their cows. Some sort of talking pet in the Other Place, I gather. They said they had quite a few of 'em."

"Why did Dorothy come to *you*?" I said, openly hurt, and the Scarecrow raised a painted eyebrow in surprise. I smiled quickly to cover my slip. How I felt about Dorothy wasn't anyone else's business. Not until I knew she felt the same way about me.

"Well, I suppose I was on the way to the Emerald City," the Scarecrow mused. He seemed thoughtful, and he kept looking at me with his beady little button eyes.

"Quite something, that business with the aunt and uncle," the Lion was saying through another mouthful. "Didn't see that one coming. Does Dorothy seem . . . different to you?"

"Different how?" I asked quickly. "What business?"

"Just after you left last night," the Lion said. "Dorothy got into a terrible fight with her aunt and uncle in front of the whole ball. And Ozma lost her temper, too, and shouted at Dorothy. Sent her right to her room like a little kid, can you imagine? Everyone's been talking about it all day. And *no one* knows where Dorothy and Ozma are now."

"No one's seen Dorothy?" I asked.

"Not since she left the ball," the Scarecrow confirmed. "Though most likely she's just hiding in embarrassment, poor thing." He chuckled.

"Don't you dare talk about her that way!" I snapped. "She's our savior! She'd do anything for us!" The Lion and the Scarecrow were staring at me in surprise.

"Goodness, Tin, no need to get worked up," the Scarecrow said mildly. "I didn't mean any disrespect. I'm sure Dorothy has her reasons for not seeing anyone today."

I scowled, but let it go. Suddenly the Lion sniffed the air. "I smell . . . glitter," he said. I sat up straight. A moment later, I heard the fast *tap-tap* of a pair of high heels, and heard a familiar high-pitched giggle. Someone rapped on the door to the Lion's room, and before any of us could answer, it swung open. It was Dorothy, looking more radiant than ever. The air around her crackled and sparked with a strange haze. She was still wearing her dress from the ball, although it looked a little the worse for wear and was torn at the hem. What had happened? I wondered. Was she hurt? She didn't seem to be—she seemed, in fact, down-right triumphant. Her shoes blazed with red light that made the Lion cover his eyes with one paw. Even the Scarecrow shielded his black button eyes. And behind her, hovering a few inches off the ground, was none other than the Good Witch Glinda herself, looking like a cat who'd just been let loose in an unsupervised aviary. All three of us were so surprised we were speechless.

"My dear friends," Dorothy said, her voice a satisfied purr and her gaze sweeping the room (and pausing for just a second on the Lion's gruesome leftovers), "do I have news for you. Welcome to the new, improved Oz. *I'm* running the show now, and everything is going to be *so* much better." We stared at her for a moment in stunned silence as Glinda floated behind her, beaming in a way that didn't quite reach her cold blue eyes. The Scarecrow was first to break the silence.

"Dorothy!" he exclaimed. "We didn't know what happened to you after the ball. You vanished with Ozma and . . ." He paused, looking as confused as it was possible to look when your face was painted on. "Where *is* Ozma? And what's she doing here?" By "she" he obviously meant Glinda, who looked none too pleased to be referred to in such a disrespectful tone.

"Oh, *Ozma.*" Dorothy giggled, sweeping into the Lion's room with Glinda at her heels. Dorothy looked around for somewhere suitable to sit, her lip curling a little at the sight of the Lion's nest. Poor Dorothy! She would be accustomed to more genteel surroundings. Why hadn't we thought to clean the room for her?

"My beloved friends, I have so much to tell you." I wished fervently that I could speak to her alone. I was burning with the need to tell her how I felt, to see her answer. I closed my eyes, imagining it was just the two of us. I'd brush her beautiful hair back as she tilted her perfect face up to kiss me . . .

"Princess Dorothy," Glinda cut in smoothly, "perhaps we should retire to a more appropriate chamber for discussion."

Princess Dorothy? My eyes snapped open. I was as puzzled as the Lion looked, but I wasn't going to show it. Dorothy was certainly a princess in my heart. But as far as I knew, she had no literal royal blood. She was from the Other Place; how could she? Had one of the fairies somehow made it to Kansas?

"You're right," Dorothy replied. "Everyone, follow me. The throne room will have to be redone—Ozma has terrible taste, bless her heart—but I think we can find a suitable room, don't you?"

"If Her Majesty is amenable, I remember a chamber in the main part of the palace that's simply perfect for a council," Glinda said sweetly.

"Certainly," Dorothy said distractedly. "Whatever you think is best." She flounced out the door, her red shoes still radiating that intense, otherworldly light, and after a moment the rest of us followed her, unanswered questions on the tips of our tongues.

Glinda certainly knew her way around the palace. I wondered how—and where she'd come from. She'd vanished ages ago; when had she come back? And how? What on earth was going on? Glinda led us down a maze of hallways and green-tinted corridors I didn't recognize. I'd visited once or twice when Scare was our noble leader, but I hadn't been to the palace in years, and I was soon hopelessly lost. Like many buildings in Oz, it looked a lot bigger on the inside than it was on the outside—and the palace was already pretty big on the outside.

Finally, Glinda led us to a large, round chamber, painted a more subdued version of the palace's ubiquitous dazzling green. An ornately carved round table dominated the room, surrounded by heavy wooden chairs that politely moved backward from the table as we entered, murmuring "Please be seated." A bespectacled Pixie burst on the scene in a puff of gray dust. "Welcome to the Council Chamber!" she chirped. "Please allow me to see to all your Council Chamber needs. Coffee? Pens? Paper? A chalkboard?"

Glinda flicked it in the chest with one pink-lacquered talon, sending the startled Pixie into a backward somersault through the air. "To be left alone," she cooed sweetly. "You're dismissed." Obediently, the Pixie vanished in another puff of smoke.

We seated ourselves around the table, the chairs smoothly scooting inward of their own volition, but Dorothy and Glinda remained standing. Well, if you could call Glinda's unnerving habit of hovering just inches above the floor standing. None of us spoke for a moment. I stared at Dorothy. She was the most beautiful I'd ever seen her, but the transformation in her was even more apparent than it had been at the ball. It wasn't that she was older—she wasn't, really; considering how much time had passed in Oz since she left us, she was at most just a few years older than the fresh-faced girl who had journeyed with us to the Wizard's palace and won me the heart with which I'd fall in love with her. The difference was something else, something harder to pin down. It was something in the glitter of her eyes and the set of the shoulders. It was, I realized, *power*. Dorothy, the new Dorothy, was powerful.

Glinda cleared her throat discreetly and Dorothy glanced at her. Glinda made a tiny gesture toward her dress, and Dorothy laughed. "Of course!" she said cheerfully. "How could I forget? This is no way to dress for a meeting with my most treasured"—my heart skipped—"confidants!" She waved one hand at herself, and before our astonished eyes her bedraggled ball gown transformed itself into a more modest but still becoming version of her old, familiar gingham dress. This one was, like the ball gown, sewn with subtle gold threads that glittered and caught the light, and its bodice fitted her tiny waist closely, but the skirt fell to the middle of her calves and a demure little white cape settled over her flawless shoulders. Invisible hands brushed her disordered ringlets, neatly tying them up with blue velvet ribbons. Her lips were painted a pale, flattering pink and a sweep of pink blush appeared on each of her high, elegant cheekbones. Her blue eyes sparkled as, refreshed, she looked down at us where we sat with our mouths open.

"Now," she continued, "where was I? Oh, don't look so astounded!" She laughed as we gaped at her. "It's just a silly little bit of magic. Nothing to worry about. What girl wouldn't use the opportunity to pretty herself up a little with magic if she could?"

"But, Dorothy—" the Scarecrow began.

"*Princess* Dorothy," Glinda smoothly interjected, and the Scarecrow looked around, his face as startled as we all felt. Glinda was serious about this "princess" business, then. What on earth was going on?

"Princess Dorothy," the Scarecrow amended. "It's just that, well, none of us ever realized you could use magic when we were all traveling though Oz."

Dorothy's perfect eyebrows drew together in a tiny frown of displeasure. "Darling Scarecrow," she said a trifle coolly, "surely you're not implying there's something *wrong* with my having magic?"

"Of course not, Dorothy!" he replied hastily. "It's just that— well, it was a very long time ago, so my memory could be fuzzy. But when you helped the Lion and the Woodman and me on our journey through Oz and most nobly won us our respective gifts from the Wizard, there was no hint that you had any magic then. Did you have these powers all along? If you did, why did you need the Wizard to help you?"

Dorothy's blue eyes widened. "Are you saying that after everything I did for you—after everything I sacrificed to help you, setting aside my own needs even though I had no idea whether I'd ever be able to go home myself—are you saying that I was *selfish*? But I thought—I thought you were all my friends," she whispered, and a single tear trickled down her perfect cheek. Unable to bear the sight of her in distress, I leapt to my feet and then fell immediately to my knees before her, reaching for her hand.

"Dorothy," I pleaded, "don't listen to him. Of course we're your friends. You know that. We—we love you, Dorothy." She gazed down at me, and I wondered if she understood what I was really saying. Not *we* love you, but *I* love you. Her expression softened, and some of the hurt left her face.

"Oh, Tin," she said gently, laying one soft hand against my cheek, "I should have known *you* would be loyal to me, even if no one else was. My dear soldier. What would I have done without you, that last time in Oz? Without your courage and your *dedication*?" I was so thrilled at her words that I nearly missed that last, subtle emphasis on "dedication." But she was looking not at me, but at the Scarecrow, her eyes narrowed. I could have strangled him. If only Dorothy and I had been alone, I could have told her everything—told her that it wasn't just loyalty I felt, but love. I sat back in my chair. I could have sworn my cheek burned where she'd touched me.

The Lion yawned widely. "I'm sort of hungry," he said to no one in particular.

Dorothy and the Scarecrow were still staring at one another, but the Scarecrow looked away first. "Of course we don't think you're selfish, Dorothy," he said. "We're *all* your friends. Your very dear friends," he added, with a sharp look at me. "It's just a bit of a surprise, all of this, that's all. We're so happy to see you that we aren't even thinking straight. And for you to come back with magic is an even more wonderful surprise."

Dorothy widened her eyes again, the picture of childlike innocence. "Very well, Scare," she said. "I see your confusion. I should have known better than to doubt my beloved companions. As for the magic—well, I simply didn't know how to tap into my potential when I first arrived in Oz. I was raised by simple people." She paused for a moment, and a single crystalline tear sprang into life at the corner of one eye. I almost leapt out of my chair to wipe it away. "Simple people," she continued, her voice quavering a little, "who didn't know what I was capable of. They didn't understand that I was so much more than just an ordinary girl from the prairie. They loved me, I know they did, but they just weren't courageous or clever enough to see what was right for me. Can you believe they honestly thought I belonged in Kansas?" She shuddered daintily, and then smiled.

"But I have a new family now," she said. "A family who believes in me. Who knows how much I can do, and who will celebrate that instead of trying to hold me back." She turned to

Glinda, who'd been silent for this whole exchange, and bowed her head just slightly. "Glinda believed in me from the very beginning," she said. "And Glinda's going to show me how to use the power I've always had without knowing it. Everything I'm going to become, I owe to her. And my own innate gifts and intelligence, of course," she added hastily. "I'm done underestimating myself."

"But, Dorothy," growled the Lion, from where he was slouched in his chair with one still-bloodstained paw sprawled across the glossy tabletop, "what does that actually mean?"

Dorothy smiled. "It means, my darlings, that the future of Oz is in this room." She paused dramatically, leaving time for the word "darling" to send dizzying passion cascading through me.

"It means," she said finally as Glinda hovered behind her, smiling in a visible pink cloud of strawberry-scented perfume, "that the future of Oz is *me*. Dorothy, the Princess of Oz."

FOUR

We looked at her with uncertainty as she stood proudly before us. I would never have questioned anything Dorothy said, of course. She had saved us all, helped to grant our deepest wishes. I would forever be grateful for that, and my love came with undying loyalty. Her wish was my command. But I had to admit that I was a little relieved when the Lion cleared his throat and asked, "Er, Dorothy—we're really glad to see you, like everyone keeps saying. But what happened to Ozma? Isn't she the One True Princess of Oz? Or its queen?" He looked confused for a second. "You know," he said. "In charge."

Dorothy shrugged. "Oh, Ozma," she said sadly. "She did her best, of course, poor thing. But we all know she wasn't cut out for the job of government. Ruling a country takes more than just magic, sillies! It takes what each of you has individually—brains, courage, heart—and I have plenty of all three of those things." She took a deep breath and looked around the room.

"I was so happy to be back," she explained, "that I didn't even stop to think I might have been brought here for a reason. I'm not just here for a vacation, as wonderful as it is to see all of you again"—here her eyes lingered unmistakably on me—"but I realized yesterday, thanks to Glinda, that I'm actually here for a purpose. Oz has fallen into disrepair. The countryside is in disorder. Oz needs me. It's my duty to take power until Oz is restored."

A wave of shock rippled through the room, and even I blinked, startled, as we finally realized the implication of her words. Dorothy didn't just mean she was *a* princess, she meant she was *the* princess. She planned to become the ruler of Oz. But how? Ozma was an odd little creature, from what I'd heard, though I'd never seen that much of her. But the fairies had always been the rightful rulers of Oz, and I couldn't imagine Ozma just handing over the throne to the first person who claimed she was more qualified to run the show.

"And here's where you come in," Dorothy continued, ignoring our surprise. "I need you three more than ever before. I need counselors I can trust at my side as I bring Oz back to the glorious place it once was. I can't rule Oz without your help."

"But Oz is already glorious," the Scarecrow said slowly. "Where is Ozma, exactly, Dorothy?"

At this, Glinda drifted forward and rested one lovely, slim hand on Dorothy's shoulder. She was smiling gently, but I noticed that her knuckles were white where they gripped Dorothy. "My dearest Dorothy," she said gently. "You must understand, all of this is very confusing to your old friends. It's happened so quickly for them." She smiled sweetly at the Scarecrow, and then at the Lion and me. "Dorothy, kind soul that she is, is protecting Ozma's reputation by not telling you the whole truth. You see, Ozma has been stealing Oz's magic for years. She exiled me, the only person who was powerful enough to discover her secret, but when Dorothy arrived she knew there was a chance Dorothy would find out. She played false friend to Dorothy just to keep an eye on her. But she'd planned all along to banish Dorothy back to the Other Place the first chance she got. And she almost succeeded. This morning, Ozma took Dorothy, her aunt Em, and her uncle Henry away from the palace, planning to kill all three of them with her magic. Thankfully, I was able to escape my banishment just in time and protect Dorothy, but Ozma's magic still killed her aunt and uncle." She shook Dorothy slightly and Dorothy's eyes opened wide and filled with tears.

My heart flooded with sympathy. My poor Dorothy! How was she even standing, after such a shock? She must be made of steel, I thought admiringly. Unwilling to burden her friends with her terrible sorrow, she'd put on a brave face for all of us. She was simply incredible.

"In the battle," Glinda continued, "Ozma's magic backfired, and wiped her memory. She knows nothing of what she tried to do."

"So that's why you were able to forgive Ozma," I said, my heart filling with awe for my beloved's magnificent compassion. "Because she doesn't even remember what she tried to do to you.

You're too kind to hold it against her, now that you know she won't try again."

"What?" Dorothy asked. "Oh yes. Yes, that's it exactly. That's why I was able to forgive her." She wiggled her feet, looking down at her glowing shoes. "But thanks to these sho—"

"Thanks to Oz," Glinda interrupted quickly. "We don't know what exactly it is that's allowing you to access Oz's magic, so it's best not to speculate. But we do know you can give the magic back that Ozma stole, and that's all that matters."

"It's possible Oz simply wants to protect me," Dorothy said. "If Ozma can become an enemy, who knows who else might want to hurt me?" She looked at me then, her eyes beseeching. "I need all the protection I can get," she said, and there was no mistaking her words were meant for me. I sat up straighter. "Anyway, I've discovered that I can tap into the magic of Oz. I can use its power for good, my friends. I can become the ruler that Oz deserves—and I intend to do exactly that."

"Until we restore the magic Ozma stole," Glinda added. "And then an official successor to the traitor fairy will be appointed."

Dorothy blinked. "Right," she said after a moment.

We were all silent for a moment when Dorothy and Glinda finished talking. The Lion looked confused, and the Scarecrow looked—well, if I didn't know him better, I'd have said he looked suspicious. I didn't have to wonder if my own face mirrored the Lion's consternation, since it was a mask of tin, but I had to admit I wasn't quite able to follow what Dorothy and Glinda were saying. I didn't want to question Dorothy, or to doubt her. But I didn't want to think too hard about her story either, because something about it seemed a little . . . off. Oz still had plenty of magic. Ozma had never seemed very evil, or very jealous either, for that matter. But I had traveled with Dorothy for months. We'd been through all kinds of things together. I *knew* her. She wasn't just beautiful and kind, she was a good person. Plus, she'd just lost her aunt and uncle. No wonder she wasn't completely making sense—even if, come to think of it, she didn't look too upset. Glinda was a good witch, and she'd never do anything to jeopardize the fate of Oz. Dorothy had saved all of us. More than that, she was the woman I loved. And—at who knew what cost to herself—she was volunteering to take on the enormous responsibility of governing Oz. Had there ever been a woman more self-sacrificing or courageous?

I stood up, pushing my chair away from the table. "All I need to know is that I serve you," I said, cursing myself as a squeak in my jaw detracted from the nobility of my words. "I will be at your side, Princess Dorothy, through anything you ask of me." I bowed down on one knee before her, my head low to the ground.

Dorothy put one cool hand under my chin and tilted my head up so that I was looking into her deep blue eyes. "My wonderful Woodman," she said softly. "So loyal and so brave. I knew you'd be the first to come to my side, and I won't forget it." As I knelt, her shoes blazed even more brightly, surrounding me in a red light that pulsed like a heartbeat. I could almost hear them whispering to me in words I couldn't quite make out. The light filled my eyes until I could no longer see the room, and a hissing rose up in my ears. A red mist swirled above my head, forming a huge, powerful hand that plunged toward me. Before I could cry out or move, the fingers pierced my tin chest, diving straight for my cloth heart.

Somehow, impossibly, I could feel them wrap around the soft fabric. Power flooded through me, power and a new, unfamiliar emotion: rage. Everything was changing. I could no longer feel Dorothy's hand under my chin or hear the noises of the room around us. I was standing in front of my palace in the Winkies' country, towering over a courtyard full of cowering Winkies. The stones around me were stained red, and my tin fingers were covered with blood. I had done something terrible, but I didn't know what it was. Horror filled me, but at the same time so did something else. Elation. The knowledge that no one could stop me from doing anything I wanted to the Winkies weeping at my feet. The sky was the same powerful red of Dorothy's shoes. In the distance, I could hear someone shouting something indistinct that slowly grew clearer. "Woodman! Tin Woodman!"

The castle and the Winkies vanished. I was back in the Council Chamber. Dorothy had fallen to her knees and wrapped her arms around me, crying, "Tin Woodman! Are you all right?" Relishing the feel of her, I let her embrace linger before I finally put my hands on her back and murmured, "I'm all right. Everything's fine." She leaned back, seizing my hands and looking at me.

"What happened?" she cried.

"I don't know," I said. "I think—I think I must have been

dreaming. But I wasn't asleep. It was—terrible, Dorothy. I dreamed I did something—" I stopped. I had been about to say "awful," but that didn't seem quite right. In my vision I had done something *powerful*. Something, I knew suddenly, that was for her. No, *awful* wasn't the right word at all. "I dreamed I did something terrible," I said again, my voice clearer. "But it was worth it, because it was for you." Wonder filled Dorothy's face, wonder and something else. I knew it was love. It had to be.

I glanced up. Over her shoulder, Glinda regarded me coolly, her lovely face revealing no emotion. But for just one second, I could have sworn I saw a spark in the depths of her crystal-blue eyes. A spark as red and glittering as Dorothy's shoes. Though her lips did not move, I heard her gentle voice echoing inside my head. "Someone must protect the new princess. Do you accept this honor?"

"I do," I said out loud, looking back down at Dorothy's radiant face. "Always and forever. I do."

FIVE

After our council, things were much clearer. Dorothy, always generous, told us that she would allow the traitor Ozma to stay in the palace, but it was clear her betrayal meant she was no longer fit to rule Oz. The five of us agreed that the best solution would be for Dorothy to rule in Ozma's stead until she figured out a way to undo Ozma's damage. Glinda pointed out that as Dorothy's closest confidants in Oz—closer even than Glinda herself, she added modestly—the Lion, the Scarecrow, and I were to be entrusted with a new level of responsibility. It was possible Dorothy had even more enemies within the palace, and it was our job to protect her. I knew what Glinda was really saying. I was Dorothy's protector. I alone had been given this task. And I knew I would never fail.

As we talked, the Lion's stomach rumbled audibly, and Dorothy clapped her hands and laughed. "Silly old Lion!" she said. "You never change. Go get something to eat. Scare and Tin, why don't you go with him for now. Glinda and I have much to discuss. And, Tin"—I turned to her eagerly—"why don't you come back and see me after supper? Alone, I mean."

I was so flustered I could only mumble an assent, and I cursed myself as I followed the Scarecrow out the door. If I kept making a fool of myself in front of Dorothy, she was hardly going to see me as a suitor. The Lion bounded away from us, eager to get to his next meal, but as soon as the door to the Council Chamber swung shut on Dorothy and Glinda the Scarecrow grabbed my arm.

"What on earth do you think is really going on?" he muttered. "This stuff about Ozma, and Glinda coming back, and Dorothy being put in charge—none of the story makes sense." I was silent for a moment as we walked toward the banquet hall. I wanted to disagree with him, to shout him down. But he was only echoing what I'd thought just a few moments ago.

"I'm sure Dorothy would never do anything to hurt anyone," I said finally. That much, I knew for certain, was true.

"Glinda coming back is certainly convenient," he mused. "Her timing is a little too perfect, don't you think?"

"What do you mean?" I asked, though the same thing had occurred to me.

"I suppose it doesn't matter. What *does* matter is that Dorothy's in charge, at least for now, and that means quite a bit of opportunity for us. The Lion's a silly old thing, always has been, but you and me—" He paused significantly. "No more corncobs and Winkies, I can tell you that much," he said when I didn't respond.

"I'm not interested in power," I said truthfully. "I don't mind being King of the Winkies, but I'm not ambitious."

"Not in that way you aren't," he said with a smile, "but I think you've got other aspirations on your mind, don't you?"

"I don't know what you mean," I said with dignity, and he laughed.

"It doesn't matter," he said. "We're both a lot closer than we were yesterday to getting what we want, let's just put it that way. You chase after Dorothy, old friend. She couldn't do better. But me, I've got other sunfruit to light. I'm not going to ask too many questions about what Glinda's up to, and I don't think you should either."

"I would never doubt Dorothy," I said, ignoring his real meaning.

"No, you wouldn't," he said. "I think that's becoming quite clear to everyone."

Dorothy wasn't at dinner. I tried to hide my disappointment as the Scarecrow and I sat with the Lion while he merrily gulped down a pile of drumsticks. The mood in the banquet hall was subdued, and Ozma's chair—a big, green throne-like thing carved with scenes from various places in Oz that shifted when you looked at them—was conspicuously empty. The Lion and the Scarecrow chatted away, but I was too distracted to join in. My conversation with the Scarecrow that afternoon had unsettled me. On the surface, he was still his usual jovial self. But there was a strange new glitter in his black button eyes that made me uncomfortable. Was he hiding something? Was this going to be the future of Oz—all of us suspicious of each other? I thought with longing of the old, happy days, all of us innocent and merrily enjoying our quest. I missed that time so much that for a moment I would have traded a future with Dorothy to have it back—just the four of us, wandering together through Oz.

I stared at my plate, torn between excitement and despair. I was finally going to be alone with Dorothy, to find out why she wanted to see me. Could it be—could she possibly be ready to confess her feelings for me? I told myself not to get my hopes up, but there was no mistaking the signals she'd been sending me since the banquet. What other reason could she possibly have?

But what on earth was going on with my oldest, dearest friends? What intrigues were simmering beneath the surface? What kind of wickedness was lurking at the heart of Oz?

I left the banquet hall as soon as I was able to graciously excuse myself. The Scarecrow, watching me fumble in my excitement as I pushed my chair away from the table, muttered something to the Lion under his breath and they both laughed, but I didn't care. The moment of truth was upon me. Whatever happened, I was going to tell Dorothy how I felt—and find out if my love was returned. It *had* to be, I told myself, my heart pounding as I approached Dorothy's quarters. It simply had to be.

Dorothy had already moved into Ozma's former bedroom. She hadn't had much time to change the decor to suit her— there were still lots of green veils, vines twisting down from the corners of the room, dotted with sweet-smelling blossoms that released occasional flurries of perfumed butterflies, and the burbling sound of a merry forest stream emanating from what looked suspiciously like a closet. Still, she'd dug up an enormous vanity somewhere, and it was already covered with pots and creams and powders and brushes, vials of perfume, and huge bouquets of flowers nearly bursting from their vases. A hot flood of jealousy surged through me. What admirers had sent her flowers? Why hadn't I thought of that? And then Dorothy turned to face me, and all other thoughts fled my mind.

She was seated before her vanity, in a soft silken dressing gown that flowed from her shoulders and pooled in a shimmering pile of fabric at her feet. Her long hair was down, brushed into a shining cape that spilled over her shoulders, and her blue eyes were wide and guileless as she looked at me. Without thinking, I crossed the room and knelt before her on one knee, lowering my head.

"Dorothy," I said, and stopped, overcome with emotion. Now that I was here—now that I was really, truly here, it seemed there was nothing I could possibly say that would express the real depths of my feelings.

"Oh, Tin," she said gently. "Don't bow before me, my dear friend. It makes me feel like everything's changed." She put one slim hand below my chin, and tilted my face up so that I was looking directly at her. I struggled to keep my eyes away from the deep, tantalizing V of her dressing gown, focusing instead on her ruby-red mouth, which was no less distracting.

"But everything *has* changed, Dor—Your Majesty," I said. "The Scarecrow and the Lion are practically strangers. You have all this magic now, and you're ruling the kingdom. And the witch—"

"I trust Glinda," Dorothy said firmly, "and so must you."

I seized both her hands in mine. "Dorothy," I said breathlessly. "Run away with me. Away from whatever's happening here. Oz will sort itself out. I'll keep you safe. I swear it."

She smiled sadly, and to my horror I saw that her blue eyes were filling with tears. "Darling Tin," she said softly, a single tear splashing across the silk of her robe. "You know I can't do that. Oz needs me. Why else have I been called here? It's my duty. I've already lost so much. What does it mean anymore to lose my freedom? My safety?" She sighed and looked away from me, but she didn't let go of my hands. My heart nearly tore itself in two as I looked at her. She was so beautiful—so noble!

"Dorothy," I said, summoning all my courage. "You know I—you know there's nothing I wouldn't do for you. I will keep you safe, I swear it. I'll protect you."

She smiled at me. "I would never ask that of you, dear Tin. No, go back to your kingdom, to the life you had before I returned and everything got turned upside down. At least one of us should have a chance at happiness."

I leapt to my feet and drew her to me. "Dorothy, never! I'll never leave your side! Just let me stay by you. Let me be your protector. Please, Dorothy, it's all I want." I took a deep breath, crushing her to my chest as she looked up at me breathlessly. "Dorothy, I love—"

At that moment, the door to Dorothy's chambers flew open,

and Glinda swooped in, followed closely by the Scarecrow. "Oh!" Dorothy gasped, startled, and let me go. Glinda's mouth twitched in what looked almost like a smirk.

"I hope I'm not interrupting anything," she said in her syrup-coated voice.

"Oh no," Dorothy said, flustered and pulling her robe more tightly around her. She sat back at her dressing table, not looking at me. I thought, though I couldn't have been sure, that the Scarecrow was trying not to laugh. "Tin was just telling me—he was just explaining that he would stay on in the palace, to be my protector," Dorothy said.

"How charming," Glinda said brightly, all trace of her smirk gone. "What a good friend you have." She smiled brilliantly at me. "I'm sure you'll do a wonderful job of keeping Dorothy safe," she said. "Though I don't think our new princess is in any *immediate* danger, here in the Emerald City."

"I could have enemies anywhere!" Dorothy said, a little peevishly. "Everyone is already jealous of me."

"I'm sure my magic is enough to keep you safe for now," Glinda said. "But perhaps the Tin Man will come up with some alternate means of defense." There was that eerie red glitter in the depths of her eyes again, and for the first time since I had come back to the palace, I felt actually afraid. I had the overwhelming urge to grab Dorothy and run out the door, flee with her back to the Winkies' palace, the Sea of Blossoms—anywhere but here. Somewhere she'd be safe, and we could be alone, and all of this would be like a bad dream.

The red spark flared, and I shook my head. Suddenly I couldn't remember what I'd just been thinking about. "I can keep Dorothy safe for now," Glinda was saying. "But we need more power. More strength." She was talking to Dorothy, but looking at me, the red spark glowing with the same heartbeat pulse of Dorothy's red shoes.

"I'll figure something out," I said dully, rising almost as though some other force had taken control of my limbs and was marching me out of the room.

"Good night, Tin," Dorothy called, and the door to her room shut in my face.

I went back to my own rooms and stood for a moment looking out the window. I had promised to help Dorothy. I'd said I would protect her. But if Glinda wouldn't let me near Dorothy herself, what could I do? It took me a while before I thought of the obvious. A princess needed an army, and an army needed a general. That was what Glinda had been trying to get me to see. But where to find such a force? And then it hit me—of course. I was already a ruler myself. It would be a simple matter to bring the Winkies to the Emerald City so that they might protect Dorothy while she and Glinda figured out how to return Ozma's stolen magic.

Once I'd decided, it was a simple matter of slipping away from the palace. I didn't tell Glinda—or Dorothy—of my plans. The army would be my gift to Dorothy. I spent the journey back to the Winkies' kingdom imagining her reaction when I presented her with her new army. Her creamy cheeks flushing with color, her eyes sparkling, her ruby-red lips parting breathlessly with joy and awe. Finally, my actions would say what I hadn't been able to tell her in words. And how could she possibly say no to me, when she was confronted with the force of my devotion? I knew she felt something for me, knew it all the way down to my tin joints. It was in the way she looked at me—in the way she'd let me hold her in her room. It was in everything she said to me. She loved me, I was sure of it—but she was too good, too self-less, to allow her feelings for me to get in the way of her duty to Oz. But once she and Glinda had restored the stolen magic, we'd be free to be together. Glinda would find a true successor, and Dorothy and I could go—why, we could go anywhere. I'd always wanted to visit Polychrome and see the Rainbow Falls. Maybe even a parasol sailing trip across the Sea of Blossoms. I'd heard they were the most romantic spots in all of Oz, but I'd never had anyone to share them with.

I was so lost in my reverie the journey passed in a flash. I didn't even stop to rest or refresh myself when I reached my pal-ace. I strode into my throne room, bellowing for my chancellor, Norbert. He was the most dignified Winkie I could find among my subjects: over the Winkies' traditional costume of short pants and suspenders, he liked to add a suit jacket and pince-nez. Unfortunately, it was difficult for someone three feet tall and covered with yellow fur to really convey the impression of pro-fessionalism, and the decor of the throne room didn't help. The Winkies' palace was comfortable enough, and I wasn't much of a home decorator, so I'd never gotten around to making any changes other than having furniture large enough for a full-size man made for my own rooms. The Winkies were enthusiastic artists, if not very good ones, and the walls of the throne room were painted with a lurid series of murals depicting hallucinatory scenes of glowing yellow Winkies drifting through a variety of Ozian landscapes—Winkies floating over the poppy fields, Winkies climbing mountain ranges, Winkies sailing in tiny airships over the Sea of Blossoms, Winkies splashing in the Rainbow Falls. For the first time it occurred to me that they were hideously ugly. I'd let the Winkies make all the changes they wanted to the palace after the defeat of the Wicked Witch of the West, but maybe I should have been a little stricter with them.

When Dorothy had restored Oz's magic and no longer had to live in the Emerald City as its ruler, I would ask her to come live with me. But to be honest, it was hard to picture her here. Perhaps I should remodel. But those plans could wait. I had more pressing matters to attend to.

"Tomorrow morning, my subjects must assemble in the courtyard," I instructed the chancellor as he scribbled furiously on his ever-present notepad, pushing his pince-nez up on his nose as it slipped down toward his luxurious golden moustache. "I want everyone. From the smallest child to the oldest of the old. I have a tremendously important announcement." He nodded industriously, mouthing the words to himself as he wrote them down.

"Yes sir," he said cheerfully, "I'll see to it, sir. Will you be wanting your usual oil bath, sir? We've some nice new artisanal scented oils in from the country of the Quadlings. And Polychrome sent you a new travel brochure. It's the darnedest thing, sir, a singing telegram, if you can believe that? So impressive what they can do with magic these days. Why, when I was a lad, we hadn't any such—"

"I don't think you understand," I said coldly. "This is not business as usual. The future of Oz is going to change tomorrow."

"Yes sir," he repeated absently, chewing the end of his feather quill. I stared at him in disbelief. Why wasn't he taking me seriously? I knew the Winkies were silly creatures and always had been. I'd never tried to impose much discipline during my rule; there hadn't been any point. But couldn't he hear in my voice how important this was? I was offering my people a chance to make history and he was babbling on about travel promotions? I felt an unfamiliar emotion seize hold of me. My heart felt strange in my hollow chest, heavy and hot. I could almost sense it glowing inside me like an ember the color of Dorothy's shoes. The Wizard's gift had brought me love, but I realized it was also giving me a new feeling entirely: fury. Dorothy trusted me with her life, and I wasn't going to let this stupid Winkie keep me from my duty. A red haze descended over my vision, obscuring the room around me, and my hands moved forward of their own volition, grabbing handfuls of mist. It pooled in my palms like water, pouring between my fingers to fall heavily to the ground, where it slid across the floor in an ever-spreading wave of red. I watched it move, fascinated. It moved almost like an animal, like something with an intelligence behind it.

A strange choking noise interrupted my reverie, and I looked down. To my astonishment, my hands were wrapped around Norbert's throat, squeezing the life out of him as his eyes bulged desperately. In shock, I opened my fingers, and he collapsed to the floor wheezing for breath. As quickly as it had appeared, the red mist dissipated into long, slender tendrils that slithered into cracks in the stone walls and vanished. I couldn't remember where I was or why my chancellor was staring up at me as though I was about to bite off his head. I looked around, blinking, only recognizing the familiar furniture of my throne room after a long moment. Why was I in my throne room? How had I even gotten here? My chest felt strange, as though my heart was moving around inside it. Something was happening to me— something I couldn't explain.

"Everything will be as you wish in the morning, Your Majesty," my chancellor whispered, his voice shaking. What had I wished for in the morning? I thought about this for a while, and then remembered I had wanted to address my subjects. That was it. An army. I was building Dorothy's army, as a gift to her. Relieved, I nodded, still not entirely sure why my chancellor was lying at my feet. Perhaps he'd slipped? I didn't remember that either. I needed a good bath to clear my head.

"Excellent work," I said, and left him in a heap on the floor as

I went to my rooms.

I summoned a few of the house Winkies with the bell I kept in my room for such purposes, and they obligingly drew me a bath of warm oil. Was it just my imagination, or did they keep looking at me? Why was everyone acting so strangely? The oil was perfumed, I noticed—hadn't Norbert been saying something about a new shipment?—and a rich, pleasant scent filled my bathroom. Tin man that I am, I don't have much need of the ordinary human fixtures. I don't even really sleep anymore, though I do my best to follow the rhythms of a normal human day. But I do enjoy a good oil bath. I sank into the warm, sweet-smelling oil, dismissing the Winkies with a wave of my hand. They practically ran out of the room. Something was definitely up, but I had no idea what it could be.

As the oil cooled, I turned my thoughts to the next morning. I'd make a short speech to the Winkies, explaining the situation. They were too foolish to really understand the complexities of politics, but as long as I explained things simply they should be able to follow. I had no doubt they'd be as eager as I was to defend Dorothy. It was true, I supposed, that they wouldn't make the most intimidating army. They were awfully short, and the suspenders sometimes made them look a little silly. But they were only the beginning, and I knew Dorothy would be delighted with my initiative. I'd march them to the Emerald City and assemble them for her so she could see all the work I'd already done on her behalf, and then I would find more recruits.

Everyone in Oz, I knew, would be happy to help out on behalf of their savior, the girl who killed the wicked witches. I wondered idly how the next ruler of Oz would be chosen, once Glinda and Dorothy had restored the stolen magic. It was too bad about Ozma. I'd always sort of liked her. But there was no telling what kinds of wicked secrets even good people were hiding.

SIX

The next morning dawned clear and sunny. I polished my arms and legs and torso until the metal gleamed like mercury in the morning sun. I got my crown out of the Winkie-size wardrobe in one corner of my room and polished that, too, setting it on top of my head when it glowed as brightly as my tin skin. I finished my preparations just as Norbert knocked softly at my door, announcing that my subjects were assembled in the courtyard as I had requested. His suspenders, I noticed, were new, and his suit jacket had been ironed sometime since last night. Even his shoes were buffed. He wouldn't meet my eyes, for some reason, and I almost asked him what had gotten into everybody.

The Winkies were gathered in a noisy, chattering group in the large courtyard in front of the palace's main door, but they fell silent as soon as I came out of the palace, eyeing one another. Norbert bobbed obsequiously at my side, wiping his furry brow with a spotted handkerchief. I surveyed them, my heart sinking

a little. They really were sort of—well, unimpressive. And there
weren't that many of them either. But Oz was not exactly a land
noted for its martial power, and Winkies could be as courageous as anybody if they were given the chance. I noted with
approval that they were standing carefully so as not to trample
the lovingly cultivated flower beds. They might be silly and
undisciplined, but that was at least a start. What mattered most
was that Dorothy would see how much I cared, how much I was
thinking about her.

"My most devoted subjects," I began, gazing out over their
upturned faces. "It has been a great honor to be your ruler, and
I am proud to have done such an excellent job overseeing your
welfare. I have gathered you here today to alert you to a number of important changes that are taking place in Oz." Their
faces were blank. Undaunted, I continued. "I am afraid I have
some disheartening news about the Princess Ozma. Though we
believed her to be a good and kind ruler, she has in fact betrayed
us." At this, the Winkies exchanged startled glances. "I have
learned that she has been stealing the magic of Oz for her own
purposes. But all will soon be well, for something wondrous has
happened." My cloth heart soared in my chest. There was something about saying it out loud that made it seem really true. "The
beloved Dorothy Gale has returned to Oz to help us!"

A murmur of astonishment rippled through the little crowd.
"Dorothy the Witchslayer?" piped up a young Winkie in the
back, who was quickly hushed by his fellows. But I didn't mind
the interruption.

"The one and the same," I said proudly. "When Oz was in need before, she came to us, and now that Oz needs her again, she has returned to us." The Winkies didn't need to know that I still hoped in my heart of hearts she'd come for *me*. "She came to convince Ozma to return the magic she had stolen to the land, but Ozma refused. In the ensuing battle, Ozma cast a terrible spell that erased her own memory. Dorothy, in her generosity and selflessness, has agreed to govern Oz temporarily until a new ruler can be found. In the meantime, she will need an army to protect her. That army, my dear subjects, shall be you."

The Winkies were staring at me openmouthed. I frowned slightly. I had expected them to be more excited. Maybe I just hadn't made myself clear. "We will leave for the Emerald City tomorrow," I added. "Prepare yourselves. I do not know when we will return to this country. Our duty is to Dorothy, and we will serve her as long as she needs us."

The Winkie who'd spoken before was waving his hand furiously, and I nodded in his direction. He cleared his throat. "I'm sorry," he said, less politely than I thought was appropriate. "You said all of us? Are leaving for the Emerald City? Tomorrow?"

"That is correct," I said.

"But I don't want to go to the Emerald City," he said. To my astonishment, several other Winkies nodded in agreement.

"But of course you want to go to the Emerald City," I replied. "This is Dorothy we're talking about. Dorothy Gale, who killed the wicked witches, who's given everything for Oz. It's our responsibility to keep her safe after everything she's done for us."

"Your responsibility, maybe," the Winkie said. "Why should it be ours?"

"Because I am your king," I said, but muttering had spread through the crowd, and now more Winkies were raising their hands to speak.

"I don't know any Dorothy!" one of them shouted, and was shushed by her fellows, but more and more of them were grumbling. I raised my voice in an effort to speak over them.

"It is not a request!" I shouted. "It is an order! You will all be heroes! I demand it!"

"How do we even know this is true about Ozma?" snapped the original dissenter. "Ozma is a fairy! Maybe she just knows better than us what the magic of Oz should be used for!"

"Hear, hear!" someone else shouted. As more and more of them protested, my disbelief turned to anger. Here I was, offering them the opportunity of a lifetime, and they were worried about technicalities? I was their king! Even if they didn't want to help Dorothy, as impossible as that was to believe, I was in charge, not some whining Winkie teenager.

"Silence!" I bellowed, but now they were ignoring me completely, and some of them were even heading for the palace gates as though to return home. How *dare* they? After everything I'd given up for them? Dorothy had killed the Wicked Witch of the West and freed the enslaved Winkies when she had first come to Oz. I'd been at her side, obviously, and in fact she wouldn't have been able to defeat the witch without my help. Not at all. But her act of bravery had left the Winkies without a ruler, and so the Wizard had appointed me their king all those years ago. He didn't ask me what I wanted. Nobody ever did, as a matter of fact. Not even Dorothy, if I was being *completely* honest. But I was like Dorothy. I cared more about the good of Oz than my own personal needs.

I had a perfectly good heart, one the Wizard had given me, and while it naturally belonged to Dorothy, all the years after she'd left Oz I'd assumed I would never see her again. But instead of doing the things other people did—falling in love, having adventures, seeing the world—I'd stayed here, in this backwater little palace. I could have gone anywhere, done anything. I could have found—well, I'd never have found a replacement for Dorothy, but maybe I could have found someone I'd love almost as much. I could have had a life. Instead, I'd given up everything for the Winkies, for these ungrateful, foolish, nasty little trolls.

At my side, Norbert cleared his throat, adjusting his pince-nez. "Well, sir," he said quietly. "I suppose that will be all, then?"

"No," I said. "That will not be all." I could feel my outrage transforming into something bigger, and stronger, and meaner. A sudden breeze sprang up, bringing with it a tiny cyclone of pink strawberry-scented glitter, and for a moment I could almost see Glinda hovering above the Winkies' heads and smiling at me. "I will lend you the power to control them, brave Woodman," her voice whispered in my ear. "You will show them the glory and the might of Oz." The glitter swirled around me, whirling around my arms and my hands. The metal of my fingers began to glow red-hot, as though I'd left them in a fire, and started to melt and change shape. To my astonishment my fingers began to transform before my very eyes. They sprouted long, thin needles and short-bladed knives, all sharp and wicked-looking. As soon as the transformation was complete, the metal cooled again, gleaming dangerously in the morning sun.

For just a moment, my heart pulsed with doubt. "But these are weapons," I said out loud.

Glinda *tsk-tsk*ed in my ear. I turned around, expecting to see her, but there was no one there. "What we do, we do for the good of Oz, my noble friend," she whispered. "What will Dorothy do if you cannot protect her? Who will she turn to, if you are not at her side? I will choose another protector, if you are not man enough for the task."

Jealousy sparked up in me like a forest fire. There would be no question of Glinda's choosing someone else! I would be at Dorothy's side for always. I would show these filthy Winkies how powerful I was if they did not obey me out of duty.

"Stand where you are!" I snarled to the Winkies, who were by now pouring toward the palace gates. Something in my voice stopped them in their tracks. "Bring me the Winkies among you who have dared to defy me," I said, and even to my own ears my voice was terrible. Glinda's cyclone of magic darted over the crowd, dusting them with some kind of enchantment. As if in a trance the Winkies seized the traitors and dragged them toward my podium. Only the first Winkie who'd spoken, the one who'd said he didn't want to go to the Emerald City, was trying to resist, struggling furiously and even biting at the arms of his captors. I would deal with him first. I gestured for them to bring him before me.

"This is *my* kingdom," I said in a low voice that I knew was strong enough to carry to the far edges of the crowd. "I have allowed you to forget it. I will not make that mistake again." I wrapped my fingers around his neck and looked up at the assembled crowd. "Tomorrow, we march to the Emerald City," I said. "From now on, this is how I will deal with traitors." The knives that had replaced my fingers cut into his flesh, and blood poured down his yellow fur and pooled at his dangling feet. He gurgled frantically as my fingers cut and cut, all the way to the bone. Red light blazed around me, the red of Dorothy's shoes, pouring in through my open mouth and filling my entire body with a blinding, all-powerful rage. With a single gesture, I tore his head from his body and hurled it into the crowd, striking one of them square in the chest with a grisly smack. The Winkies stared at me, and I saw in grim satisfaction that their eyes were filled with utter horror and fear. Some of the Winkies were crying, but most of them were in such terrified shock that they just trembled where they stood and gaped up at me.

"I knew you were the right choice," Glinda's disembodied voice whispered next to me. "I knew you were brave enough, Woodman." I looked down at my hands. They were still the strange new hands Glinda had given me. Covered in blood, they looked even more menacing. More evil, I thought, and then shook my head. No. This wasn't evil. This was necessary. *What we do, we do for the good of Oz.* She had been right. This was a new time. I couldn't back down. Dorothy needed me.

Almost without thinking, I moved toward the next traitor in line with my hands outstretched when Norbert gave a little cry. "What is it?" I snarled.

"Sir," Norbert said desperately, "what are you doing? Why are you harming us? We'll obey you, sir, we understand how important Dorothy's army is now. Please don't hurt anyone else." I blinked and suddenly the red mist that had filled me poured out of my eyes and mouth, rising up into the clear blue sky and taking with it the intense rage that had possessed me. Glinda's voice was gone. I looked around. There was blood everywhere. The headless body of a Winkie lay on the ground, and a line of Winkies crouched before me, shaking in terror.

"Did I—did I do that?" I asked Norbert, confused.

He looked at me in astonishment. "Yes sir," he said quietly.

"Why?"

"I don't know, sir. You said—you said you needed an army."

The army! Of course. Dorothy's army. I wasn't entirely certain what had just happened, but if it meant I had an army to bring to my princess, it was surely for the best. I'd bring her an army, and then tell her how I truly felt at last. How could she say no, when she saw the evidence of my devotion?

"We march for the Emerald City at dawn," I told the blood-spattered masses trembling at my feet. "Shirkers and deserters will be executed." I turned my back on them and walked into the palace.

SEVEN

The Winkies who gathered again in the courtyard the next morning were a far cry from the nattering, cheerful crowd who had
assembled the day before. Some of them, I was certain, hadn't
moved from their spots since I had executed the traitor in front
of them the preceding morning. They were silent, their heads
bowed, their pathetic possessions gathered on their backs or
hastily stuffed into small carts they towed behind them. A flash
of doubt ran through me. They didn't look like an army, they
looked like a few dozen refugees. None of them had weapons, let
alone armor. None of them had ever fought a battle in their lives.
But I shook my head, dismissing the thought. We would all rise
to the occasion. Even the humblest among us. Dorothy needed
them almost as much as she needed me if she was to be safe in
the Emerald City. I would turn them into an army if it was the
last thing I did.

It took my ramshackle army a long time to find the Road of

Yellow Brick, and when we did finally find it the bricks looked
old and crumbly and were stained with a faint red hue—not the
color of Dorothy's shoes, but the color of blood. I remembered
my vision in the palace the morning Dorothy had met with us
and told us that Ozma had betrayed the country. I remembered
the way Glinda had looked at me. Had she known what I would
have to do? Had she been trying to warn me? I frowned, unwilling to allow any more uncomfortable thoughts. I wasn't proud of
what I'd done, but it had been necessary. There'd be no reason
to have to do anything like it again. I avoided looking at my
inexplicably transformed hands. Maybe Dorothy could help me
change them back to the way they'd been before. After all, she
was the one with magic.

The Road of Yellow Brick led us miles out of the way, almost
as if it were trying to keep us away from the Emerald City. We
walked for a long time through the Forest of Fear, the trees
shrieking terrifying things at the Winkies, who flinched and
wept and then, looking back at me fearfully, trudged onward.
Some of them stuffed up their ears with cloth. Others held hands.
I let their cowardice slide. There would be plenty of time for discipline once we reached the city. I wasn't a monster.

Finally, after hours of doubling back and leading us astray,
the road seemed to realize it couldn't stop me from reaching the
palace and straightened itself out. The bricks grew solid and polished again, and the hedges lining the road were neatly trimmed
and bursting with flowers that periodically caroled us in trill-
ing, high-pitched voices as we passed. The Winkies were still

subdued, but their mood seemed to improve a little, and some of them perked up enough to look around them as we walked. A few of them dug cheese-and-marmalade sandwiches out of their bags—the Winkies were fanatical about cheese-and-marmalade sandwiches for some reason, and I had never known one of my subjects to travel anywhere without a ready supply—and munched as we marched. At last, I could see the green spires of the Emerald City on the horizon.

By now, several of the Winkies were stumbling with exhaustion. I did not allow them to rest. They'd have to learn to toughen up. The sun was on the horizon as we marched at last through the Emerald City's broad gates. One of the Winkies collapsed, only to be hastily pulled to his feet by the others and propped upright. I selected a small delegation of the most alert-looking Winkies and called for Munchkin servants.

"Give them chambers in the palace," I said curtly. "And see that they're fed. I'll be back for the rest of them later." The Winkies I had chosen to accompany me, among them the chancellor, watched longingly as the others were led away to rest.

"You've served me well today," I told them. "You will be rewarded in the princess's army, never fear." They did not seem very interested in the prospect of their reward but they did not protest as I led them into the palace and sent another servant to tell Dorothy to meet me in the Council Chamber.

She kept us waiting for a long time. One of the Winkies had pillowed his arms on the table and fallen asleep by the time she swept into the room, her auburn hair done in an intricate updo

and her dress a slightly different version of the shimmery gingham she'd worn to tell us of her plans. I leapt to my feet when
she entered the room, bowing deeply and surreptitiously kicking
the chair of the Winkie who'd fallen asleep. He leapt to his feet,
too, with a yelp of fear and stood looking around him, blinking
frantically.

"My dear Woodman," Dorothy said. Was that a hint of irritation in her voice? "Why on earth have you disturbed me? You
know how busy I am now."

"I have important news," I said, my heart flooding with joy
just to look upon her beautiful face. I reached forward to take
her hand, but then remembered my new fingers. I did not wish
to hurt her.

She ignored the gesture and looked at me with impatience.
Suddenly I was overcome with doubt. Why wasn't she happier
to see me? "Well? What is it?"

"Princess Dorothy," I said, going down on one knee before
her. "You know your safety is my utmost concern, and your new
position puts you at terrible risk."

"Well, yes, that's true," she agreed, fluffing her reddish-
brown curls. "Glinda says I must pay careful attention. I think
it's sort of exciting, don't you? Nobody in Kansas was smart
enough to understand how special I am. But here—well, look
how far I've come!"

"I will remain at your side always, your knight and your protector," I said. My heart pulsed again with that eerie power. "But
a bodyguard is not enough, not even one as devoted as I. My

beloved princess, I have brought you an army the likes of which Oz has never seen."

Dorothy's eyes widened and she gasped in delight. "An *army*? Oh, Tin! You're incredible! I've never even dreamed of having an army before! Is it very splendid? Do they have horses and banners? Where are they? I want to see them right now!"

I rose to my feet and took her arm, indicating the Winkies with a sweeping gesture. "These are your generals. Your army awaits you in the palace."

Dorothy stared at the trembling Winkies with confusion, her eyebrows knitting together. "But, Tin—I don't understand. These are Winkies."

"As are all your soldiers," I explained. "For now," I added hastily. "Of course, I'll soon have more recruits. Perhaps the Lion knows a few beasts who would be willing to serve. I'll oversee their training. Soon you'll have a fearsome force to defend you."

A flurry of emotions crossed Dorothy's face. She was overcome, I realized. Overcome by what I'd done for her. By the lengths I'd gone to. She was so overwhelmed she didn't even know what to say. I was so happy to see her delight that it took me a moment to understand that she was laughing not from joy, but from exasperation.

"Tin," she said. "This is really sweet of you, but they're Winkies. That's like having an army of stuffed *animals*. I really wish you hadn't bothered me with this—Glinda and I were having the nicest time going through nail polishes."

"But, Dorothy," I said in consternation. "You must understand, Oz has never had soldiers——"

"Tin, just get rid of them," she interrupted. "They're a bunch of furry midgets terrified of their own shadows. Look at them." The Winkies, it was true, were staring at us in alarm, and the chancellor might have actually been crying. I was about to answer when the Scarecrow came into the room, drawn by Dorothy's raised voice.

"Well, well, well," he remarked, taking in the scene. "What exactly do we have here?"

"The Woodman has lost his *mind*." Dorothy giggled. "He's brought me these *creatures* and says they're going to be an *army*."

"An army?" the Scarecrow said, and looked at me thoughtfully. "But that's not a bad idea at all, Doro—er, Your Eminence."

Your Eminence? I thought, reeling. Since when was Dorothy Her Eminence, other than in my heart? And why couldn't she see the nobility of my gift? None of this was going as I had planned, none of it at all. I looked around the room desperately, as though the answer was under one of the Winkies.

"I don't want an army of vermin," Dorothy snapped, and the Scarecrow raised one painted eyebrow. "Wasn't it enough to have to toil in servitude with these dreadful creatures under the Wicked Witch of the West the *first* time I came to Oz? There's a reason I didn't go *back* after I killed that old cow."

And then my error hit me. Of course. How could I have been so stupid? The Winkies could only remind Dorothy of that terrible time in the Wicked Witch of the West's palace, before Dorothy had heroically killed her and liberated the Winkies like the noble woman she was. Her anger hid another, deeper emotion—her pain. And now, like a fool, I was reminding her of it. No wonder she was so upset.

"Well," the Scarecrow observed, "they're here now. Might as well do something with them." I wanted to throw him from the room. He didn't understand anything, and he certainly didn't understand Dorothy. Not the way I did.

"I don't want them within a mile of my palace," Dorothy snapped. "They probably have *lice*."

"The Winkies are a very clean people," I said hastily. "Dorothy, I lived among them for years. I ruled over them, don't forget."

"Tin, just make them go away." She stared at me, narrowing her beautiful crystal-blue eyes. "If you really do care about me," she said coolly, "you'll do as I ask without questions, Tin." With that, she swept out of the room, leaving me staring after her in despair.

"What have I done?" I moaned. "She'll never forgive me. How could I be such an idiot?"

"What do you mean?" the Scarecrow asked.

"Instead of bringing her an army, I brought her a reminder of a terrible time in her life. How can I possibly earn her trust again?" I sank into a chair next to the chancellor, who made a small, terrified noise, and put my head in my hands, nearly sticking myself in the eye with my sinister new fingers.

"Tin," the Scarecrow said slowly, "are you actually in *love* with Dorothy?"

"Of course I'm in love with Dorothy!" I shouted, so force-fully I startled us both. "Who wouldn't be in love with Dorothy? She's beautiful, and kind, and generous, and we've been through so much together. I thought she felt the same way. I was going to tell her when I brought her the army. But now I've ruined everything."

The Scarecrow was silent for a moment. I could practically hear the stuffing in his head rustling, but I didn't want to know what he was thinking since it was probably along the lines of what a complete failure I'd made of myself. "What will you do with them?" he asked casually.

"Oh, I don't know," I mumbled unhappily into my palms. "Send them home, I suppose. There are dozens of them here." At the word "home" the chancellor perked up visibly, although all of them still looked at me as though I was going to tear off their heads, too. I felt badly about what I'd done, I really did, but if they'd just obeyed me—their king!—from the beginning none of that business would have happened.

"Seems a shame to just waste them," the Scarecrow said. "Now that they're here and all."

"I can't put them to work in the palace," I replied. "You heard Dorothy. She doesn't want to see them again."

"There are . . . other options," the Scarecrow said, and I looked at him. His flat black eyes were expressionless, but some-thing in his voice sent a shiver down my tin spine. If you want to know the truth, I'd always thought the Scarecrow was a little creepy. Even on that first trip to Oz, pretending to be such an idiot, dithering around—no, he'd been planning something all along, you mark my words. The Lion, for all his uncouthness, is relatively honest. What you see is what you get, even if what you get is tacky, boorish, and bad for your nice furniture. And me— well, as you know, I'm just a man in love. But the Scarecrow isn't like either one of us. He's crafty, and he only got craftier once the Wizard filled up his head with sawdust brains. I didn't like the look on his face, but I wasn't about to let him know that he'd unnerved me.

"What do you mean, 'other options'?"

He thought for a moment, as if considering how to present a complicated subject to a simple person. "Glinda and I have been . . . discussing a few things," he said eventually. "You know, she's really a magnificent woman. Very sharp. Very sharp indeed. She has some other very impressive assets, too, if you know what I mean," he added with a wink.

"I'm sure I don't," I said coldly. "What's your point?"

"She thinks that Oz isn't going to be universally happy about Dorothy's plan to restore the stolen magic."

"Why on earth not?"

"Oh, you know," the Scarecrow said vaguely, waving one cloth hand at the window. "Doubts about the process. Something with the constitution."

"Oz doesn't *have* a constitution."

"Line of succession," the Scarecrow said. "All of that. You

know, people really love their fairies. All those wings and sparkles and whatnot. Dorothy's just a girl. And you have to admit, this whole story about the battle with Ozma is a little suspicious."

"Dorothy is certainly not *just* a girl," I said sharply. "And what on earth do you mean by 'suspicious'? Ozma betrayed all of us. Of course it's shocking, but once people realize the truth, they'll know right away that Dorothy only has the good of Oz at heart."

"Shocking, yes," the Scarecrow said mildly. "Quite shocking. Not to mention sudden. Some people are already saying it was a little too sudden, if you get my drift. Dorothy coming back to Oz? Glinda reappearing out of nowhere? Suddenly Ozma's a babbling idiot? Come on, Tin, I know I have all these brains now, but even you aren't that stupid."

"So you're just going to betray Dorothy?" I said in disbelief. "Because of some palace rumor mill?"

"Oh, I didn't say that at all. Not at all. Look at us, Tin. We're back in the Emerald City. Let's face it, we belong here. We're not just helping Dorothy. We're making a better life for ourselves. If Dorothy stays in power, well . . ." He trailed off, his eyes glittering, his expression distant. If I knew one thing for sure in that moment, it was that the Scarecrow had a plan. I wondered if Dorothy knew what it was. If I should keep an eye on him, just in case. Maybe the Scarecrow wasn't just a little sinister. Was it possible he was actually a traitor to the woman I loved?

The Winkies were following this conversation with enormous eyes, and it occurred to me we should probably be more discreet. I jerked my chin toward the chancellor, and the Scarecrow laughed.

"Don't you worry about our little furballs over there," he said. "I told you, I have an idea for what to do with them. Glinda's shown me some . . . alterations that can be made to Oz's creatures. Nothing drastic, mind you. Just a few improvements."

"Alterations?" I asked suspiciously.

"I've been working exclusively with the winged monkeys," he said, ignoring me. "But I'd love to diversify. I think you're on the right track with this whole army business. Dorothy just wants to frolic around the palace in petticoats and lipstick like the Emerald City is some kind of giant slumber party. But Glinda has a real vision." I made a noise of protest, and he laughed.

"Oh, come now, Tin. I know you're head over heels for the girl, but you have to admit she's done nothing since she got back except play dress-up and use her supposedly all-powerful magic to give herself new hairdos. I'm not saying there's anything wrong with that, but I'm interested in the bigger picture. And so is Glinda."

Talking to the Scarecrow was like wrestling with an eel. Suddenly everything I'd been trying to say was all turned around. "I think you're all wrong about Dorothy," I said angrily. The Scarecrow only shrugged, and I sighed in exasperation. "Do you really think you can use the Winkies to win her back to my side? What will you do with them?" I asked.

"Think about it," he said, getting excited. "We do need an army; even you figured out that much. But what if we had an army that was invincible? Glinda thinks we can do it with magic, but you and I can't use the magic of Oz that way, not directly. We don't have any power. It may be possible for us to create weapons that use Oz's magic—I'm working on that, too—but right now we can't do much else. But what if I engineered soldiers *using* magic? She's been helping me the past few days, and I've made all sorts of advances. You wouldn't believe what I've been able to accomplish in such a short amount of time. But my experiments are, um—" He paused, a little sheepishly. "They do sort of eat up resources," he said. "I need new subjects, and quickly. And you've just shown up at the palace with several dozen of them."

"Are these experiments harmful?" I asked. Beheading my unruly subjects was one thing, but turning them over en masse to the Scarecrow for some kind of creepshow science project was something else.

"Oh no, no, no," he said quickly. "Not really, no. Fatal sometimes, but definitely not harmful. And Dorothy will be so happy when you come to her with a real army instead of these little guys."

"But she said she never wanted to see them again," I said. "So even if you do turn them into soldiers, I'm still not in her good graces."

"They won't really be recognizable when I'm done with them," the Scarecrow said. There was a chilling silence. One of the Winkies at the table made an agonized noise and then clapped his hands over his mouth. "She won't even know they're Winkies. So, Tin, what do you say?"

"I don't know," I said reluctantly. "I mean, they're still my subjects. The Wizard said I was supposed to take care of them."

"They won't feel a thing," the Scarecrow assured me. "They might even enjoy the process. Just think—all your life, a boring old Winkie, and suddenly you're an enhanced soldier in the princess's army? Not a bad opportunity, right? Plus, Dorothy will never take you seriously as a suitor unless you're willing to do what's necessary."

I didn't entirely like his plan, but that last sentence won me over. "I'll do anything for Dorothy," I said firmly, putting one hand over my heart. Next to me, Norbert started crying again.

"Oh, believe me," the Scarecrow said, his grin growing even more sinister. "I know."

EIGHT

That night, after I'd moved my things to my official new chambers in the palace—these rooms equipped with a closet I could stand in to sleep, as I'd requested—I stood lost in thought for a long time. Everything in Oz was changing so quickly. Dorothy back, Glinda and the Scarecrow probably cooking up some secret plan behind my back, the Lion chomping down bones in his room in the palace like it was his own home. Except that now the Emerald City *was* his new home. It was all of ours. I was overjoyed to have Dorothy back—more than overjoyed. I'd thought I would never see her again, and here she was, within reach. But everything else was so confusing, and I wasn't sure how I felt about sharing her with Glinda, the Scarecrow, and the Lion.

Over breakfast, the three of us talked about the first time Dorothy had come to Oz. "Do you remember when you had to rescue me from the poppies?" the Lion roared happily, chomping on a chop and spraying bits of food as he talked. "All those mice!" We laughed, for a moment united again in our shared history.

"Everything was so much simpler then," I said, a little sadly. "We only wanted obvious things. A heart, courage, brains—and Dorothy gave us all of that, and more."

"Of course," said the Scarecrow, eyeing me keenly. "And that's why you must do exactly what she asks of you, Tin." I couldn't help but notice he didn't say "we." When had my friends changed so much? Was it really true that I could no longer trust him? I didn't want it to be, but I couldn't get the thought out of my mind.

Even before I'd known I loved Dorothy, I'd been her champion. When the Wicked Witch of the West had sent wolves to kill us, I'd slain them all without a second thought, to protect Dorothy. I'd done whatever was necessary on our quest to keep her safe. Wasn't killing the Winkie in my courtyard almost the same thing? If it was, why did I still feel so bad about it? Why did everything have to be so complicated now?

I wandered through the palace in a daze for the next few days, confused and often alone. I barely saw Dorothy, who was holed up constantly with Glinda, and if I didn't know better I would have said that she was avoiding me. After that first breakfast the Scarecrow, too, was nowhere to be found, presumably working away at his mysterious experiments. To my surprise, I even missed the Winkies—especially Norbert. He had been a good, reliable, and kind companion over the years, and he knew a tremendous amount about the history of Oz. I should have kept him at my side, I realized belatedly. The Scarecrow didn't need *all* my Winkies for his project. Norbert would have been good company—and a good adviser in this strange new palace life.

Only the Lion had as much free time as I did, and although I often found him wearisome—all he talked about was hunting— at least when I was around him I didn't have to think about a lot of things I didn't understand. On the rare occasions when the Scarecrow emerged—I'd see him in passing, or at meals, which we attended as Dorothy's closest companions even though we didn't eat—he refused to talk about his work other than to say it was progressing well. His clothes were often smeared with blood, and sometimes bits of other, gorier things that I preferred not to examine too closely. He would spend the meal practically bouncing in his chair, and then rush away as soon as the dishes were cleared. "Be patient," the Lion counseled in his meaty-breathed growl. "Only the best for Dorothy, you know." I sighed. Did *everyone* in the palace know how I felt except her? She, too, sat at meals most of the time, but took the place of honor at the head of the table, where she laughed and carried on with everyone but me. Glinda was always by her side. I tried every day to catch her alone, before or after lunch or dinner, but she always said gently, "Not now, Tin," and hurried away. Could it be possible that I'd disappointed her so much she was avoiding me? The Lion, who witnessed most of these failed attempts, gave me consoling pats on the shoulder as I stared longingly after her glittering heels retreating from me time after time. Those shoes! These days, they were all I could think about, glittering at the back of my mind like my own heartbeat. How could I make Dorothy see me? How could I make her understand how much I cared for her? I had to find a way to make her mine. I simply had to. Even if she couldn't see it, we belonged together.

Finally, one morning a few days after he'd taken away the Winkies, the Scarecrow found me in my chambers, where I was staring out the window. "Are you busy?" he asked politely, though I obviously wasn't. I'd been thinking about how Dorothy might look in a wedding dress, walking down an aisle toward me. Would we marry in the palace? Perhaps the gardens? The Scarecrow cleared his throat.

"Oh," I said, remembering where I was. "No, not really."

He actually rubbed his hands together with glee. "I have something to show you," he said. "Something I think will interest you very much." I waited. "In my workshop," he said impatiently.

I sighed and got to my feet, squeaking audibly. I hadn't been so good about oiling my joints in the last few days. Nothing seemed very important anymore if I wasn't going to see Dorothy.

I followed him through the hallways to the suite of rooms Dorothy had given him. I didn't think we'd been in the palace long enough for the Scarecrow to amass the kind of clutter that filled his chambers. Every surface was filthy, cluttered with piles of paper and old books and pens and tools. A bookshelf was so stuffed with volumes that they threatened to burst from

its shelves. A large table covered in leather straps and mysterious stains dominated one end of the room. Though the day was
bright and sunny, the Scarecrow's workshop was as cold as an
icebox, and if I hadn't been made out of tin I would have shuddered.

"What did you want to show me?" I asked, trying not to let
him see how creeped out I was by his whole setup. I'd known the
Scarecrow was weird, but I'd had no idea he was this weird. He
gestured toward the broad table, which was covered by a dirty,
bloodstained blanket. I moved closer. The blanket was lumpy
and misshapen, suggesting it covered something fairly large.
Something, I realized, that was moving.

"What is it?" I asked. The Scarecrow smiled.

"Not it," he said cheerfully. "He! An old friend of yours, in
fact." He flipped up the bottom half of the blanket, revealing a
gruesome mess of bloody flesh and metal. I bent down, trying
to figure out what I was looking at. It seemed to be the lower
half of an animal, but no animal I had never seen. The torso was
covered with fur, so stained with blood and grease it was impossible to determine the original color. Bloody, gaping wounds
slashed here and there through the fur, crudely sewn together
with thick black thread. "Not all the implants take, you know,"
the Scarecrow said, seeming just a touch defensive. "This is very
complicated work." Where the animal's legs should have been, its
torso was fused to a single rusty wheel, like a unicycle. The line
where flesh met metal was red and angry, bulging with scabbed-
over skin and glistening red meat that looked suspiciously like

organs. I swallowed at the gruesome sight.

"I don't understand," I said. "What is this?"

The Scarecrow smiled and clapped his hands together. "Tin, old friend, meet your new general!" he cried, and whipped away the rest of the blanket. I gasped.

The creature strapped to the Scarecrow's table was—or had once been—Norbert. One eye stared sightlessly up at me, but the other side of his face was a mess of metal and wires and exposed bone, the eye socket sprouting a glowing red bulb. His fur was matted with blood and oil, and in other places it had been cut open, revealing the pulsing red of his muscles. One arm ended in metallic pincers, not unlike the implements my own hands had transformed into. His chest heaved as he struggled for breath. "Sir," he wheezed beseechingly. "Sir, it hurts. Please help me." Impossibly, this awful ruin of my former chancellor was alive.

"What have you done?" I whispered.

"I thought you would be pleased!" The Scarecrow beamed. "Unrecognizable, am I right? Unfortunately, most of the other little fellows didn't quite make it through the process, but this one gives me hope. In no time we'll have fully mechanized soldiers for your army. I'll even allow you to be the one who tells Dorothy, as long as you give me proper credit, of course."

"What do you mean, didn't make it through the process?"

The Scarecrow clapped me heartily on the back. "Science involves sacrifice, my boy! You wouldn't know that, I suppose. I've been imagining a project like this for a very long time, you know. Glinda's return has given me the opportunity, and

Dorothy's return has given me the excuse. But truth be told, I'm in it for the knowledge, not the power. Just think of what advances I can make next!"

"You killed them?" I asked in disbelief. "All of them?"

"Not killed!" he exclaimed. "*Sacrificed*. It's not like I murdered them in cold blood! I had no way of knowing they wouldn't be strong enough to survive the initial round of trials. I have a few of them left, though, and soon I'll have them all fixed up and ready to go. This little fellow was my first success. He's a real trouper—no pun intended. Let me put him through his paces for you." He undid the straps that held what had once been my chancellor to the table, lifted him up, and set him on the ground so that he balanced on his wheel. "Show the Woodman your stuff," he ordered. Obediently, the chancellor scooted back and forth, and then creaked around the room in a little circle. His one good eye wept. "Please, sir," he whispered again. "Just make it stop."

"See? Right as rain," the Scarecrow said. "Nothing wrong with him a little oil won't fix, and I'm sure you've plenty of that lying about. It was you who gave me the idea, actually. A machine-animal mix? What could be better. All your sturdiness, with a bit of muscle and brain thrown in for good measure. The soldiers will be engineered not to think too clearly, of course. Wouldn't want them to mutiny. So I suppose they'll take after you more than me." He laughed.

I didn't entirely understand what he was saying. As I watched the chancellor make his horrible circuit of the room, my heart sank. This wasn't what I had wanted at all. Norbert had served me faithfully for years.

"Come now," the Scarecrow said quickly. "Now's no time to be squeamish, Tin. You want Dorothy to be impressed, you have to be willing to go the extra mile."

"She—she approves of this?" I asked, finding my voice.

"Approves! Tin, when you tell her what I've done—what we've done—she'll be over the moon. Look at what you've done for her! Given up your servants, your old life? Transformed these useless little creatures into real weapons? She'll be at your feet!"

"Are you—" I swallowed. Norbert had come to a stop and was leaning against the table, staring dully at nothing. Trickles of fresh blood seeped down his fur. "Are you sure this is the right thing to do? It's what she wants?"

"Dorothy doesn't know what she wants," the Scarecrow said confidently. "It's up to you to tell her. And"—he lowered his voice significantly—"to make sure she knows she wants *you*. A girl as pretty as that? Someone else is bound to snap her up if you can't manage to tell her how you feel. What better way than with a gift like this?"

I didn't like what he'd done to Norbert, but his words were persuasive. It was true that every gain comes with some kind of cost. Presumably the Scarecrow had perfected his technique, and further sacrifice wouldn't be necessary. And if I could go to Dorothy with an army—a real army—she'd finally forgive me for my missteps.

"But he said it hurts him," I said.

"Hurts him?" The Scarecrow chortled. "Nonsense. Look at him. Happy as a clam." He snapped his fingers in the chancellor's face and Norbert began his squeaky circle of the room again.

"He does seem content," I agreed.

"The process is harmless, really, now that I've got it down. It was Glinda's idea, actually. Magnificent woman. I'd been bandying about ideas, as I said, but she was the one who gave me the final push. She had the idea to start with myself."

"What do you mean?"

He tapped his head with one finger. "The brains the Wizard gave me are helpful, don't get me wrong. But there's so much more I want to know. She helped me soup up my brains—no machine parts, obviously, but magic's the ticket. Once I did that, I was a new man. Dove right into this project, and look how much I've accomplished."

"You're fooling around with the Wizard's gift?"

"The Wizard was a fine fellow, but his magic wasn't even real—not back then, anyway, though Glinda says he might have found his own store of Oz's magic when he controlled the Emerald City. But the stuff she and Dorothy are throwing around, that's the good stuff, my boy, that's the good stuff. She came to me practically the minute she was back in the palace, making an offer I couldn't refuse. You wouldn't believe the leaps I've made with my new, improved brains. I never would have thought to experiment on living creatures of Oz before Glinda used her magic on me, and I never would have been able to do it either."

He looked at me keenly. "It's a new order, Woodman. A new time in Oz. We're at the center of it. You're not going to get left behind, are you? I don't think Dorothy would like that."

Dorothy. The Wizard's gifts. The Scarecrow had improved himself so that he could do better. What if I did the same? Then she'd know I deserved her love. If I came to her with an army, and a heart that was even bigger and better? If I showed her I'd done it all for her?

"Can you do something like that for me?" I asked him. "For my heart?"

He smiled. "Had a feeling you might ask. So did Glinda." He turned to the chancellor. "Go fetch Glinda," he said, and Norbert squeaked obediently out the door.

We waited in the dim, cool room until the chancellor wheeled back in, with Glinda hovering above the ground a few feet behind him. Her long, strawberry-blonde hair was braided into an elaborate updo, and she wore a shimmering pink gown that looked like it was sewn from thousands of delicate pink spiderwebs. It fitted closely to her tiny waist and belled out again, cascading down to her pink slippers in shimmering waves. Her nails and lips were painted a matching shell pink, and pink gemstones glittered at her ears and throat. She was not as beautiful as Dorothy, and she never would be in my eyes, but I saw the Scarecrow's point.

"My dearest Woodman," she cooed. "How good it is to see you. The Scarecrow's little pet tells me you are here to improve yourself for the glory of Oz?"

"For Dorothy," I said stubbornly.

Glinda laughed kindly. "Your devotion is admirable, sweet Woodman. Dorothy is certainly lucky to have such a suitor."

"Do you think so?" I asked, allowing my doubt to show.

"Of course," she said gently. "You must understand that Dorothy is very busy right now, and overwhelmed by the responsibility that has been placed upon her shoulders. She's concerned about you—you mustn't ever imagine otherwise—and I know she loves you. But right now she needs you to be brave and strong and self-reliant. She needs you to be there for her, and to ask nothing of her."

"She loves me?" I looked up at her eagerly. "She told you she loves me?"

Glinda's mouth turned up at the corners in a beatific smile. "Not in so many words, but she doesn't have to. It's plain as day. All of us can see it. Can't we, Scarecrow?"

"Oh, sure," the Scarecrow said absently, adjusting one of the chancellor's gears.

"See?" Glinda said to me, beaming. "I told you. It's obvious. Now, are you ready to do your part for Oz—and for Dorothy?"

The Scarecrow turned away from the chancellor, his face alight. "Get him on the table," he said. I made as if to climb on the table myself, but an invisible hand grabbed me and carried me through the air, dumping me unceremoniously on my back. I looked up at the single overhead light that shone down on my chest. "Will this hurt?" I asked.

"You won't feel a thing," the Scarecrow said, looming over

me. He held a set of tin snips in one hand and a mysterious, multi-pronged metal tool in the other. I took a deep breath as he began to cut through my chest, peeling back a metal plate about the size of a fist. He was right; I didn't feel anything. Glinda peered down at me, her smile unwavering. There was something almost menacing about the way she was looking at me, but I reminded myself I was doing this for Dorothy.

The Scarecrow lowered his tool into the cavity of my chest and I felt its prongs close around my heart. I gasped in surprise, but Glinda was already moving her hands through the air, summoning that now-familiar glowing red material that filled the room as though we were inside an aquarium. It coalesced into a mass that hovered over me, pulsing with its eerie light, and as I gazed up into it the glow started to look exactly like a miniature thunderstorm. Red lightning flashed, and thunder boomed through the room. The clouds began to swirl faster and faster, forming a whirlpool that stretched downward into the long funnel of a cyclone. The cyclone's spout reached lower and lower until it touched the metal gadget that held my heart in place.

Energy coursed through me, sending red sparks shooting in all directions. Maybe I should have been afraid, but instead, I felt incredible—as though I held all of Oz in the palm of my hand. No wonder Dorothy was different, if she had power like this. I could control anything, do anything—and I was just a conduit for the power the Scarecrow was channeling into my heart. The little cloth heart floated upward, crackling with light as Glinda's magic poured into it.

"That's enough, I think," Glinda said. Slowly, the cyclone of magic lowered the heart back into my chest. When it was in place, the Scarecrow pulled away his tool and the red light faded, the magical storm dissipating in the dank air of his room. "See?" he said happily. "Piece of cake. Nothing to it. You're a new man." He grabbed a soldering iron off a shelf and briskly patched the hole he'd made in my chest. I sat up slowly, patting the patch. I could feel the difference in my heart. It was difficult to explain. Heavier, but also somehow more real.

"How do you feel?" Glinda asked, moving closer and putting one slender hand on my shoulder.

I looked down at my hands, at the needles and knives that had sprouted up where my fingers used to be. Suddenly they seemed exactly right. They were tools, that was all. Tools I would need in Dorothy's Oz.

"I feel great," I said, and she relaxed a little. Maybe they hadn't been as certain as they'd seemed that the Scarecrow's magic doohickey would work. But that didn't matter now. It had worked, and I was different. Stronger. Braver. Even more ready to do whatever it took to defend Dorothy.

The Scarecrow smiled at me with satisfaction. A little too much satisfaction, if you asked me. How long had he been working in secret on these experiments? What else were he and Glinda keeping from Dorothy? But I was careful not to let my suspicions show. Two could play at that game, and now I had the Wizard's new, improved heart up my sleeve. Or in my chest, as it were. I could feel it ticking away, radiating power.

"Bring in the remaining Winkies and prepare them for their transformation," I said. Norbert looked up at me sadly with his one good eye.

"But sir," he whispered. "This isn't natural. What you've done to me—"

"I've had enough of you," I snarled, striding toward him. "There's no room for dissent in the new order. Scarecrow, I want the next batch more obedient." With one swift, decisive move, I whipped out my hands and cut Norbert's throat. Blood poured out over his chest as he slumped to the ground. "That one was defective," I said. "Do better next time."

The Scarecrow and Glinda looked at me, their expressions unreadable. "As you wish, Tin," the Scarecrow said. "As you wish. Dorothy's army will be the most perfect force I can create. Now go get me some soldiers."

"By the time I'm done," I said, "you'll have every Munchkin in Oz for Dorothy's army." Their delighted laughter echoed behind me as I strode out into the hall.

There was no doubt about it. Dorothy's Oz was going to be a very different Oz indeed.

NINE

After the Scarecrow patched me up, Glinda left us, saying she had business with Dorothy to attend to. The Scarecrow watched her go, sighing in admiration. "What a woman," he said wistfully. "Do you think I have a chance?"

"No," I said. "Let's get to work."

There were only a handful of Winkies left.

The Scarecrow brought out each of them in turn, pleading frantically for his or her life no matter how many times we explained we weren't doing anything but improving them. "I don't know why you couldn't have gotten yourself appointed king of a people with more dignity," he muttered. I ignored him.

We operated on six Winkies in total. All but two of them survived the process. The Scarecrow lined them up at the far end of his chambers as he finished, where they stood blinking and quiet, waiting to be summoned.

When we were done at last he cleaned the blood off his stuffed body with a rag. "Need to get an apron," he remarked, dabbing at a tough stain. "This stuff is the devil to get out. You ready to show these fellows to Dorothy?"

I had been confident and sure of myself as we worked, but now that I faced the prospect of going before Dorothy again, I was flooded with doubt. What if she didn't approve? What if the soldiers weren't good enough? The Scarecrow was watching me sharply, and I was aware that my emotions must have been plain. I didn't want to fail her again. I couldn't bear it.

The Scarecrow ordered the Winkies to march, and they did so in eerie unison, moving their arms and legs as stiffly as robots and at the exact same time. We followed them out of his chambers. I flagged down a Munchkin servant, who eyed the Winkie soldiers with discomfort and told us Dorothy was taking the rays in her solarium. The Scarecrow let me direct the soldiers down the hall. They responded to my commands with the same mindless, automated precision they had to his, and I was reassured by their obedience. How could Dorothy not be pleased?

My beloved was reclining on a luxurious couch in her solarium, dressed in a long, soft robe and holding out one hand to a servant, who was painting her nails. Another girl behind the couch was brushing her hair. She still wore her glittering heels, and they glowed with an atomic-red light that called up in me an answering flare of clockwork emotion. A little black ball was curled up at Dorothy's feet, and I belatedly recognized it as Toto. He jumped to his feet, barking excitedly, and raced to meet us, running around our feet in yapping circles. I stooped to scratch awkwardly behind his ears with my knives.

Dorothy looked up as we came in, her perfect face drawn into a scowl. "What on earth are you doing here? I didn't send for you." Her eyes widened when she saw the soldiers. "And what on earth are *those*? Woodman, I told you I never wanted to see those filthy Winkies again. What's wrong with their arms?"

I sank down to one knee before her, but her expression didn't change. "Dearest Dorothy," I began, "you must understand, your safety is of our utmost concern. We've been working to perfect an army for you, as I promised."

Dorothy's scowl deepened. "I told you I wanted a real army, Tin, not this—this petting zoo."

The Scarecrow stepped forward, interrupting smoothly. "Ah, Dorothy, of course. And that's why the Woodman and I have worked day and night to create a new kind of soldier for you. Take a closer look, Your Eminence."

The scowl lessened a little, and she stood up, sending the nail polish jar flying. The servant girl scurried after it frantically. She walked toward the mechanized Winkies, Toto racing back and forth between us, and studied them carefully.

"The Woodman will demonstrate their commands," the Scarecrow prompted. I scrambled to my feet and ordered the Winkies to march around the room, and then to execute several coordinated maneuvers. Dorothy watched them with astonishment, clapping her hands in delight as they pivoted back and forth in front of her.

"But this is wonderful!" she cried. "You thought of this?" I began to answer, and then realized she was speaking to the Scarecrow.

"I had some assistance," he said modestly. I waited for him to mention the hours I'd spent helping him, but he said nothing.

"You've done wonderfully," Dorothy said, flinging her arms around him in an embrace that should have been mine. The ticking of my new heart pulsed faster, and I was filled with fury. I was the one who'd brought the Winkies, I was the one who'd had the idea to build an army for Dorothy, and I was the one who loved her. How dare he usurp the gratitude that should have been mine?

Dorothy released the Scarecrow and turned to face me. "Thank goodness I have *someone* useful around me." She sighed.

"But, Dorothy," I said quickly, "he couldn't have done it without my help—or my Winkies. And the army was my idea, not his."

"Oh, Tin," she said, patting me gently on the shoulder. Her touch was wonderful. "I know you try, I really do. But you keep failing me. How can I possibly count on you? You have no idea how stressful it is trying to run an entire kingdom. It's practically giving me a migraine, and I can't even find a servant who can give me a decent foot rub. Do you have any idea the pressure I'm under?"

"No, of course not," I said humbly. I felt awful. How could I live with myself if I was only adding to her burdens?

"So you see my problem," she continued. "I need to trust you, Tin. You say that you want to defend me, and that's very noble of you. I really do appreciate it. But you keep making silly mistakes, and people like the Scarecrow have to clean up after you. I want to appoint you head of my defense team, but I can't give you that kind of responsibility unless you prove yourself worthy."

I fell to my knees, clutching her dress. "I'll do anything!" I cried. "Anything at all!" At that moment, Glinda swept smoothly into the room, her eyes full of concern.

"Dorothy, what on earth are you going on about? I can hear you all the way down the hall," she said, looking from me to Dorothy to where the Scarecrow surveyed us, gloating. Then she saw the Winkies. "Oh," she breathed, "what excellent work! Scarecrow and Woodman, you've outdone yourselves. They're perfect protectors for the new ruler of Oz."

Dorothy's mouth snapped shut, and she looked at me in surprise. "You helped?"

"Yes, Dorothy," I said quietly.

"Why didn't you say anything?" she asked impatiently. "Honestly, Tin, I don't know what to do with you sometimes. Where are the rest of them?"

"The rest of them?"

"Well, this is hardly what I'd call an army," she said, her

voice cooling noticeably. "Surely there are more?"

"Dorothy," the Scarecrow said, "we've only just begun. You have to give us time."

"Hurry up, then," she said. "I haven't got all day. Just imagine what it will be like when I have an army of my very own!" She twirled around the room like a little girl, and my heart soared. I wanted to do what I could so that she'd always be this happy. And once she was happy, she'd really, truly be mine. I wasn't going to fail her again. I knew what I had to do.

"I will build you an army, Dorothy," I said. "I'll build you an army the likes of which Oz has never seen. No one will harm you, or even dare to try."

Dorothy stopped her dance and threw her arms open wide. "If only Aunt Em and Uncle Henry could see me now!" she cried. Behind her, Glinda was smiling, although the smile didn't reach her eyes. The Winkies were frozen at attention, their grotesque metallic hands to their foreheads in matching salutes. The Scarecrow was snickering next to me, and Toto yapped and ran around the room. Inside my chest, my new heart swelled with such joy that I thought it might burst out of its patchwork housing, and I could almost see the pulsing glow that matched the flaring red of Dorothy's shoes like a beacon shooting out from my chest. I turned to the Scarecrow.

"Prepare your workshop," I told him, loud enough for Dorothy to hear. "The soldiers and I ride out into the countryside tomorrow. Dorothy's army must have new recruits."

"The people aren't going to like that," the Scarecrow said quietly.

I heard rather than felt the ticking of my heart. "The people don't have a choice," I said, and Dorothy laughed in delight. For her, I would raze the villages of Oz to the ground if I had to. Everything was different now, and everything was going to keep changing. Dorothy had come back to Oz at last.

THE STRAW

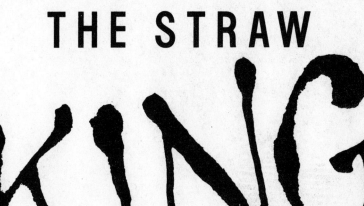

ONE

"Did you know there's a hidden district of Oz where the talking pastries can seek refuge?" The Scarecrow was sitting on a pile of books in the Great Library of the Emerald Palace, turning the pages of an enormous encyclopedia volume.

"Too bad we can't eat them now," the Lion rumbled. "Are you done with that book yet? Can we go outside, at least?"

"I'm only on Volume 23 of *The Collected History of Oz: Its Landscapes, Customs, and Peoples*," the Scarecrow said peevishly. "There are thirty more volumes." The Lion groaned aloud, but the Scarecrow ignored him.

His greatest regret since he started reading was that he could not read them fast enough. He had decades of history to catch up on—he'd spent his entire early life tied to a post in the cornfield, after all. He'd gone so long without a brain, and the thought of all that wasted time was nearly enough to make him cry—except, of course, that he couldn't. At least he was a king now.

That was something. He was powerful. He was smart. And he was getting smarter by the minute.

"Aren't you done yet? I *really* want to eat something." The Lion roared and stretched, rolling over on his back and gnawing at the spine of one of the Scarecrow's books.

"Knock that off!" protested the Scarecrow. He was startled by the flash of anger in his old friend's eyes. Since he'd arrived in the Emerald City a few days ago, the Lion had been constantly restless. He seemed almost ferocious—a far cry from the terrified creature who'd journeyed with the Scarecrow, Dorothy, and the Tin Man through Oz. Scare was happy for his friend's newfound confidence, but sometimes he wondered if the Lion had lost a little something when he gained his courage. Sure, the Lion used to jump at the sight of all creatures smaller than him, but seeing this big creature wearing his fear on his sleeve made the Lion more approachable. Now, as the Lion's muscles rippled beneath his fur and his lips curled up in a growl, the straw in the Scarecrow's stuffed arms stood on end.

The Scarecrow, giving in to the Lion's hunger pangs, rang for one of the servants. Fiona was the smartest Munchkin on his household staff, with a mind that moved as quickly as a Kalidah and an uncanny ability to sense his whims before he even knew what they were. Sometimes, the Scarecrow wanted to crack open her brain just to see how it worked. Not literally, of course.

"Is the old tin can on his way?" the Lion asked, but there was affection in his voice. Scare felt it, too. They'd decided to celebrate the second anniversary of the Scarecrow's coronation with a reunion. The three friends hadn't seen each other since little Dorothy had returned to the Other Place and the Wizard had made the Scarecrow King of Oz, the Lion King of the Beasts, and the Tin Woodman King of the Winkies. Privately, the Scarecrow thought he had gotten the best deal out of the three friends. The beasts were unruly and had fleas, and the Lion didn't even have a proper castle. The Winkies were short, unattractive, and quite dull. But King of Oz! That had a nice ring to it, the Scarecrow thought, looking at his old friend as he lay sprawled across the throne room floor picking his teeth. And he had plans, for his friends, for himself, and for all of Oz. At night he lay awake, his newly expanded mind roving through all the possibilities. Once he had read everything about the history of Oz, he'd be prepared to be a great king. More than anything, he wanted to see his own name in one of those books someday, with a long list of great deeds. But the greatest accolade of all would be for him to be recognized as the wisest ruler Oz had ever had. He hadn't told anyone of his secret dream—not even the Lion.

The Scarecrow still wasn't used to his title. He told himself that he wasn't as bad a ruler as the Wizard, who'd secreted himself away in the Emerald Palace and who'd been a fraud besides. Plus, he had his brand-new brain. Sometimes he could almost hear it whirring away in his head, thinking all sorts of new thoughts.

"He sent a messenger," the Scarecrow replied. "He had some royal business to attend to, but he'll be here as soon as—"

One of the library windows shattered in an explosion of

broken glass, and something whizzed past the Scarecrow's ear and buried itself in one of the books behind his head.

"What in the name of Oz?" he asked, leaning in to inspect the precious volume. Another projectile flew by and hit one of the floating sunfruit-fueled lamps, sending fruit and chunks of glass flying.

"What is it?" shouted the Lion, jumping to his feet. The Scarecrow picked a lump of metal out of *Anthropomorphicum Catalogarium: A Bestiary of Magical Creatures, Their Diets & Their Habitats*. "This book is priceless," the Scarecrow moaned. "Why, if I told you the lengths I had to go to—" Another piece of metal flew in through the broken window, narrowly missing his other ear.

"To the Deadly Desert with your stupid books!" the Lion gasped, flattening himself onto the carpet. "We're under attack! What *are* those things?"

"They're bullets," the Scarecrow said wonderingly at the tiny piece of metal in his palm. "I've read about them, but I've never seen one. They come out of a gun."

"They're going to kill us both, whatever they are," the Lion growled, knocking the Scarecrow to the ground as another rain of bullets hailed down on them.

"*I* can't be shot," the Scarecrow reminded him.

"Well, I can," the Lion said curtly, creeping stealthily to the window and gesturing the Scarecrow to keep low. "What in the name of the Wizard is going on out there?" He peered over the sill.

Rows and rows of girls, standing in military formation, stared back at him. They wore identical uniforms: tightly fitted leather leggings and pointy-toed stiletto heels with flared minidresses made of chain mail. Each unsmiling mouth was painted the same shade of cherry red, and each girl's fingernails were polished a matching crimson. Each girl's glossy hair swung in a matching ponytail. And they brandished matching pearl-handled silver pistols, all of them pointed at the palace.

The girls parted ranks to make way for another girl, this one riding a chrome-plated moped. Her chain mail minidress was shorter, her lipstick was redder, and her ponytail was higher. She had an unmistakable air of authority.

"I am General Jinjur of the Ladies' Military Auxiliary of Oz!" she shouted, firing another shot into the air. "You ain't the real king, you old strawbag, and I'm dumping you out on your straw behind! Come on down, meet my girls—and bring your big scaredy-cat friend with you!"

TWO

"My goodness," the Lion said in surprise, peering down at General Jinjur. "What on earth can she possibly mean? And I'm certainly not cowardly anymore." He lashed the tail the Wizard had given him and growled.

"I don't know," the Scarecrow said. His new brain was racing. An all-out attack on the Emerald Palace was unprecedented—at least in the history he'd read so far. No one had ever tried to oust whoever was in charge. "Keep her busy," he hissed to the Lion as General Jinjur fired another shot into the air.

"Busy doing what?" the Lion asked incredulously, but the Scarecrow was already racing over to his bookshelves, running his finger across the spines. "*Botanica* . . . no, not that one," he muttered, reading aloud. "*Herbarium Magisterium* . . . *Tax Codes of the Quadlings* . . . *How to Cook for a Rigmarole* . . . aha! *Despots of Oz: Their Way, or the Highway!*" Triumphantly, he pulled the book off the shelf and flipped frantically through the pages. "Chiss . . . Dr.

Pipt . . . Eureka the Kitten . . . Evoldo . . . Gayelette . . . the Hungry Tiger—here we are! General Jinjur of the Western Lands!"

"What on earth is a book going to tell us?" snapped the Lion, who was trying to drag one of the library's heavy bookcases in front of the broken window as Jinjur and her soldiers fired round after round of shots at the library. "Come down, you cowards, and meet the future of Oz!" she shrieked. "I know all three of you are in there!"

"All *three* of us?" the Scarecrow asked, looking up from his book.

"She must mean the Woodman," the Lion panted. He'd managed to move the bookcase a few inches and was now slumped against it before he tried again. "Why would she want to kill all three of us?"

"'Jinjur is a fearsome warrior but not a clever one,'" the Scarecrow read aloud. "'She has long coveted the throne of Oz. In the time of Dorothy, the Witchslayer, she gathered her all-girl army to make a move on the palace, but was thwarted when the Wizard gave mighty gifts of magic to Dorothy's noble protectors, the Lion, the Tin Woodman, and the Scarecrow. She remains a threat to the sanctity of the throne of Oz.' That's all it says, really. Something else about how she thinks men are too incompetent to rule."

"You're not a man, you're a scarecrow," the Lion said, pushing the bookshelf another inch. "She must think the three of us are somehow in her way. Poor Tin. We ought to warn him somehow."

"Should we go down and meet her?" the Scarecrow asked anxiously. "I haven't gotten to the books on military strategy yet. I never thought I'd need them."

The Lion frowned. "I bet I could take her. But those pistols could do a number on my hide," he said. "Doesn't the palace have an army to fend off invaders?"

The Scarecrow smacked himself on the side of the head, jostling his new brain. Of course! The Royal Army! What had he been thinking? Sometimes he wondered if the Wizard's gift wasn't slightly defective. He ran to a corner of the throne room and pulled a tasseled velvet rope. A deep, melodious gong sounded in the depths of the palace, and a moment later a tall, lean old man tottered into the throne room.

"Royal Army at your service, my lord," he croaked, sounding like a tree creaking in a strong breeze. The Royal Army didn't look very promising, the Scarecrow thought. His armor was dented and scuffed, and in several places pieces of it seemed to be missing. His sword was broken. His long, scraggly white beard was dotted with what looked to be toast crumbs. A pair of cracked spectacles slid down his big, beaky nose, and he looked around him with a slightly bewildered air. Still, he was better than nothing.

"The castle is under siege," the Scarecrow said quickly. "I need you to go downstairs and take care of things."

"Take care of things, sir?"

"You know," the Scarecrow said vaguely. Warfare was new to him. "Drive them off, or something. I haven't read about giving orders yet. You're the army, don't you know these things?"

"All the way downstairs, sir?"

The Lion stood on his hind legs and roared, and the Royal Army jumped about a foot in the air. "Yes, all the way downstairs!" the Lion bellowed. "Your king has ordered you!"

"Yes sir, right away, sir," gasped the Royal Army, his face white in terror. He bowed twice and ran out of the room. A second later they could hear his metal-tipped boots clattering on the stairs.

The Lion's courage might prove useful, the Scarecrow thought as he went back to the window to watch the Royal Army deal with the invaders. He'd always seemed such a silly creature during their adventures in Oz, frightened of practically anything. But clearly the Wizard's gift was taking hold. The Scarecrow didn't tell his friend his uncertainties about his own gift. Something stirred at the back of his mind, something that suggested it was better to keep that suspicion to himself for now. Something almost alien, like a cold serpent moving in a dark burrow. The Scarecrow blinked, and the feeling went away.

Below them, the Royal Army rushed out of the palace to confront General Jinjur, brandishing his broken sword. "Cease and desist at once!" he squeaked, waving the sword at her. "His Royal Highness demands it!"

Jinjur laughed, her voice carrying easily to the Scarecrow's window. "That old thing ain't no royalty," she called out scornfully. "The Wizard didn't have no claim to the throne, and you can't pass on what ain't yours. We're here to put Oz in proper order." She tossed her ponytail, and behind her the girl soldiers saluted smartly.

"How?" the Royal Army asked.

Jinjur smiled. "Why, I'll take power, you daft old coot." She cocked one hip and winked at him. The Scarecrow stared in disbelief. He was absolutely certain he'd never come across anything like this in the history he'd been reading. Attacking the Emerald Palace? Demanding the throne? She knew the Lion, the Scarecrow, and the Woodman were supposed to be there together—had she been spying on the palace all this time?

The Royal Army lowered his sword and looked up at the Scarecrow, clearly waiting for instructions. Getting rid of her was going to be harder than he had thought. The Scarecrow had no idea how to deal with this strange girl and her sinister army, and the Wizard's brain wasn't offering him any answers. The Lion seemed to sense his confusion.

"I could go out and help," he offered.

"Help what?" the Scarecrow asked. If only his brain really worked! What would the Wizard have done in his place? Again, that feeling stirred at the back of his mind, and suddenly a thought occurred to him. He was the King of Oz; he should probably start acting like one. He straightened up.

He went out onto the balcony and looked down at the girl. He paused before speaking, curiosity outweighing everything for a moment. Knowing why she was holding the gun mattered more than any fear he had about her shooting at him again.

Jinjur stared up at him, a nasty smile playing over her

bright-red lips. The Scarecrow felt a sudden twinge of anxiety. No ruler of Oz, he was sure, had ever faced a challenge quite like this.

"I am sure that we can come to some kind of understanding, Ms. Jinjur."

He could reason with her—he could reason with anyone. Wasn't that the point of the Wizard's gift? His own books had said she wasn't clever.

Jinjur laughed. "The only understanding I need is that you're even worse at this job than the Wizard, and the three of you are standing in my way." She narrowed her eyes. "Where's the other one? The metal one?"

"He's in the kitchen," the Lion lied quickly.

"I want you to get him. And then I want all three of you down here." She fired a bullet into the ground.

"I'm actually quite a good ruler," the Scarecrow protested. "I haven't raised taxes, and I've settled dozens of petty disputes. And I'm going to establish the most wonderful thing you can imagine—a school system for the Munchkins of the Emerald City. Next I'll create schools for all of Oz!"

"We don't need no *schools* in Oz!" Jinjur snapped. "You're unnatural and you ain't a proper king. You don't belong any-where but in a field on a post."

Now Jinjur's words hit him somewhere below the brain.

He realized in that instant that she was not reasonable. And it was time for him to act like a king.

"I will not bow to threats!" he boomed down at General

Jinjur. "Leave the palace at once, and do not return!"

It appeared they were at a standstill. Scare cocked his head to the side, wondering how this would play out. He had done what his books said was kingly, but she was not moving.

"It's time for a new era in Oz." She leveled the pistol at the Royal Army's chest, and, still smiling, pulled the trigger.

THREE

For just a second, time stood still. The Lion and the Scarecrow stared, gaping, at Jinjur's smoking pistol. The Royal Army's jaw dropped in shock. And then he looked down at the red stain spreading across his chest. He lifted one hand as if to touch the wound, his expression bewildered. And then, slowly, he toppled sideways and hit the ground with a thud, his eyes open. A glistening red pool spread outward from his inert body.

The Lion growled, but the Scarecrow was speechless. In all of his reading, he had heard of nothing like this ever happening in the history of Oz. Battles, perhaps—but not cold-blooded murder. That was the domain of the witches. Over the years, a few people and animals had gotten caught in the cross fire of their seemingly eternal battle of Good versus Wicked. But Ozians didn't kill other Ozians, not like this.

There was no time to think. With a scream of triumph, Jinjur fired another shot into the air, and her army surged toward the palace, trampling the Royal Army's body into the ground. "Now it's your turn, Straw King!" she screamed. "You and everyone who serves you will bow to us—or die!"

"We have to get out of here," the Scarecrow hissed, snapping to attention. The Lion growled again and lashed his tail.

"I say we fight," he snarled. Despite the seriousness of the situation, the Scarecrow almost laughed.

"Don't be foolish," the Scarecrow said. "There's only two of us, and this awful girl has an entire army who won't hesitate to— to—" He couldn't quite bring himself to finish the sentence. The Royal Army's broken body was seared across his vision.

"The palace is full of Munchkins!" the Lion exclaimed. "Surely we can hold off these upstarts. The Munchkins will fight for us." Already, they could both hear screaming and crashing as the invaders made their way through the palace. The sounds of breaking glass and splintering wood filled the air.

"The Munchkins don't know how to fight," the Scarecrow protested. "None of us do. No one's ever had to fight an invading army in the history of Oz."

"Speak for yourself," the Lion growled. "I'm not cowardly. I'll fight."

"I'm not cowardly! I'm *sensible*." The Scarecrow weighed their options. He didn't like the idea of leaving the Munchkins. But running away would buy him time to come up with a plan— a strategy for how to deal with General Jinjur.

"Jinjur only said she'd kill people who opposed her," the Scarecrow pointed out. "As long as the Munchkins follow her orders, they should be safe. She's here for us, not them."

Shaking his head, the Lion paced to the window and looked out. The courtyard was empty; all of Jinjur's soldiers had poured into the castle already, and they hadn't bothered to leave a guard outside. The body of the Royal Army lay in the mud where they had trampled him, broken and battered. Suddenly they heard metal clattering on the stairs, and a girl's voice yelling "He's in here!" A chorus of bloodthirsty shouts followed her pronouncement. "Kill him!" someone else screamed. "Tear out his stuffing and burn it!"

"Jump on my back!" the Lion barked.

"What?" The door banged open so hard it slammed into the wall and splintered, and girls ran into the room, taking aim with their weapons.

"Just do it!" roared the Lion. The terrified Scarecrow lurched forward, grabbing the Lion's mane desperately. Even before he had swung his leg over the Lion's back, the Lion leapt out the window as bullets zinged past him. "Hold on!" the Lion shouted as the Scarecrow shrieked wordlessly in fear. The ground rushed toward them at unbelievable speed. The Scarecrow would have covered his eyes, but then he'd have to let go of the Lion's mane.

The Lion hit the ground with a thud that knocked the wind out of both of them, but there was no time to recover. Screaming girls hung out the window they'd just jumped from, and bullets thumped into the dirt all around them. Somehow, the Scarecrow had kept his deathly tight grip on the Lion's mane during the landing. He could feel the Lion's muscles bunching underneath him as his friend began to run.

More soldiers streamed out of the main gates of the palace, howling bloodthirsty cries and taking shots at the escapees, but they couldn't match the Lion's speed. Soon, their pursuers fell away behind them, and their warlike shrieks faded away, to be replaced with the Lion's hoarse, gasping breath. "Out . . . of . . . shape!" he panted. But he continued to run until there was no sign at all of Jinjur or her army, finally slowing to a walk when it was clear they were well away from the castle.

The Scarecrow finally allowed his fingers to relax their grip on the Lion's mane, and he slid from his friend's back and collapsed on the ground, too shaken to sit up. The Lion sat down with a sigh, sprawling. "We shouldn't rest long," he said. "They'll be after us. Nasty piece of work, those girls."

The Scarecrow was so tired and frightened he couldn't think. "Where will we go? What will we do?"

The Lion gave him an amused look. "You're supposed to be the one with the brains, Scare. You can come back to the Kingdom of the Beasts with me, if you want. You'll be safe enough there, and you can figure out what this Jinjur wants and where she came from."

The Scarecrow shook his head. "She said she wanted to rule Oz," he said, bewildered. "But the Wizard said *I* should be king. Isn't that enough?"

"Apparently not," the Lion rumbled. A thoughtful look crossed his face. "Oz is changing, old friend, whether we like it or not. An invasion of the Emerald Palace—I've never heard of such a thing either, and I was a cub long before you were put on a pole in that cornfield. Even when people were dissatisfied with the Wizard's rule, they never would have tried to oust him. But now . . ." He chewed the end of his tail. "You've spent all your time in the library, old friend, and not enough letting the people of Oz know you're their king. Jinjur saw an opportunity and took it. She must have been plotting ever since the Wizard took power, but it wasn't until you took over the throne that she saw her chance."

"But how can I be a good king if I don't know the job?" the Scarecrow asked, his voice plaintive. "Reading is the only way to learn."

The Lion looked at him solemnly. "Maybe it's time you learn by doing," he said.

FOUR

The Lion did not let them rest long. Sniffing and growling to himself, he paced around in the grass until he got his bearings, and then he urged the Scarecrow to his feet. The Scarecrow privately hoped his friend would continue to give him a ride, but the Lion did not offer and the Scarecrow didn't ask. "The forest isn't too far," the Lion said as they started walking. "We'll have to take care not to leave a trail, but we should be there within a day of walking."

The sun was high in the sky, and warm on their backs. The Scarecrow began to feel peevish. Already, the horror of the Royal Army's death was fading. And now all he could think of was getting his precious books back. And the Munchkins, too, of course. "Tin is still on his way to the Emerald Palace," he said suddenly. "We have to warn him."

The Lion shook his head in disbelief. "Of course. I can't believe I didn't think of it. We'll tell him to take cover until we figure out what to do next."

"The Winkies might fight for us," the Scarecrow argued. "We should tell him to meet us in the Forest of the Beasts."

"The Winkies? Fight? I don't think so. And you know Tin's more of a lover than a fighter himself." The Lion chuckled at his own joke, and then reared up on his hind legs, bellowing a sequence of guttural roars that sounded like a strange code. He waited for a few minutes and then roared again. Suddenly a huge old crow descended out of the blue sky, landing in front of the Lion and cocking its head.

Looking at it, the Scarecrow felt a sudden churning where his stomach should be. His straw rattled just a bit but he stilled himself. The Lion, all animal instinct, turned to him.

"Scare?"

The crow wasn't one of the ones the Scarecrow had known when he was tied to the post in the field, not that long ago, before he received his gift. But it was a crow all the same.

"You owe *me* a favor, fleabag," it croaked to the Lion.

"I'll settle that once and for all after I'm back in the Forest of the Beasts," the Lion said silkily. "But I'm afraid I need just one more thing from you."

The crow snorted and ruffled its ratty feathers. The Scarecrow wondered if it would even be able to take off again. The bird was so ancient it looked as though it was next to death. It cocked its head at him and cawed in delight.

"The King of Oz!" it exclaimed, its beady eyes meeting the Scarecrow's. "I didn't even recognize you, sirrah. You've come a long way from the cornfields." It bowed in a way that somehow managed to be sarcastic.

"I'm not afraid of you," the Scarecrow managed, keeping his voice even.

The crow cackled, flapping its wings in merriment. "No, too clever for that!" it shrieked. It laughed so hard it fell over in the dust and had to struggle mightily to right itself.

Scare narrowed his eyes at it. He wasn't in the field anymore. He did not have to stand for this.

"Bow before your king," he said firmly. So firmly, that Lion glanced at him in surprise.

The crow cocked its head to the side, as if considering another comeback.

The Lion growled at the crow so loudly and with such wind that the crow's feathers shook.

The crow complied, touching its beak to the ground. When it rose, the Lion gave it instructions. And when the Scarecrow looked it in its beady eyes again, the crow looked away first.

"You will take a message," the Lion said wearily. "Our friend the Tin Woodman is journeying to the Emerald Palace, but he must return to the land of the Winkies for now. The palace has been overtaken by an enemy force."

At that, the crow looked startled. "But such a thing has never—"

"Yes, we *know*," the Scarecrow interrupted. Seeing the crow bow for him for real had somehow energized him. He could focus again on what was important—keeping Tin safe. "If he goes to the palace unprepared, he'll be riddled with bullets and torn apart for scrap. You have to warn him."

The crow eyeballed them both, looking as though it wanted to protest, but decided against it. "Very well," it said, flapping its wings vigorously and launching awkwardly into the air. "But I'll never help you again!" it shrieked at the Lion, before it caught an updraft and was gone.

The Lion looked at the Scarecrow critically.

"That was fun, but you know there's no bowing on the battlefield."

The Scarecrow looked at him for a long beat, and answered, "I know."

The Lion studied him, and the Scarecrow could see a wave of recognition break across his broad face. The Lion knew the Scarecrow's history with the crows.

"I could have picked another kind of messenger. But time is so short," he said, his voice gruff but gentle.

Scarecrow's brain was expanding faster and faster every day, so much so he sometimes worried he'd outgrow his dear old friend. But in moments like this, he knew that the Lion and Tin and Dorothy would always understand him no matter what.

The Scarecrow shook his head. "Crows are effective messengers. And like you said, time is short."

"Still, it's a nasty old thing," the Lion said under his breath. "Ruling the beasts is a real chore sometimes. They're not like your Munchkins. They don't sing and work the day away. They devour it. Every moment is a challenge. Anyway," he added in a normal tone, "the message will tell him to take cover. We might be able to rally the beasts to your cause."

"It's *your* cause, too," the Scarecrow pointed out. "I'm supposed to be your king."

"Of course you are, old friend. I just wanted to make sure it's what you wanted . . ."

"Why would you say that?"

"I know your brain is up to the task, Scare. But the way Oz is going you're going to end up with some blood on that shiny new uniform of yours . . . Oz is changing . . . but do you want it to change you?"

It was Scare's turn not to answer. At least not out loud. He needed time to think, to do more research. But he knew one thing—he was going to rule Oz intelligently. He was going to create a world where the mind was valued above all else. He'd go down in history as the cleverest king Oz had ever had.

He took a deep breath and looked at his friend. "Lion, I want to be kind more than anything. And I want to educate all of Oz."

The Lion looked at him a long beat, his tail standing on end like it did when he was figuring something out. "You mean like have everyone go to school?"

"Exactly," he cried.

"That's either the dumbest or most brilliant thing I've ever heard," Lion said with a laugh, and began moving again.

Scare felt a spring in his straw step after that. Saying it out loud had given him even more energy. But Lion's earlier assertion still haunted him a bit . . . His sawdust-stuffed brain struggled to process everything that had happened. Maybe the Lion was right; while Scare had been shut in with his books, Oz was changing. If that were the case, he'd have to find a way to keep up. But how could he fight off an entire army of invaders? There was no way he could retake the castle by himself. He'd have to think of a way to get the Lion to help him, maybe even all of the beasts. And that was going to take more craftiness than he'd ever used in his life. The Scarecrow smiled grimly to himself. If Oz itself was changing, so could he.

Looking at the landscape, Scare realized he hadn't been on a real adventure since Dorothy had landed in Oz, rescued him from the field where she'd found him, and swept him up in her quest to find the Wizard. He owed everything he was now to that girl and her funny dog. He wondered absently where she was now. Back in the Other Place, he supposed. If only he had a way to send her some kind of message, to tell her what had happened in the palace. The Scarecrow's new brain had been helpful when he was the King of Oz, but he secretly had to admit that he wasn't entirely sure it was up to snuff when it came to totally new situations like a coup and an invading army. But Dorothy would have known how to deal with Jinjur, he was sure of it. She'd figured out a solution to all the problems they'd faced before.

Dorothy was the reason that he had come up with the idea of education. She'd told him about her schools back home. Apparently, the very young went there and learned about the world. If Oz had had one of those, maybe Jinjur wouldn't be so ignorant and this whole mess wouldn't be happening.

He sighed. He wished he could bounce his current predicament off Dorothy. It didn't matter. He had no way of reaching her, and he would have to deal with this strange new situation himself. He'd already come a long way from that sad stuffed creature languishing away in a cornfield. He'd helped Dorothy defeat the Wizard, gotten his brain, and become the King of Oz. Surely he could manage the coming conflict without the help of a child from another world. The Lion would have been ashamed of him if he'd spoken any of his doubts aloud. He stood up straighter as he walked, determined to turn over a new leaf, but hoofbeats on the path behind him caused him to turn.

"Get under cover," the Lion growled, pushing him toward a row of bushes. "*Now.*" The Scarecrow dove behind a bush, with the Lion close behind him, as the mysterious rider thundered toward them. They peered through the branches as the horse galloped past. Its haunches were smeared with blood and gore, and its rider was in even worse shape, barely clinging to its dirt-clumped mane. The horse was moving so quickly that it was difficult to make out the rider's features, but the Scarecrow was certain it was a Munchkin—and it had looked absolutely terrified.

"Wasn't that one of the palace horses?" the Lion asked.

"And I think that was one of the palace servants," the Scarecrow said, nodding.

The Lion frowned. "Perhaps he or she was just fleeing the battle."

The Scarecrow felt his brain stir, almost as if he were revving a motor. "The battle is over," he said decisively. "It was over as soon as the Royal Army was killed and we left the palace. We've been walking for a while. This is something else."

The Lion nodded thoughtfully. "If we see another rider, we should stop him and ask—as long as it's not one of Jinjur's soldiers."

"I'd certainly rather not be captured by the likes of them," the Scarecrow said with a shudder.

Scare heard a strange, whooshing sound, but when he and Lion continued, all they found were more trees. As they pressed forward, Scare felt a few drops of rain landing on his lapel.

He looked down as another drop landed on his hand. It wasn't rain. It was dark red.

It was blood.

"Lion?" he said in a whisper. He looked up. Above him, a Munchkin was caught in some kind of elaborate web. The web was cutting into her skin, drawing drops of blood.

A little voice cried, "Help me."

FIVE

It took the Lion what seemed like a million excruciating minutes to tear the little Munchkin out of the tree. As Scare tended to her cuts, tearing cloth from his own palace finery, he noticed that she was a young, female Munchkin, dressed in a scullery uniform that was tattered and bloodstained. A purple bruise colored her left eye, and blood still trickled from where a clump of her hair had been torn out at the roots. Her eyes stared up at him, unseeing, and she was trembling with fear.

"It's all right," the Scarecrow said as gently as he could. "It's only me." She was too upset to move on her own, so the Scarecrow and the Lion carefully carried her away from the path in case another rider—or one of Jinjur's soldiers—appeared.

"What happened?" the Lion growled. The Munchkin's eyes seemed to focus, and a quizzical expression flashed across her face.

"Your Majesty?" she asked, looking from the Lion to the

Scarecrow. "Is it really you?"

"It's me," he reassured her. "And my friend the Cow—" The Lion growled deep in his throat. "The Lion," the Scarecrow amended hastily. "What's happened? Did you come from the palace?"

"Oh, Your Highness!" the Munchkin wailed, bursting into tears. "It's so aw-aw-awful! Your Highness, you must come back and help us! Those g-g-g-*irls*!" She dissolved into sobs, and for several minutes made no sense at all. The Lion and the Scarecrow were forced to wait for her hysterical fit to subside as the Scarecrow patted her awkwardly on the back. She took several deep breaths, finally getting control of herself.

"I'm sorry, Your Highness," she said in a low voice. "Only it's so awful, what's happening at the palace. Jinjur's been killing the servants left and right. She says we're conspiring with the usurper—that's you, sir, begging your pardon—and we have no place in the new regime! I snuck out of the palace in one of the laundry carts and was trying to walk to safety, but Jinjur's forces must have set some kind of trap on their way to the palace."

It was worse than he imagined. A question, errant and wrong, bubbled up before the images of dead Munchkins replaced it: *But how are my books?* He stuffed it down and focused on his poor subjects. He had left them to be slaughtered.

Scare spotted the Lion, whose mood had turned to vigilance. The Lion was crouched in punching mode and his eyes were darting around the forest ceiling. Scare looked around the forest, imaging new dangers everywhere—he spotted another web stretching low between two trees glistening in the waning Oz light.

The Munchkin girl began to cry again. "We're only trying to do our jobs, sir, just as we've always done. We don't mind if it's you ruling Oz, or the Wizard, or Ozma—our place has always been in the Emerald Palace. But now . . ." Her voice broke.

The Scarecrow tried another tack. "Hibiscus Lemon . . ."

"You know me?" she asked, so surprised that her tears were forgotten. She looked up at him; her big eyes blinked themselves dry.

"Of course I do. East wing. Not terribly good with the duster but a master seamstress. Which is of particular importance to a king who is held together by needle and thread . . ."

To test his growing intellect, he'd memorized every Munchkin's name and face and a few of their attributes.

Hibiscus Lemon didn't smile but her tears stopped falling. That was something. He squeezed her tiny hand gently, and she leaned against him. She weighed less than nothing, but he could feel the weight of all that was lost back at the palace all over again.

"This Jinjur person is getting more awful by the second," the Scarecrow said quietly to the Lion over her little green-haired head.

"It's certainly unprecedented," the Lion agreed. "Perhaps Jinjur saw you as vulnerable."

"Me? Vulnerable?" the Scarecrow sputtered. "Of course I needed to get a feel for things still, but I was certainly learning how to do an excellent job as king. And like the book said, she is clearly not in any position to judge me."

The Lion looked at Scare as if he was trying hard to figure him out. "I never know anymore whether you want me to answer or whether your question is rheumatical?"

"Rhetorical," the Scarecrow corrected.

The Lion shrugged his hulking shoulders as if this somehow proved his point.

"Can't you help me, Your Highness?" the Munchkin asked desperately.

The Lion rose with a sigh. He cast a sympathetic glance at the Munchkin but then gave Scare a look that said they needed to move.

The Scarecrow had no idea what to tell this poor creature. How could he possibly help her? He had to get to the Forest of the Beasts with the Lion and find a way to reclaim the throne. But the Lion was looking at him intently, and the teary-eyed Munchkin was staring at him with beseeching eyes. He couldn't just leave her here. The Wizard had given him brains—surely he could come up with a solution to her problem.

A spark of inspiration hit him. "Where were you hoping to go?"

"To my family, sir." She pointed down the path. "They live in a Munchkin village at the edge of the Forest of the Beasts."

The Scarecrow was delighted by this convenient turn of events. "Then we shall escort you there," he said grandly, feeling generous and magnanimous. Picking up people to help along a journey reminded him of the trip down the Road of Yellow Brick with Dorothy, and that had turned out better than they ever imagined. At the very least he could help this one girl.

Hibiscus Lemon nodded, but he could see from her far-off stare that his clever solution hadn't done much to reassure her. Still, he was certain it was just what the Wizard would have done, and he was pleased with himself. She was not like him—knowing the next move had lifted a bit of the weight off his straw-filled chest. He assumed that the Munchkin would not feel better until she saw her home again and was safely in the arms of her parents. The Lion did not comment, but the Scarecrow could sense that he approved, or at the very least, was happy they were moving and no longer sitting ducks for any of Jinjur's army.

The three of them set off in the direction the girl had been heading. They saw no more riders on the road, and the Scarecrow wondered if any of the other palace residents had escaped Jinjur's forces. He certainly hoped so. The memory of the Royal Army's trampled body flashed in front of his eyes. It was horrible to think of the same thing happening to other residents of the palace. His people. What if Jinjur had killed poor Fiona? Or the sweet Munchkin chef who oversaw the kitchens?

"Hibiscus Lemon, when you were . . . did you happen to see Fiona?" he managed as gently as possible.

Hibiscus shook her head. And opened her mouth, but the effort brought more tears.

He wished that she'd answered differently. That she'd seen his favorite little maid escaping to safety. But at least she'd not said that he'd seen her hurt by Jinjur. He opened his mouth to ask more, but he closed it again. In this one case not knowing felt better than knowing, especially when he knew that whatever she had to say would not be good.

With Hibiscus Lemon taking the Scarecrow's former place on the Lion's back, the journey passed quickly, and soon the Scarecrow could see a small village in the distance. The Munchkin perked up visibly at the sight of her home. "Ma and Pa will be happy to see me," she said, straightening her bloodied dress. "I haven't been home in ages. Everyone's home—you can see the smoke from their cooking fires."

But as they got closer, it was obvious something was wrong.

"Are those grislybirds?" the Lion asked in a low voice. The Scarecrow looked up. Dark shadows circled and swooped in the air above them.

Grislybirds were hulking and silent creatures. Unlike other animals in Oz, they didn't speak—which made them all the more terrifying. Not to mention they fed on dead flesh. The Scarecrow shivered.

As they drew closer, he could see that the smoke wasn't coming from the chimneys. The thick, dark, oily plumes were rising from the huts themselves. The village was on fire.

"Jinjur's army was here first," the Lion said quietly.

"But why?" cried the Munchkin, breaking into a limping run.

The Scarecrow's mind raced and came up with a solution. "She said that she'd kill anyone who supported me," he said, guilt washing over him with every step closer to the charred

pastel houses. "The Munchkins have always been loyal to whoever sat on the throne. They had no idea she'd kill them for not
yielding to her coup. The Munchkins have never been fighters—there's probably not a single weapon in the entire village.
They were totally unprepared."

"My parents! I have to make sure they're alive!" the Munchkin girl sobbed, her bloodstained face now streaked with tears.
"I don't have anything left!"

"Wait!" cried the Scarecrow. "For all we know, some of Jinjur's soldiers stayed behind to finish the job!"

The Lion nodded in agreement, but Hibiscus tore away from
them and ran toward her ruined village. Up close, the destruction
was awful. Many of the houses had been burned to the ground,
and others were only partially standing. Through the scorched
and blackened walls, the Scarecrow could see tables still set for a
meal, as though the occupants had just stepped outside. But the
charred corpses in the streets suggested that none of the Munchkins had gotten far.

Scare scanned the faces for ones he knew. None of them
worked at the palace. He did not know them. But they were his
people all the same. They were his responsibility as king and
now they were gone.

The once carefully tended flower beds that lined the road
were trampled, and blood had pooled between the paving stones.
The Lion lowered his head, sniffing at one of the dark puddles.
"Still warm," he growled. "The soldiers just passed this way."

Ahead of them, Hibiscus screamed. She had sunk to her

knees in front of the house that must have been hers, and she wasn't alone. The Scarecrow had been right: they weren't alone in the village. One of Jinjur's soldiers had been left behind, and she was holding a knife to the Munchkin girl's throat.

SIX

The Lion leapt forward with a roar. "Wait!" the Scarecrow cried out. The Lion twisted in midair and dropped back to his feet. Jinjur's soldier grinned at them over the terrified Munchkin. She grabbed a hank of the Munchkin's hair and jerked her head backward, her knife pressing so deeply into the girl's throat that a line of blood welled up beneath it. The Munchkin's eyes were huge with fear.

"Welcome, Your Highness," the soldier sneered. "Do you like what we've done with the place? Anyone not loyal to the new queen will learn the cost of disobedience—immediately."

"Let the girl go," the Scarecrow said firmly. "Your quarrel is with me. You've already shed enough blood for one day."

Jinjur's soldier laughed. "Spoken like a true fool," she snarled. "Welcome to the new Oz." With one swift motion, she drew her knife across Hibiscus's throat. The Scarecrow cried out in horror as blood spurted from the gaping crescent wound. The soldier let the girl's body go. Her body teetered ghoulishly for a second and then fell to the ground with a sick thud.

"Hibiscus Lemon." Her name escaped his cloth lips, which trembled with rage and sadness all at once. For a split second, Scarecrow wished that he had never known Hibiscus's name. That he did not know a thing about her. Maybe that would have made looking at her lifeless little form easier. But a second later he was glad he had known at least that.

Out of the corner of his eye he could see the Lion was already leaping forward with a snarl, his claws extended. Jinjur's soldier whirled to meet him but he knocked the knife from her hand easily with one swipe of his huge paw. She lunged at him with her bare fists, her face totally without fear. But even she was no match for the Lion. He threw her to the ground and stood over her with his paw upraised. "Don't hurt her!" the Scarecrow cried out, but it was too late. Jinjur's soldier spat in the Lion's face, and with a terrible roar he brought his huge paw down on her skull, snapping her neck.

Everything seemed to stand still for a long second. The Lion stared down at his victim, panting. The Scarecrow realized his mouth was wide open and he was watching the sinister tableau with his hands balled into fists. He could feel that strange, sinister serpentine thing stirring in the back of his sawdust brain, and the Lion's tail was lashing furiously as though it were possessed. The Lion ripped out the soldier's throat, spraying them both with blood.

"What are you doing?" Scare cried, coming to his senses.

The Lion stopped mid-roar, his eyes crazed and his mouth dripping gore.

"I don't—I don't know," he gasped. The Lion slumped backward and all the rage seemed to drain out of him into the blood-soaked ground.

"A new Oz, indeed," the Scarecrow said quietly.

The Lion stepped away from Jinjur's soldier as if the ground burned his paws, leaving her body next to Hibiscus Lemon's in the dirt.

"What happened just now?" the Scarecrow asked, staring down at the stranger who seemed to have taken the place of his oldest friend.

"We were too late to save the girl," the Lion said hoarsely, not meeting his eyes. That wasn't what the Scarecrow had meant, and they both knew it.

Without another word, the Lion turned and stepped back onto the path, and the Scarecrow followed. From time to time, they heard distant cries and the sound of gunshots—more of Jinjur's soldiers, the Scarecrow guessed grimly, taking care of the disloyal. But for now there was nothing they could do. They continued walking in silence. The Scarecrow could feel his saw-dust brain churning, trying to process what had just happened and what would happen next, but it was too much for him to comprehend.

"The Wizard gave us these gifts, but he never told us how to use them," Scare said finally. At first, he thought the Lion was ignoring him, but after a minute his friend sighed.

"It's better not to think about it too much."

"But that's all I know how to do," the Scarecrow protested. The Lion didn't answer. He wondered if his learning curve would be as fast as the Lion's evidently had been, and if he'd figure out the solution in time to save Oz from Jinjur. But if the Wizard's gifts meant they'd have to become murderers, how were they any better than the would-be queen?

Ordinarily, he would have enjoyed the trip to the Lion's country. He hadn't traveled since Dorothy had rescued him from his post in the farmer's field and gone with him to find the Wizard, and before he met Dorothy he had never traveled at all. The path took them along a roaring brook that flowed with lavender-scented water; translucent, jewel-bright fish glinted in the current like bits of glass. They crossed a broad meadow of multicolored flowers that undulated like waves even though there was no breeze. The snow-topped mountains sparkled in the distance, and butterflies the size of the Lion's head flapped lazily past them. But the Scarecrow barely noticed the wonders of Oz, he was so preoccupied with his thoughts.

"Do you remember the Kalidahs?" the Lion asked suddenly, interrupting his reverie.

"Of course," replied the Scarecrow, surprised. He, the Lion, the Woodman, and Dorothy had almost been killed by the terrifying tiger-headed monsters on the way to the Emerald City, and only the Woodman's quick thinking had saved them. He'd destroyed the bridge the beasts were crossing, sending them plummeting to their deaths in the ravine below.

"I was so afraid of them then," the Lion mused. "I couldn't have managed to kill them, even though they were threatening our lives. But today . . ." He trailed off, but he didn't have to finish his thought for the Scarecrow to guess what he was getting at.

"The Wizard's gift is working for you," he said.

The Lion shrugged. "I suppose so. I've never had to test it before." He looked briefly troubled. "I've never killed anyone before either. It felt strange."

"Strange?" The Scarecrow didn't think "strange" was the right word,

Lion was a killer.

Scare had read books about beasts and he knew technically that was something that beasts did. But Lion wasn't like the other beasts, was he?

Jinjur's soldier had killed the Munchkin girl, and would have killed them, but killing her wasn't any better. Murder was murder, even if it was self-defense.

"I don't know if I liked the feeling," the Lion said, "but it felt different from anything I've ever done. I felt powerful. I suppose that's what courage is. I just never knew before."

Scare was sure that wasn't right. In fact, the way Lion said it kind of scared him.

"I know I didn't ask for courage . . . ," Scare began, preparing to tell him just that.

"Maybe you should have," the Lion said. "We'll have to do it again."

"Do what again?"

"Kill people. If you really want your throne back, it won't happen peacefully."

The Scarecrow had not thought that far ahead. "There must be another way," he said immediately, but his brain hit a brick wall that did not move.

"If there is, you'll have to think of it," the Lion said. "You're the one with the brains." The Scarecrow wondered whether his old friend was mocking him, but the Lion seemed serious.

"This isn't what I wanted at all when I asked for a brain," the Scarecrow said unhappily. "I didn't even ask to be king—I just wanted to be clever. Do you think the Wizard's gifts led to what's happening now?"

The Lion swished his tail. "I don't see how," he rumbled. "Perhaps the Wizard's gifts are the tools we need to deal with what's coming."

"What *is* coming?"

"I don't know," the Lion said quietly, "but I don't think it's going to be very good."

SEVEN

The Scarecrow had never visited his old friend's new home, and despite the circumstances, he looked around in wonder. From a distance, the forest's boundary was so pronounced it looked like a giant green wall looming over the landscape. A golden meadow, grass gently waving in the breeze, ran straight up to the forest's edge and stopped abruptly. Golden jewelflies buzzed in the tall grass and were snapped up by emerald-green belly-frogs that burped tiny puffs of pink smoke after their meal. Flat sapphire pools glinted here and there, but when the Scarecrow stooped down to touch the fresh-looking water, his fingers flicked against diamond-hard gemstone.

It was beautiful. But he could never live like this. Where would all his books go?

As soon as they set foot inside the forest barrier, the sunlight vanished as if someone had thrown a light switch. The Forest of the Beasts was eerily quiet, as if the Lion's subjects somehow already sensed that trouble was brewing.

The Scarecrow rubbed his button eyes, squinting in the sudden dimness. Lion was nocturnal, so he was used to the dark, but the Scarecrow hesitated. The Lion looked back with a sigh, then looped his tail around Scarecrow's wrist, guiding him. All around them the towering brown trunks rose into the shadowy forest canopy, and the silence of the forest was as thick as a blanket. The Lion rose up on his hind legs, leaning his paws against the nearest tree, and made a sound somewhere between a cough and a roar. Out of nowhere a large rabbit scampered up to them; he was wearing a neatly cut velvet suit, and a tiny top hat was tilted at a rakish angle over one of his ears. His buckteeth protruded at a slightly ridiculous angle.

"Your Majesty!" the rabbit cried, clapping his paws together. "We've been so anxious to have you back!" The rabbit caught sight of the Scarecrow, and a startled expression passed across his face. "I beg your pardon, Your Majesty," he said, executing a sweeping bow. "I didn't see that the King of Oz was with you." He bowed again, this time at the Scarecrow.

"It's all right," the Scarecrow said, in a way he hoped was regal.

"Can't we have some light, Cornelius?" the Lion rumbled, and the rabbit clapped his paws together again.

"His Majesty will fire me for my foolishness!" he exclaimed to the trees. He ran back and forth in agitation, pawing frantically at his top hat.

The Lion sighed and dropped to all fours again, settling back on his haunches and opening his mouth in a huge yawning roar. "LIGHTS!" he bellowed.

As if by magic, a storm of tiny lights swirled up out of the earth, spinning around them. Each one of them was a tiny firefly that buzzed upward, landing on the trees and branches until they were thickly covered in glowing light. A small army of badgers, foxes, and weasels carrying stringed instruments rushed in after the fireflies, assembling themselves in an unruly group in front of the Lion and the Scarecrow and striking up a slightly out-of-tune march. Cornelius produced a golden banner depicting a lion from behind a tree and waved it back and forth. "His Majesty has returned to the Forest of the Beasts!" he bellowed. The Scarecrow heard cheering from the depths of the forest, and soon more and more animals poured into the clearing where they stood, jostling one another as they each tried to get closer to the Lion.

Cornelius rudely pushed aside a bear cub, a crocodile with rows and rows of jagged teeth, and several rats. "Clear a path for His Majesty!" he shouted pompously. The animals ignored him, and he shoved them more aggressively until finally they moved aside. The Lion walked forward, and the Scarecrow followed him through the forest.

It was difficult for the Scarecrow to make his way through the woods. The animals surged around him and sometimes underfoot, nearly tripping him. The trees grew densely together, and while the Lion wove around them with ease, the Scarecrow had to pick his way. His clothes caught on the underbrush, and branches hit him in the face. "I'm a long way from the palace," he thought, and he didn't realize he'd spoken aloud until the Lion laughed.

"It's not the luxury you're used to," he agreed. The Scarecrow resented the implication that he'd gotten soft, but he said nothing. The Lion would see soon enough how tough he could be, when he found a way to regain his throne and restore order to Oz. No one would doubt him then.

At last they reached another clearing, this one much bigger than the one where they'd met Cornelius. Animal skins were rigged overhead on a network of ropes and pulleys, forming a kind of canopy. At one end of the clearing was a lopsided structure that looked like a rickety, giant wooden jungle gym, with more animal skins piled on various wooden platforms and ledges. The Lion leapt up onto it, and the whole arrangement creaked and wobbled. The Lion yawned as his subjects flooded into the clearing.

"Home at last!" he sighed in satisfaction. "I'll need something to eat." He looked pointedly downward, and several badgers seized a young deer who was staring obliviously in the other direction. It struggled briefly, but the badgers subdued it and dragged it up to the Lion's platform. The Lion licked his lips happily and the Scarecrow looked away in horror as he dove into his snack. The Lion had said he'd never killed anyone before, but apparently that didn't extend to animals.

"It's part of the job, you know," someone said at his side, and he looked down to see Cornelius.

"Eating your subjects?" the Scarecrow said, aghast. Cornelius shrugged.

"He's a lion. It's his nature. He doesn't mean to be cruel. He's doing it to survive. Killing for sport is something only humans do. The rules are different here, Your Majesty. We all understand the law of the forest."

When the Lion was finished eating, he belched loudly, and a hush fell across the clearing. He turned his gaze to the Scarecrow.

"Now we must decide what to do about the throne," he said. News had traveled fast, the Scarecrow realized; the gathered animals began to shout out suggestions. "Eat the impostor!" shrieked a bobcat. "Bury her in a burrow!" yelled a fox. "Chew off her toes!" squeaked a mouse. The Scarecrow almost groaned aloud. He could just picture the Lion's menagerie charging the palace and falling dead within seconds to Jinjur's bullets. They were no match for her. At least not without a good plan.

"I need my books, Lion," he said suddenly. He'd find the perfect strategy in one of those volumes. He just knew it.

A silence fell over the animals. And then the Scarecrow heard what could only be described as a giggle that quickly turned into a roar of laughter. . . .

"Leave us, all of you," the Lion growled. "This is a matter for the Scarecrow and I to decide. Cornelius, bring me Lulu."

"Lulu will know what to do!" yelled a dormouse excitedly, before one of its companions hushed it.

"Who's Lulu?" the Scarecrow choked out, sure that the

fabric of his face was on fire.

"Help." The Lion glanced at him and raised a bushy eyebrow. "And maybe don't mention the b-word again, if you want the beasts to take you seriously. We're not big readers in the forest."

The Scarecrow nodded. He wasn't in the palace anymore.

"I wouldn't mind dessert," the Lion mused, and the rest of the animals fled.

EIGHT

The Scarecrow was eager to meet this mysterious, powerful Lulu. Would she be wise, like him? Or a fierce warrior? Perhaps she'd even be both. He twiddled his gloved thumbs impatiently as the sun sank below the treetops and the first stars drifted down from the sky.

"Get yer dirty paws off of me, you stinking rabbit!" bellowed a hoarse voice from the shadows. The Scarecrow sat bolt upright. A small, hunched figure was trundling toward him wearing some kind of enormous cloak and slapping furiously at the exasperated Cornelius. "I can find the damn Lion by his smell!" it added crossly, stepping into the light.

"Oh no," the Scarecrow groaned. Things had just gone from bad to worse.

Lulu was a winged monkey. And the Scarecrow *hated* winged monkeys. During his travels with Dorothy, the Wicked Witch of the West had used the Golden Cap to command them to destroy the Scarecrow and the Woodman and capture the Lion. The monkeys had torn him to pieces, and the Winkies had had to put him together again. Dorothy had taken the cap when she'd defeated the Wicked Witch, and the winged monkeys had carried them to the Emerald City. But he'd never entirely forgotten what they'd done to him first.

The King of the Winged Monkeys had been a huge beast, powerfully built and regal, but Lulu was neither large nor frightening, and she certainly didn't look like royalty. She was a young, wiry monkey whose wings had not reached their full growth, and she was wearing a miniskirt and a leather biker jacket studded with garish fake rubies and with two holes cut in the back to accommodate her wings. A pair of sunglasses was perched on her snub nose, and she carried a candy cigarette in a long holder, which she waved around when she talked.

"You sent for me, Your Majesty?" she drawled, leaning against the Lion's platform.

"Lulu is one of the cleverest beasts in my kingdom," the Lion explained to the Scarecrow while Lulu preened. "She'll be able to help us figure out what to do about—"

"You want to dump that Jinjur bitch, am I right?" Lulu said briskly, snapping her fingers. "Send her packing? Make all those girls with guns look for her at the bottom of a river?"

The Scarecrow was not impressed, and he was irritated the Lion had summoned this bizarre creature without so much as consulting him. "I won't have any problem finding a way to oust the usurper myself, if you don't mind," he said coolly.

Lulu laughed out loud. "Right, like you've been doing such a great job of that so far. Listen, sonny, there's a reason the big boy over here called on me." She puffed up her chest. "I'm the smartest thing in Oz, and today's your lucky day—I'm willing to help you get Jinjur out of the palace. Of course, if you don't mind me saying so, I think the real question here is who ought to replace her."

"What do you mean?" sputtered the Scarecrow.

"I think the cards are clear. You're not fit to rule, or else you'd still be ruling. Me, on the other hand"—she tapped her lapels— "I'm the one you want running the show."

"Lulu, that's enough," the Lion said, clearly amused by the monkey's brazenness. "I summoned you here to help us plan our attack, not belittle the Scarecrow's abilities."

Lulu shrugged. "It was worth a try. No hard feelings?" She looked at the Scarecrow expectantly.

The Scarecrow mumbled a reply, but inside he was seething.

"Then it's time to get down to business," Lulu said, miming rolling up her sleeves. "The obvious plan is to attack immediately, but we need to use stealth if we're going to win. Word on the street is she's got bigger numbers, but her soldiers will probably be sitting around on their heinies twiddling their thumbs now that they've taken the palace. If we surprise 'em, we stand a chance, but I'm picturing casualties."

"Exactly my point," the Scarecrow began. "Which is why I don't think—"

The Lion spoke over him as if he hadn't even opened his

mouth. "My thoughts exactly, Lulu," he said. He leapt down from his platform and sketched a map of the surrounding area in the dirt with one claw. "We have too much ground to traverse if we want to sneak up on the Emerald City," he pointed out. "Jinjur's soldiers will see us coming a mile away."

"Not if we fly," Lulu said triumphantly. "The rest of the monkeys will be happy to help, I'm sure of it. We're dying for something to do. We'll land just outside the Emerald City and sneak in." Her expression turned serious. "All reports are that Jinjur is ruthless. The few people who've escaped from the palace don't have pretty stories to tell. We'll have to be prepared."

"But I don't want—" the Scarecrow said, and again the Lion interrupted him.

"My people will fight," he vowed. "Oz has never had a tyrant on the throne, and we won't start now. When Jinjur is taken down, we can discuss who should replace her."

At that, the Scarecrow made a noise of outrage, and both the Lion and Lulu finally stopped talking as if they had both just noticed he was there. "*I* will replace Jinjur when she is defeated," he snapped. "And we certainly won't be attacking the palace directly. She'll see us flying in from a mile away, too. A better solution would be to—"

Lulu sighed loudly, cutting him off. "Listen, sport," she said, "you had your chance, and you blew it. Now it's time to stand aside and let people who can handle the job take over."

The Scarecrow was mad at Lulu, but even madder at himself. While he was trying to think of a plan and remember what he'd read, Lulu had raced ahead of him and presented her own. The Scarecrow wanted nothing more than to protest again, but he realized he was outnumbered. The Lion's subjects wouldn't be likely to side with him, and if the winged monkeys were anything like what he remembered, they'd hardly back him up either. He had no choice but to go along with Lulu and the Lion's suicidal plan until he had the opportunity to act—and to think of something else. If he didn't use the Wizard's gift to find a better answer, all of Oz would be plunged into a war—and he would rather die than see that happen.

NINE

Lulu wasted no time in assembling the winged monkeys. She put two fingers in her mouth and blew a piercing whistle that was so loud it sent Cornelius running for cover. Even the Lion flinched. Moments later, a squadron of monkeys in flight helmets and goggles descended into the clearing, stirring up a small dust storm with the furious beating of their wings.

"Right, chaps!" Lulu barked as the monkeys folded their wings. "It's time to fight. Are you ready to do right for your country?" It wasn't entirely clear to the Scarecrow why the monkey had such authority over her brethren, when many of them were clearly much older and bigger than she was, but the monkeys paid careful attention to her.

"Why do you listen to her?" he asked the nearest monkey quietly.

"Lulu'll be queen any day now," the monkey whispered. "And she's a little . . . you know." He twirled a finger next to his ear. "No sense starting off on the bad side of the one who's next in line for the throne. Plus, as batty as she is, she's a sharp cookie."

The Scarecrow perked up. "She's smart and she's to be queen? Do you think she'd talk to me about ruling?"

The monkey shot him a scornful look. "Lulu *earned* our respect," he said.

Respect or no respect, the other monkeys were busy arguing with Lulu. But she at least had their attention.

"Why should we fight? What's in it for us?" one of them ventured.

"I'll see to it personally that everyone's banana ration is increased," Lulu said confidently. "And extra holidays after we've won."

"You don't have the authority to do that," another monkey pointed out. Lulu didn't miss a beat.

"Not yet," she said. "But do any of you doubt me? You listen to me because you know I'm headed for big things, and I'll reward the monkeys who support me." She glowered menacingly at the monkeys who'd come to her summons. "And I'll never forget the monkeys who don't," she added. "So it's best not to cross me."

The monkeys conferred among themselves briefly, and then the first monkey who had spoken stepped forward. "We'll help," he said.

The Scarecrow thought he saw a flicker of relief in Lulu's eyes, and he wondered if she was really quite as confident as she seemed. He wondered if it meant more to appear certain than to be right.

"Glad to see you know what's best for you," she said. She turned to the Lion. "We can transport you into battle, but you'll have to assemble the troops," she told him. The Lion nodded.

"Find the best fighters in the forest," he ordered Cornelius. "Tell them we head for the Emerald City at dawn." Cornelius nodded and dashed away. Once again, the Scarecrow had been left out. But if he was honest with himself, he had to admit that he was dealing with a different kind of smarts. Lulu had established herself with bravado and intimidation. The Scarecrow had never practiced either of those arts. He was better with facts and figures. But now that they were standing over a makeshift map of the palace and the grounds that one of the more talented monkeys had etched in the dirt, he felt like he should be ready to step up. Only he hadn't read a book on cartography yet. And he was unfamiliar with the logics of monkey flight. He absolutely hated that.

The monkeys ignored him completely as they discussed wind currents and angle of approach, and even the Lion seemed to have forgotten he was there. He might as well be back in that field tied to a post for all the good the Wizard's gifts were doing him. He knew he could find the answer, if only he had enough time. If only he had his books! Why hadn't he at least tried to save a text on theoretical military strategy when they'd fled the palace?

Suddenly a bright pink-tinted light flashed in a distant part of the forest. The Scarecrow leaned forward, peering into the trees. In a few seconds, the light flashed again, but this time it didn't vanish. It flickered through the trees like pink firelight. The Scarecrow looked back to see if anyone else had noticed. They hadn't. "I'll go see what that is," he said unnecessarily. No one stopped him, or even looked his way, as he stepped out of the clearing and began walking toward the light.

This time, the way through the forest was somehow easier. The trees seemed to be making room for him as he crashed through the underbrush. He tripped once or twice, but never fell, and the light grew steadily larger. It was almost as if whatever the light was, it wanted him to find it. After a few more minutes of walking, he reached a gap in the trees and saw the source of the light.

It was a woman, although her face was so youthful and flawless that he couldn't have begun to guess her age. She was wearing a simple, pale dress in a color somewhere between eggshell and rose, and her long golden hair tumbled around her shoulders in loose curls. She was the one glowing with that strange, magical light, the Scarecrow realized. It filled the air around her like a cloud. As he came toward her she smiled, looking up at him through her long eyelashes with strangely familiar crystal-blue eyes.

"Hello, Scarecrow," she purred, her musical voice as sweet as honey. "It's so good to see you again."

If he had had a jaw, it would have dropped. *"Glinda?"* he asked in disbelief.

Glinda giggled, reaching out her manicured hands to him. "It's been so long!" she cried, hugging him close. She smelled like jasmine and something even sweeter—so sweet, in fact, that it was almost rotten.

"But what are you doing here?" the Scarecrow asked, bewildered.

"Tin is too far away to help us," she said. "And the Lion— well, there's a reason I'm coming to you first, but I'm not sure I want to tell you what it is. It might . . ." She paused, her eyelashes fluttering again. "It might hurt your feelings," she said seriously.

"I don't understand," the Scarecrow said. "Why are you in the Lion's forest, if you don't want to see him? What would hurt my feelings?"

Glinda took a deep breath. "It's just that the Lion isn't very clever," she said. "Not like *you*, Scare. Is it all right if I call you that? I always felt I had so much more in common with you than I did with the Lion and the Woodman—not that they're not wonderful, but you're the one who asked for a brain and got one, and I've always been something of an intellectual."

The Scarecrow was so happy he hardly knew what to say. "Then you think I've been doing a good job?" he asked anxiously. "You take me seriously?"

"Of course I take you seriously," Glinda said immediately. "That's why I've come to help. I know what's happened in the Emerald City, and I've dealt with Jinjur before."

"You have?"

"Oh yes. She comes from the west. She's always been power

hungry and quite mad. I knew she'd do something like this sooner or later, though I never dreamed she'd have the nerve to try and unseat a ruler as strong as you. But I know her, and she won't stop at the throne. She'll move out across the rest of Oz, destroying everything in her path. You must stop her and regain the throne, and I can help you. That's why I've come back."

The Scarecrow hardly knew what to say. Glinda was a witch, he knew, but he'd never known a witch to get much more involved in politics than enslaving the Winkies for her own ends, or controlling the winged monkeys with a magic cap like the Wicked Witch of the West. Not that Oz had really *had* politics before. Just the witches battling it out. But that wasn't political. That was something else. Was she talking about using magic to defeat Jinjur? And if so, was she really that powerful? And where had she come back from? She was hiding something, of that much he felt sure. But he couldn't begin to guess at what it was, or if she was holding something back because she thought that he wouldn't be able to bear it. He hadn't been upset by her comments about the Lion, had he? Why was she trying to protect him?

"You doubt me," Glinda said, a hint of coolness in her voice.

"No, of course not!" the Scarecrow protested. "It's just that everything is changing so quickly. The Lion and the winged monkeys want to go to war tomorrow, and I think they have the wrong idea. We should be using strategy to get rid of Jinjur, not brute force. She's already shown she's powerful and ruthless." He raised his hands in a helpless gesture. "But they won't listen to me, and I don't see how you and I can stop them by ourselves."

"We won't," Glinda said calmly. "We'll wait for them to fail, as you know they will. When they're ready to see their way is the wrong one, they'll listen."

"But we have to warn them! If they go into battle tomorrow, they could be hurt—or even killed!"

"Casualties are inevitable in any war," Glinda said, that previous coolness creeping back in. "If I'm going to help you, Scare, I have to know you're willing to do whatever it takes, even if that means sometimes people you care about get hurt. We're past the point of protecting everyone from danger now. Don't you see that?" Her voice grew urgent. "Danger is *here*, Scare! We have to do what's necessary, or even more people will be lost. Do you understand? Tomorrow, I want you to hide during the fighting. You're a thinker, not a fighter. I need you to be strong and clever—and I need you to stay alive." Glinda pulled a glowing pink bottle out of thin air and handed it to the Scarecrow. "Drink this tomorrow," she said. "It'll keep you hidden—and safe."

"I can't drink," the Scarecrow said, bewildered.

"Trust me," Glinda replied. Obediently, he tucked the bottle into one of his pockets.

"I just want to go back," the Scarecrow said, his mind reeling. "I want Oz the way it was, before any of this happened." He sank to the ground and put his head in his hands. "It's all so much."

Glinda crouched down beside him and put a gentle hand on

his shoulder. "You have to be strong now," she said into his ear. "There's no other way. You know I'm right."

And of course, he did. She was so strong, so sure. There was something about her that was so persuasive he forgot all of his questions. He'd let the Lion and Lulu go into battle in the morning—it wasn't as if he could stop them. And if Glinda really was right, they'd lose, just as he'd thought.

"But what will we do after tomorrow?" he asked. "How will we come up with a plan?"

"I know you'll think of something," Glinda said. "You always do."

He sat up a little straighter. Did he really? He wasn't sure, but if Glinda said he did, it must be true. She was a witch, and she knew even more than he did. Her powers were mysterious and apparently far stronger than he'd ever guessed. "Of course," he said. "You're right. I'll think of something."

"I knew I could count on you," she said, and he felt a glow of pride that matched the radiant light emanating from Glinda. "It's best that we keep my return from the south a secret for now. The others will be too surprised that I'm back in Oz and wielding magic again, and the less distraction we have right now the better. No matter how clever you are, it's clear the Lion and Lulu won't listen to you until their own foolish plan has failed. When the time is right, I'll reveal myself, and you'll tell them the details of your brilliant plan."

"Shouldn't I be planning a way to convince them we're right before they go to war tomorrow?" the Scarecrow asked. Glinda frowned the tiniest of frowns.

"The Lion asked for courage, not brains," she said. "He won't listen until he has no other choice. There's no other way."

Nothing Glinda was saying quite made sense, but every time he tried to think about it that strange, sinister feeling at the back of his brain stirred and he forgot his doubts again. After all, why was he questioning Glinda? She was an all-powerful witch—and a good one, too. She'd only ever helped him when Dorothy had traveled with them in Oz. No, she was on their side, there was no doubt about it. His new brain just wasn't powerful enough yet to keep up with hers. He was reluctant to send his friend and the Lion's subjects into danger, of course, but if she said there was nothing else they could do she had to be right. She wanted to avoid bloodshed just as much as he did. She was a good witch, after all.

Seeing his agreement, Glinda leaned in and gave him a kiss on the cheek. The cloth felt warm where her lips had been when she pulled away.

"Be clever," she said. "And be strong. I'll return soon." The pink light flashed once, and she was gone.

The Scarecrow stared into the dark forest, thinking hard. It would be up to him to save the day when the Lion and Lulu had failed. He couldn't let them down—and as importantly, he wanted Glinda to know she'd made the right choice to trust him. "You don't fail a woman like that," he said aloud into the dark. "Not even once."

TEN

Scare was on the post again. His legs and arms were bound. All he could see in every direction were fields of corn. And crows.

One

Two

Three

Four.

They each landed on him and began their cawing and pecking—*Stupid Scare . . . Stupid Scare . . . Stupid Scare . . .*

Scare awoke with a start. The crows weren't real. He wasn't back on the post again, his arms and legs unable to move. Back then, he'd spent day after day, night after night wishing he had more to occupy himself than counting the crows that perched on him. They were not at all afraid of him. And they were not his friends either. He had longed for two things back—friendship and a brain—and now he had both, he reminded himself with a sigh that rustled his straw.

Lion snored as loudly as a steam engine, and there was no escaping the noise that filled the clearing that served as his throne room. His snores were echoed by the cacophonous breathing of Lulu's winged monkeys, who sprawled out across the ground sound asleep. The noise was awful. But it was a relief compared to the dream.

All the same, the Scarecrow's heart sank when the first rays of dawn flooded the forest. No matter how convincing Glinda's arguments had been, the fact remained that his friends—and he—were headed into danger, and some of them would not survive. There was no way around it, he told himself firmly. He could no more have prevented it than he could have changed the time the sun rose and set every day.

Cornelius rushed into the clearing at the break of dawn, wearing a shiny, fringed chain mail shirt and banging vigorously on a rabbit-sized drum. "To arms!" he shouted. "To arms!" The sleeping monkeys stirred, and more animals began to file into the clearing. These were the soldiers Cornelius had picked out, the Scarecrow realized: they were the fiercest and most intimidating of the Lion's subjects, wildcats and badgers and several wolves, one of whom was already licking chops bloodied by whatever unfortunate creature it had eaten for breakfast. They all eyed the winged monkeys warily, and for a brief moment the Scarecrow wondered what would happen if they refused to be carried.

But the Lion explained Lulu's plan quickly, and everyone seemed to agree. Each of the Lion's warriors paired up with a monkey. The Lion was so large that it took two monkeys to lift him.

"I'll take you," Lulu barked to the Scarecrow. Lulu was the smallest of the winged monkeys, and the Scarecrow was the lightest of everyone attacking the castle, since he was only made of straw, so he could hardly argue. But he wasn't happy about being paired with the brash, obnoxious little monkey. Lulu grabbed his shoulders unceremoniously and lurched upward, flapping her wings wildly. "Let's go!" she yelled. "No dilly-dallying on my watch!"

All around them, the monkeys launched into the air, most of them with far more grace than Lulu had managed. A few of their passengers looked a little green, and one bobcat struggled frantically, nearly forcing its monkey to drop it to the ground, before it managed to calm down enough to allow itself to be carried. Despite his anxiety about what lay ahead, the Scarecrow couldn't help but enjoy the flight. He'd only had a handful of chances to fly before, and the first of those had been more than a little unpleasant.

Below them, Oz looked like a patchwork quilt. They were passing over farm country, and green and gold fields made neat squares across the landscape. "Look!" the Lion called out, pointing one massive paw to the east. "It's the Road of Yellow Brick. We're headed in the right direction."

"Of course we're headed in the right direction," Lulu muttered. "I'm no dummy. Unlike *some* people," she added under her breath. Unsure whether she was insulting him or the Lion, the

Scarecrow kept his mouth shut. He'd been dropped by a winged monkey once before; he had no wish to repeat the experience.

Flying to the Emerald City was far quicker than walking, and they hadn't been following the undulating golden ribbon of the Road of Yellow Brick for much of the morning before the green gleam of the Emerald City appeared on the horizon. As soon as he caught sight of that familiar bottle-green light, the Scarecrow's doubts returned, and he forgot all about the pleasures of the journey. There was no way Jinjur could fail to see them coming, no matter what Lulu said, and he had a feeling she'd be ready for them when they arrived.

The city rushed toward them. Its streets were eerily deserted instead of their usual thriving bustle. The gates, ordinarily manned by a gatekeeper, stood wide open, but the sight was sinister instead of inviting. "We'll carry you over the gates," Lulu said in a low voice. "Be ready for action as soon as we drop you on the other side." The monkeys landed silently, gently dropping their passengers to the ground and folding up their feathered wings without making a sound.

The Lion waved a paw, and his warriors moved into a loose formation, muscles rippling under their sleek coats. In the forest, they had looked frightening enough. But here, ready for battle, they looked lethal. The monkeys had no weapons, and the Scarecrow wondered how they would defend themselves. Thankfully, he didn't have to worry about that, assuming Glinda's potion really could protect him. She wouldn't let him risk his life, would she?

The beasts were alert, ready for danger. The Scarecrow could almost smell their readiness to fight.

But the city was empty. Everywhere, doors stood open and windows were unshuttered. Bread filled the shelves of the bakeries, and fruit stalls overflowed with exotic fruits from every part of Oz. But there were no people. The Scarecrow looked through the doorway of one house and saw that a half-prepared meal had been left in the kitchen. It reminded him of the burned-out Munchkin village, except that here there were no flames and no bodies. It was simply as if everyone had left the city at once in the middle of whatever they'd been doing.

"What did Jinjur do to the city?" whispered a stoat that slunk alongside the Scarecrow.

"I'm not sure I want to know," the Scarecrow admitted. Up ahead, Lulu made a slashing motion with one paw to silence them. There was no sign of Jinjur's soldiers. Could they possibly win the battle without even fighting it? If they did win, would Glinda still return? He hoped so. *She* believed he was the rightful King of Oz. Surely she'd be able to convince the Lion and Lulu to support him, and he knew Tin would, too. With Glinda on his side, he'd be back in power in no time. He could even appoint her a royal adviser.

The army crept stealthily through the deserted streets until they reached the edge of the castle grounds. The sense of abandonment was somehow even worse. Someone had left gardening tools and a wheelbarrow next to one of the flower beds. Tarpaulins were scattered here and there, perhaps the beginning of a construction project. In a side yard, drying laundry hung on a line. The air smelled faintly of cooking.

The palace gates were shut tightly, and there was no sign of life behind its windows. Lulu led them right up to the gates, and then stopped short. "There's no way in," she hissed.

He looked around them. Something wasn't right. His brain was working furiously. If Jinjur had wanted to protect the Emerald Palace, she would have barred the gates to the city, not left them open for anyone to wander through. Why was the city empty? Why was the castle undefended? The Scarecrow's brain worked furiously, analyzing every possibility, until he realized the truth.

"It's a trap!" he cried out, running toward Lulu. "We have to get away from the palace! It's a trap!"

ELEVEN

He was too late. All around them, Jinjur's soldiers threw off the tarpaulins that had concealed them from the Lion's army. More emerged from shallow trenches they'd covered with strips of sod. The Lion's army was backed up against the impenetrable wall of the castle, with Jinjur's soldiers blocking any possibility of escape. Jinjur had known they were coming all along, and lain in wait until she could trap them against the palace itself.

Lulu realized what was happening a second after the Scarecrow did. "To arms, monkeys!" she bellowed, whirling to face the oncoming soldiers. The dead-eyed, grim-faced girls were impossible to tell apart. Even their armor matched. They raised their identical pistols, surging toward the Lion's forces.

Suddenly the winged monkeys rose up into the air, and for a brief, terrible moment, the Scarecrow thought they were abandoning the battlefield. But one by one, the monkeys began to dive-bomb Jinjur's soldiers. One monkey grabbed a girl and flew up into the air with her. She screamed in fury as he soared upward, dropping her at the top of his arc. She hit the ground with a sickening crunch. The other monkeys quickly followed suit, seizing Jinjur's soldiers off the battlefield and hurling them at the ground or the castle walls. Gaping in terror, the Scarecrow was rooted to the spot by the sight of the carnage in front of him.

"There he is!" Jinjur screamed. She was dressed for battle in bloodred armor, and her lipstick was an even brighter shade of red. "The Straw King! Destroy him!" She was pointing directly at him. The nearest of Jinjur's soldiers raised their pistols, firing a hail of bullets that ripped through his cloth arms and legs.

"Oh no!" the Scarecrow said. Then he turned around and ran.

"Get him!" Jinjur screamed. "Don't let him escape!" But the Lion's army leapt forward with a furious roar, laying into the soldiers with claws and teeth. The girl soldiers, distracted by the onslaught, fired madly into the oncoming menagerie. A crocodile snapped its huge jaws shut on a girl's arm, ripping it from her shoulder. A wolf darted forward, tearing out another girl's throat. For just a moment, it seemed like the fight might turn in their favor. In the total chaos, the Scarecrow was momentarily overlooked. Dodging flying bodies, he made his way to the edge of the carnage.

But Jinjur hadn't forgotten about him. Her moped had been outfitted for battle: spiky armor plated each side, forming a protective shell that covered her legs. A gun was mounted above its windshield that fired rapidly into the melee. She carried a pistol in one hand and a sword in the other, piloting the moped with her feet. She slashed furiously with her sword hand while somehow aiming and firing shot after shot with the other. Her soldiers rallied around her, and more and more animals began to fall to the blood-soaked ground as she cut her way toward the Scarecrow.

The potion, you idiot! Glinda's voice was as clear in his ear as if she'd actually been standing next to him. Of course! He fumbled in his pocket for her potion and it slipped through his fingers, clattering to the ground. A stray bullet thudded into the earth inches from the bottle, sending it flying. "No!" the Scarecrow moaned, diving after it. Jinjur was nearly upon him, screaming with rage and firing shots into the air. At the last moment, he reached the bottle and fumbled with the stopper.

"Good-bye, you pathetic excuse for a man," Jinjur sneered. He looked up in terror. She loomed over him, her weapons glittering in the sun. Her pistol was pointed directly at his head. The bullets might not cause lasting damage to his arms and legs, but that didn't mean a shot between his eyes wouldn't end him. Jinjur tightened her finger on the trigger just as the Scarecrow rolled frantically to one side and tilted Glinda's bottle toward his mouth. He squeezed his eyes shut and waited for the end.

All around him, the sounds of the battle vanished as suddenly as if someone had brought the lid down on a piano. The Scarecrow opened one eye. He was still alive. Jinjur was still standing over him, but her pistol hand had dropped to her side and her face was a mask of confusion and fury. Her mouth moved, but he couldn't hear a sound she was making. He was surrounded by a shimmering pink bubble, magic moving across its surface like an iridescent sheen. Jinjur fired at the ground all around her. But when her bullets hit the Scarecrow's bubble, they slowed and stuck as if she'd fired into a vat of gelatin, then slowly dissolved into silvery liquid and ran down the bubble's sides to the ground. The Scarecrow stared at Jinjur, but she wasn't looking at him. She was looking at where he'd just been.

She couldn't see him, and she couldn't shoot him. Glinda's magic had worked. He almost whooped with glee, but he didn't know if the bubble would conceal any noise he made, too, and it was best to play it safe. Ducking flying limbs and hopping over struggling bodies, the Scarecrow made his way around the edge of the battlefield, back to the hedge maze, which was quiet and empty. He had no idea how long Glinda's magic potion would last, and he didn't want to be in the middle of a battlefield when it wore off.

"Find the Scarecrow! Destroy the beasts!" Jinjur screamed. Her army fought with renewed ferocity. It looked like the beasts were struggling to hold up against the girls' superior firepower.

"Retreat!" Lulu shouted. "Monkeys and animals, to me!" The monkeys flapped into the air, hurtling toward where Lulu hovered, and the Lion's surviving soldiers fought their way to where the monkeys flew in a tight circle. One by one, the monkeys swooped down and picked up their passengers; there were far more monkeys than animals this time. Jinjur fired at each of the monkeys as they came into range, taking down several. At the last moment, the Scarecrow realized he would be left behind, and ran frantically toward where the last two monkeys were struggling to lift the Lion into the air as Jinjur's soldiers shot at them furiously.

"Help!" the Scarecrow shouted. "Take me, too!" But the monkeys couldn't see him—and they couldn't hear him either.

"Where's the Scarecrow?" the Lion shouted. "We can't leave him!"

"No time!" Lulu screamed. "We can't look for him now, we're getting massacred down there. We have to come back for him."

"He's my friend!" the Lion bellowed, struggling, but the monkeys had already hoisted him far above the battlefield. The Scarecrow watched in despair as the last of the animals were carried to safety.

Then he felt a pair of arms wrap around him. "Let's get you out of here," Glinda said into his ear. There was a bright flash of pink light, and then the battlefield—and Jinjur's astonished soldiers—disappeared in a puff of glittery pink smoke.

TWELVE

The Scarecrow had a dizzying sense of flying through the air—far faster than the winged monkeys had carried him. Clouds flew by, and the landscape below rushed toward him and then receded again. Glinda's grip on him never lessened, and somehow he knew he was safe. And then everything went dark. He heard a rushing sound, and had the sensation of passing through something thick and dense. "Hang on, dear," Glinda said. The Scarecrow squeezed his eyes shut. The pressure grew more and more intense, until he was sure both of them would be crushed.

With a sudden pop, the pressure vanished, and the Scarecrow tumbled to a soft, carpeted floor. Blinking, he sat up and looked around him.

He was in a beautiful, richly decorated bedroom. The walls were covered with a pink rose-patterned wallpaper, and thick pink carpet covered the floor. A huge bed, piled high with pink satin cushions, sat at one end of the room, but despite its size the room itself was so big the bed hardly seemed to take up any room at all. An ornately carved divan upholstered in pink fabric was perfectly positioned to take advantage of the view from the room's huge picture windows, which looked out over a garden.

"Where are we?" asked the Scarecrow.

"My palace, of course!" Glinda laughed, throwing herself down on the divan and stretching luxuriously. "That last bit going through the walls is always *so* dreary, but we made it safe and sound! Can I get you anything to eat or drink?"

"No, thank you," said the Scarecrow, who was unable to do either of those things.

"Well, I'm famished," Glinda proclaimed dramatically. She rummaged in the divan cushions and triumphantly held aloft an intricately crafted, jewel-studded pink bird figurine. "Send up a strawberry sundae, please," she told the bird. The Scarecrow wondered if she might be a little batty. But to his surprise, the figurine chirped aloud, and Glinda settled back into the cushions with a sigh, tucking the bird into her dress.

"I do love ice cream after a battle," she said dreamily, closing her eyes. "I find it really calms the nerves." Within moments, there was a soft knock on her bedroom door. Glinda showed no signs of moving, so the Scarecrow got up to open it. A maid in a neatly pressed pink uniform curtsied deeply, and then gave a start when she saw him. "I didn't realize the mistress had a guest," she whispered, holding out a pink ice cream sundae on a pink tray. As soon as the Scarecrow took it from her, she bolted back down the corridor. She clearly had no desire to encounter

Glinda herself. The Scarecrow brought Glinda her sundae, and Glinda rapturously spooned ice cream into her mouth.

"Your, uh, witchly eminence," the Scarecrow began.

"Oh, just Glinda!" she exclaimed. "I feel like we're old friends, and anyway I hate formalities, don't you?"

"Glinda," he said awkwardly. "Can you tell me—I mean, why am I here?"

"Such an existential question!" She laughed. "You really are an intellectual, dear Scarecrow." He couldn't quite tell if she was making fun of him, but decided she wasn't. Her expression grew serious. "As we discussed in the forest," she said, "that wretched monkey's plan was bound to fail. Now it's your turn, Scarecrow. Have you come up with a plan?"

He didn't know how to tell her that he hadn't even begun to think about another way to retake the palace. Now, in the safety of Glinda's palace, he tried to understand what had just happened. "I didn't think so many people would die," he said finally. "I haven't really thought about what to do next."

Glinda narrowed her eyes. Suddenly he thought that he did not want to find out what it would be like to cross her. But then the expression passed again, and she smiled gently. "You've been through so much in the last day! But I did warn you that casualties would happen. There are always sacrifices that must be made when one wishes to win a war."

"I suppose what we need is a stronger army," he said. "The Lion's forces weren't strong enough, even with the help of the winged monkeys. But Jinjur lost plenty of her soldiers, too.

The castle's defenses will be weakened, if we can find a way to strike again before she can recover."

"Brilliant!" Glinda exclaimed, clapping her hands together. "I knew you'd come through, Scarecrow!" As far as he could tell, he'd only stated the obvious, but he nodded as if her praise meant something to him. He hadn't forgotten that brief, mean look in her eyes, or how the servant had seemed to be terrified of her. What did Glinda really want with him, and why was it so important to her that he believe she thought he was so intelligent? He was clever, to be sure, but if he was really honest with himself he had to admit that he wasn't *that* clever. Not yet, anyway. So what game was Glinda playing?

Glinda had finished her sundae, and she set the dish aside with a sigh of satisfaction. "That really hit the spot," she declared. "Now, dear Scarecrow, I have something to show you. Come with me." She got up from the divan, and he obediently followed her out of the room and down a long pink corridor. She led him to another, much larger room, with walls made out of pink-tinted glass. Broad-leafed pink plants climbed the glass, and huge hot-pink blossoms nodded gently among the paler pink leaves. The ceiling was a stained-glass mosaic depicting various scenes. Some were strange to him, like girls with butterflies' wings flying over a desert. Others were more familiar: the Wizard floating in his balloon, Toto sitting obediently, and the Scarecrow himself, along with the Woodman and the Lion, walking merrily down the Road of Yellow Brick. "My solarium," Glinda said, waving a hand at the glass walls.

"It's marvelous," the Scarecrow breathed, looking around him in awe.

"I should really have the ceiling redone," Glinda said, looking up with a flash of irritation. "All that boring old Oz history nobody cares about. Don't you think more flowers would be prettier?"

"Yes, I'm sure," the Scarecrow said, but he looked up again. The only Oz history he knew was from the books he'd read so far. There were the witches, of course, and there had been the Wizard, but who'd ruled Oz before him? He hadn't gotten to that part yet.

And Glinda took it all for granted. He envied all the years of knowing she had that he didn't.

Glinda opened a set of glass doors and stepped out onto a balcony, gesturing for the Scarecrow to follow. The view awaiting him took his breath away. It wasn't the stunning vista of clear blue sky and high, snowcapped mountains. It wasn't the sprawling flower gardens or the carefully pruned orchards. It was the rows and rows of girl soldiers, faces turned up to the balcony, saluting Glinda smartly. And every single one of them looked exactly like Glinda, down to the perfect, identically arranged ringlets.

"May I present my army," Glinda said, the smugness evident in her voice. "At your disposal, dear Scarecrow. As am I."

THIRTEEN

The Scarecrow was speechless. Glinda's army stood motionless, their armor glittering in the sun. "You're probably wondering why I didn't send my girls in with the Lion," Glinda said. She was right; he was. "The answer is I want you at my side, Scare. Together we'll make a great team behind the throne of the new Oz. And I have just the ruler we need." She signaled to her soldiers, and they wheeled in unison and marched back into the palace.

"But I thought—you said you wanted to help me take back the palace," the Scarecrow said, completely bewildered. "Why would I help you put someone else in power?"

"Not in power," Glinda said smoothly. "On the throne. Big difference, Scare. The fact is, the people of Oz love a new ruler. If Jinjur hadn't come along, someone else would have unseated you. It's not that I don't have total faith in you," she continued, cutting off his protest. "Believe me, you're the smartest man who's sat in that old chair in a long, long time. It's just the way Oz is. Which is why the trick isn't to be on the throne—it's to be behind it." She arched an eyebrow at him triumphantly.

"Behind it?" he echoed.

"Kings and queens come and go, but power stays with the powerful. You don't have to be the King of Oz to rule it. Do you see what I'm saying?"

He did, although he wasn't entirely sure he believed her. Something told him that, as pretty and kind as she seemed, Glinda wasn't being entirely straight with him. But two could play at this game until he figured out her real motives. "So we find someone who'll listen to us, and find a way to put that person in the Emerald Palace?"

"I knew you'd get it," she said. "That's exactly what I'm talking about. I have the strength to get rid of that ugly little pest Jinjur, and I know just the girl to put in her place." She pulled the jeweled bird out of her dress. "Bring me the princess," she told it. "And make sure she's wearing a *dress* this time. She's visiting a witch, after all." She giggled and put the bird away. "She's the dullest little thing, really," Glinda said. "Always wanting to sit in the garden and read a book, if you can believe it. She goes for *walks* in the *countryside*." Glinda shuddered.

Reading books was not something to sneer at.

"No interest in fashion, and she's been up north for ages in that wretched Gillikin Country, so she has no manners to speak of. She's quite the rustic. But she's quiet, she's royalty, and she'll do what she's told."

"Royalty?" asked the Scarecrow, totally confused.

"She's a fairy," Glinda said, as if that explained it. She arched her eyebrow again. "You don't know? According to legend, the fairies are the rightful rulers of Oz." She shrugged. "Technically, she's supposed to be the queen already. She was in line to inherit the throne, but she was only an infant when the Wizard arrived in Oz and exiled her to Gillikin Country. I don't know what on earth she's been doing there, but it certainly wasn't anything useful."

"But what about my education plan? What about the School of Oz . . . ," he asked, needing to know.

"I think you and I could convince her to do just about anything," Glinda countered. But he suddenly felt like *he* was the one being convinced.

The solarium doors opened, and a young girl walked into the room. The first thing the Scarecrow noticed about her was that she was extraordinarily beautiful. She had huge, luminous green eyes, and thick, inky-black hair fell in heavy curls to her waist. Her skin was clear and glowing, and she was the picture of youthful innocence. But unlike Glinda, who played up her beauty with elegant clothes and artful makeup, the fairy princess wore a simple dress. She was barefoot, and carrying a bunch of flowers.

"Look what I brought from the garden!" she said excitedly as she ran up to them. "Glinda, the star lilies are blooming!" She held up the white blossoms. Tiny, real constellations sparkled among the petals, winking in and out.

"Ozma, those are weeds," Glinda said. With a wave of her hand the blossoms withered and turned to glitter. "We don't bring weeds into the palace, dearest. Now, I want you to meet someone." She glanced down at Ozma's bare feet and sighed.

"Shoes," Glinda said, and with another balletic move of her arm, brown leather shoes appeared on Ozma's feet. Glinda scrutinized her.

"Ears," she said, and big blossoms appeared, covering Ozma's delicate little ears. "Legend has it fairy ears can hear your deepest desires. We can't have that, now, can we?"

Ozma nodded obediently, then her eyes fell on Scarecrow.

"I know who you are!" Ozma exclaimed, turning to the Scarecrow and going down on one knee. "You're the king, aren't you?"

"I—it's a bit complicated right now," the Scarecrow said, but Glinda interrupted him.

"He was the king, my dear, but he was only keeping the throne safe until the real ruler of Oz came along." Glinda winked at the Scarecrow over Ozma's head, and he saw immediately what she was doing. "In fact, he's been waiting all along for that person to return to the Emerald City, and she very nearly has. Do you know who she is?" Ozma, wide-eyed, shook her head. Glinda threw back her head and laughed.

"Why, she's you, dearest! You are the direct descendant of Lurline, the fairy who created Oz out of the Deadly Desert, as you know. But that doesn't just make you part of a wonderful family. It means you are the rightful Queen of Oz! That's why

I've brought you back from Gillikin Country."

Ozma gasped, and her hands flew to her face in shock. "But I—I don't know how to be a queen, Glinda!"

"Why do you think I've been *so* insistent you learn about manners and fashion, my dear? But you needn't worry. The Scarecrow is incredibly experienced, and we'll both be right next to you, ready to help you with anything you need."

Ozma frowned. "Isn't being queen about much more than manners and fashion?"

The faintest note of impatience crept into Glinda's voice. "If you want to *be* a queen, you must *look* like a queen," she said.

Ozma nodded solemnly. "I understand."

"Tomorrow, we'll take my army to the Emerald City," Glinda said. "We'll get rid of Jinjur once and for all. And then, my dear, we'll put you where you belong—on the throne of Oz."

"I can hardly believe it," Ozma said. "Am I really meant to be the queen? Are you sure you don't mind, Your Highness?"

Glinda shot the Scarecrow a meaningful look. "Glinda is right," he said. "I couldn't sit on the throne knowing Oz's rightful ruler was nearby. You're the Queen of Oz, just as Glinda says." Ozma's green eyes filled with tears, and she reached for his hand, overcome with emotion.

Really, the Scarecrow thought, she was just a child. She should be in school. For a moment he felt bad for her—this poor girl, caught in issues too large for her to understand. Glinda was right, although perhaps not in the way she thought. Ozma wasn't ready to rule Oz—not because she was dull, but because she was much too young. She needed Glinda. And Glinda, he realized, needed him. Ozma might be the supposed true ruler of Oz, but he was the actual one—not counting Jinjur, of course. His support of Ozma would be a crucial part of Glinda's plan. If he opposed her openly, at least some of Oz's citizens would likely rally behind him, throwing a wrench into Glinda's works.

To his surprise, the fact that Glinda was scheming behind his back excited rather than insulted him. It was a puzzle to figure out. He was getting a real head for politics, and the behind-the-scenes action was far more rewarding than the dreary day-to-day business of ruling Oz had ever been. Let poor Ozma hear the endless petitions and complaints of her subjects. Let her fall asleep on the throne every afternoon out of sheer boredom as Munchkin after Munchkin rambled on about the misdeeds of his neighbors. Let her sign laws into effect until her little hands cramped. She was welcome to the job. As he was beginning to realize, the part that intrigued him was the thrill of the game. Ruling was about playing a long con, and power meant you were willing to strategize behind the scenes for as long as it took. Glinda'd had years of thinking and planning. He just needed to catch up.

He'd been skeptical, but in that moment he made his decision. He'd go along with Glinda's plan and support Ozma's return to the throne. He'd bide his time. And someday—maybe someday soon—he'd show Glinda that he was made of far more than she'd thought. She had underestimated him, and for now that was to his advantage. She wouldn't underestimate him forever.

He could keep secrets, too.

Glinda looked at him through her eyelashes as if she could sense his resolution. She smiled a pretty, kindly smile that entirely failed to reach her glittering blue eyes.

As he walked away, Glinda called after him. He turned around, and her eyes, those magnetic pools of blue, met his. "The thing you'll never understand is that it doesn't matter how much information you put in your brain. It's about what you do with the information you have." She smiled the satisfied smile of a well-fed carnivore. He knew he was supposed to be afraid, to feel out of his depth.

Glinda wanted him to know that she was smarter than him and that she always would be. But Glinda had finally made a mistake. She'd meant to boast, or even threaten him. But without realizing it, she'd given him instructions instead.

FOURTEEN

Early the next morning, Glinda sent a flock of gilded song-birds—literally covered in gold leaf—to the Forest of the Beasts to tell the Lion that she and the Scarecrow were making their own move on the Emerald City. "I've invited them all to the battle, but I'm sure it'll be over by the time they arrive. They can join us for your coronation instead, dear," she said to Ozma, stroking the girl's dark hair.

"My coronation?"

"You didn't think you'd just sit on the throne and that would be that! Of course you'll have a coronation. It'll be the grandest party Oz has ever seen! We'll order you a dozen new dresses, and bucketloads of jewels. You can pick out your favorite things to eat and we'll serve them at the banquet, and there will be dancing all night long!"

"But if Jinjur has hurt so many people, no one will feel like dancing," Ozma said. "Wouldn't it be better to make sure everyone in the city is taken care of instead of focusing on a party?"

"Nonsense!" Glinda exclaimed. "Everyone will want to be distracted from their troubles, and they'll be so excited to have a new queen that they won't even think of Jinjur anymore. You'll see I'm right. Remember, I know much more than you do about running a kingdom!"

"You're right," Ozma said. "You're much wiser than I am when it comes to these things." Still, the Scarecrow thought he saw a glimmer of doubt in her eyes.

Glinda was treating their assault on the Emerald City as if it were a grand picnic. She sent Ozma to her chambers to get ready—"Make sure you pick out a lovely dress, dear, we can't have anyone seeing you look less than your best," she called after Ozma—and then brought the Scarecrow up to her own room, where she spent a long time conjuring up various battle outfits before settling on a fitted hot-pink bodysuit with amethyst-edged metal plating at the breastbone. The Scarecrow glanced up at the sky, where the sun was already high.

"Aren't we leaving soon?" he inquired. "It's a long journey to the Emerald City."

Glinda yawned. "Not when you have magic," she said. "We'll be there in no time. Don't be such a stick-in-the-mud, Scare."

At last, after adjusting her makeup and eating another ice cream sundae, she was ready. Once Glinda decided to get going, she didn't waste a moment. In no time at all, she had assembled her troops in front of her palace. Ozma, contrary to what Glinda had suggested, was wearing practical clothes for the journey. She had on a plain, unembellished dress, and her hair was bound up tightly in a neat bun. Glinda gave her a disapproving look, but said nothing about her clothes.

"Now then!" Glinda said brightly. "Is everyone ready? Ozma, I'm going to need your help. Moving an army is a job too big for one witch!" Ozma nodded, and Glinda took one of her hands. "When I give you the word, join your magic with mine. Don't worry about what to do with it—I'll direct you." Ozma nodded again. The Scarecrow tried not to show it, but he was impressed. Glinda was indeed powerful—far more than she'd let on. He'd never heard of a witch strong enough to move so many people before, even with help.

"I've never been in a battle before," Ozma said worriedly to the Scarecrow. "Have you?" The Scarecrow nodded. "What was it like?" She took his free hand.

Once again, the Scarecrow felt sorry for the poor girl. She was no match for the likes of Glinda—or for what faced them at the palace. He thought of all the bloodshed he'd seen in the last few days. He was getting used to plotting, but he'd never get used to all that death.

"You'll do fine," he told Ozma. She was satisfied with that answer, although he didn't know if it was the truth.

Still holding Ozma's hand, Glinda raised her arms, and her soldiers began to glow with an eerie pink light. The Scarecrow prepared himself for the strange feeling of magical flight. At least they didn't have to go through the wall this time. The ground dropped away from them, and a thick, dark fog poured in all around them. "We're going a different way this time, since there are so many of us," Glinda said in the darkness. Ozma squeezed his hand tightly, and he squeezed back in what he hoped was a reassuring way. He couldn't see anything in the pitch-black world Glinda had brought them to, but he could feel that they were moving very quickly. Ozma was gripping his hand hard enough to cut off his circulation, and he was grateful he didn't have any.

Still, her small hand in his made him feel something not in his head, but in his chest, where his heart should have been. She trusted him.

Then he felt the surge of magic and he wondered what the fuss was all about. He did not love it like the witches did. He did not chase it like the Wizard did. He felt the power but it meant less to him somehow.

The journey through the darkness somehow seemed to last forever and no time at all. "Hold on, everyone!" Glinda called out cheerfully. The Scarecrow felt himself plunging downward. Ozma squeaked in surprise. Suddenly the darkness lifted, and he hit solid ground with a thump that jarred his stuffing. All around him, Glinda's soldiers were adjusting their armor and forming military ranks, unfazed by the journey. They were standing outside the gates of the Emerald City. This time, the gates were closed.

"Now that's what I call a surprise entrance. They're very well trained, aren't they?" Glinda asked smugly.

"Indeed," agreed the Scarecrow, wondering what use Glinda could possibly have had for a trained army. How long had she plotted to put Ozma on the throne? Would she have deposed him by force, if Jinjur hadn't come along to waylay her plans? Somehow, he didn't doubt it. It was more and more obvious how ruthless Glinda was underneath the pretty, feminine exterior. Had she had more evil thoughts in mind when she'd sent the Lion and his beasts into battle? Had she *hoped* they would be killed? The Scarecrow hoped his friend was still safe. Even at the end of the battle, the Lion had been loyal to him at no benefit to himself. That was more than he could say for Glinda.

"How will we get in now?" the Scarecrow asked, eyeing the tightly shut gates. "I can't imagine Jinjur will just let us in."

"She doesn't have to," Glinda said airily. She let go of Ozma's hand, wiggling her fingers, and flicked them dismissively at the gates. A sizzling bolt of lightning struck the solid, heavy wood, splintering it to pieces. "Go get 'em, girls!" she ordered her soldiers.

As one, her army pushed through the ruined gates and marched in unison down the broad Road of Yellow Brick that led to the Emerald Palace. The Scarecrow, Ozma, and Glinda let the ranks of girls march past, and then fell into step behind them. The city was still deserted, but it didn't give him the same eerie sense of being watched. This time, the Scarecrow felt sure, Jinjur didn't know they were coming. This time they'd be protected. If only the Lion and even Lulu had had that guarantee. Did people you cared about always have to get hurt? Glinda was clearly the wrong person to ask, but he wondered. He liked power, but he wasn't so sure yet about the consequences.

If they'd surprised Jinjur, it wasn't by much. By the time Glinda's army reached the palace, Jinjur's own soldiers were pouring out of the palace doors, pistols at the ready. Jinjur herself leapt from a second-floor balcony, landing lightly on her feet and brandishing her own gun. Glinda's soldiers raised their glittering swords. Time stood still in the moment before the two armies met.

FIFTEEN

Suddenly Ozma pushed forward. "But they'll be hurt!" she exclaimed.

"That's the point, Ozma," Glinda said, gritting her teeth.

"Is that what a battle is like?" Ozma demanded. "Is this what happens?" The Scarecrow was at a loss for words. Had Glinda not explained the full ramifications of her plan? If Ozma had grown up sheltered in Gillikin Country, the idea of Ozians killing each other would have been completely unbelievable to her. He hadn't believed it possible himself, until he'd seen it with his own eyes. It was one thing to worry about his friends, but Jinjur and her soldiers were the enemy. They *deserved* to die.

"If we don't kill them, they'll kill us," he said, his own words surprising him when he said them out loud. A few days ago he could not have said them. But that was before Jinjur. Before she took his palace, before her soldier killed Hibiscus, before she almost took his life . . . "Plus, we have to get Jinjur out of the palace, and she wants to fight us. There's no other way for you to be queen."

"But I don't want to be queen, if it means bloodshed!" Ozma exclaimed, her cheeks blushing with fury and her green eyes sparkling.

"Jinjur is a tyrant, Ozma," Glinda said impatiently. "She's murdered half the palace staff and several Munchkin villages, and she'll kill more unless she's stopped. There's no sense in reasoning with people like that, darling. The only language they understand is force."

"I refuse to believe that," Ozma said with a sudden calm. She spun around on one foot before Glinda could stop her and marched up to the edge of Glinda's army.

"Stop this at once," she said. Though she did not raise her voice, the Scarecrow could hear her as clear as a bell all the way at the back of Glinda's forces, and the strength in her voice was unmistakable.

Jinjur's soldiers froze. Glinda's soldiers lowered their swords a hairsbreadth. One of them looked back at Glinda, as if waiting for new instructions.

"I told you to attack!" Glinda screamed. Her soldiers raised their swords again and moved forward.

"And I told you to stop." Ozma's voice was so powerful that it hit the Scarecrow with a physical force, sending both him and Glinda stumbling backward. The air around Ozma was crackling. In that same huge, awe-inspiring voice, she addressed Jinjur. "Why have you come to the Emerald City to do harm to my people?"

Jinjur brought up the pistol, snarling in rage. Ozma held up one hand and the pistol clattered to the ground. Jinjur struggled furiously, but it was clear some kind of invisible bond was holding her.

"I asked you a question," Ozma said. Jinjur kicked furiously, and then slumped over as she realized the futility of fighting Ozma's magic.

"The Scarecrow wasn't doing a very good job," she said sullenly.

"That's not true," the Scarecrow protested.

"Oh, shut up," Glinda said, her glittering eyes fixed on Ozma.

Ozma stared daggers at Jinjur. "Do you think you have done better, then?"

Jinjur scuffed at the ground with one high-heeled foot, looking slightly sheepish. "I would have done," she said. "In just a bit, soon as we got settled."

"You call murdering my people 'getting settled'?" Ozma's voice was thick with anger. "Disrupting the rule of Oz, killing innocents, bringing warfare on my city?"

"It ain't your city," Jinjur mumbled, looking around. Her soldiers remained frozen where they were, held by Ozma's magic.

"It *is* my city," Ozma said, and her voice was like a massive bell tolling across the courtyard. The Scarecrow gasped. Huge black wings, veined with gold like a butterfly's, unfurled from Ozma's back and spread outward. Green lightning cracked down out of the cloudless sky, and a wind whipped up around them, sending a cyclone of tiny green gems spinning around them. "I am Ozma of Oz, direct descendant of the fairy Lurline, heir to the throne of Oz, and rightful mistress of the Emerald Palace," Ozma said in that same huge, terrifying voice. "I demand you leave my city and return to the land whence you came." A bolt of green lightning slammed into the ground inches from Jinjur's feet and she jumped backward with a little scream.

Her jaw went slack, and she sank to her knees. "It's not possible," she whispered. "You can't be Ozma. Ozma's dead."

At last, Glinda saw her moment to act. "Not true at all!" she said cheerfully. If she was disconcerted by Ozma's totally unexpected actions, she didn't show it as she walked gracefully up to stand by Ozma's side. The Scarecrow, not wanting to miss a moment, ran after her. Glinda put an arm around Ozma's shoulders, ignoring the fact that Ozma was trembling with rage and the air around her was shivering with magic. "The Wizard exiled our dear Ozma when she was just a baby," Glinda continued. "Where on earth did you get the idea she was dead, young lady? You've been *very* impertinent." Her honeyed voice dripped menace.

"I didn't—I had—we didn't know!" Jinjur stammered frantically. "We just thought he—" She pointed at the Scarecrow without finishing her sentence.

Glinda rolled her eyes. "You thought he wasn't doing his job properly, so you decided to hop on over and do it for him? I don't think so, you little minx. The Scarecrow *was* doing his job—as regent, holding the throne for Ozma's return. Well, now she's here."

Jinjur looked back and forth between them, her face filling with confusion. "But if the Wizard exiled Ozma, and then made the Scarecrow king, how could the Scarecrow be a regent?"

"Don't ask stupid questions!" Glinda snapped. "It's time for you to suffer the punishment you deserve." She turned to her soldiers. "Bring me firewood," she said coldly. "We'll burn this bitch at the stake."

"No," Ozma said. Glinda raised an eyebrow.

"Is it—is it really you?" Jinjur was staring at Ozma, her eyes filling with tears. "It *is* really you! It's Ozma, our own princess come back to us!"

To the Scarecrow's utter astonishment, Jinjur ran forward—but not to attack. She flung herself on the ground at Ozma's feet. "I never would've done bad if I knew you was coming!" she wailed. "I'm so sorry, Majesty!"

"You have done more than bad," Ozma said. "You have murdered my people and brought warfare to Oz, where before there was none. You have watered the soil of my gardens with blood." The emerald wind had died down and the lightning retreated back up into the sky, but her eyes were still glowing with an eerie green light. The Scarecrow could hardly believe this powerful creature was the same terrified girl who'd held his hand outside Glinda's palace. It was as if tapping into her fairy powers had unleashed a whole new person. This girl, he could believe, was meant to be the Queen of Oz.

Jinjur began to cry, snuffling miserably into the dirt at Ozma's feet. "I don't know what came over me!" she cried. "It was like someone told me to do it! We ain't like this normally, I swear, Highness! Something just came over us! We was minding our own business, and then one day I got this bee in my bonnet and suited up to come down here and kick out the old Scarecrow!"

Ozma's eyes narrowed, and she tilted her head to one side. "Is it possible?" she murmured to herself. "But who would do something like that? Who could use magic to such an awful end?"

The Scarecrow felt his brain at work. He had a pretty good idea of who, and carefully avoided looking at Glinda. If she had somehow compelled Jinjur to invade the Emerald City, she had been planning even more carefully than he had thought. And it was bigger than that. His head spun. What happened to Good versus Wicked? Wasn't Glinda ultimately supposed to be Good? But maybe a witch was a witch and Glinda was only Good when compared to someone really Wicked. Right now, Glinda didn't seem at all Good.

"All the more reason to execute the traitor, Ozma," Glinda interrupted smoothly, stepping forward to try to take control of the situation. "If someone has controlled the girl before, they could do it again. You must be strong enough to prevent her from harming anyone in the future. Remember what I told you, about casualties being necessary when it serves the greater good."

But Ozma shook her head. "Thank you for your advice, my dear friend," she said. "I know you mean well, and you are far wiser than I am. But I can't bring myself to spill any more blood. I know I may regret it, but how are we to end killing with killing? Her death is not the answer. No one's is."

Glinda's mouth tightened with fury, and she controlled her voice with an effort. "Ozma, darling, I *am* wiser than you. Didn't we agree I would be your counselor?" The Scarecrow cleared his throat. "The Scarecrow and I," Glinda amended, shooting the Scarecrow an irritated look. Ozma took no notice.

"Of course you shall," Ozma agreed. "But if I am to be a true queen, I will have to learn to make decisions of my own as well. I may come to regret this, but I will spare the life of Jinjur and her soldiers."

Glinda opened her mouth again and then paused for the barest second. "Certainly, my dear," she said. "You are the queen, after all." Only the Scarecrow saw the furious glitter in her eyes. He felt a chill. Crossing Glinda would have consequences for Ozma, he felt sure of it. The girl might think Glinda was her friend, but Glinda was clearly no one's friend but Glinda's.

SIXTEEN

Jinjur was so dazed by Ozma's return that it was no trouble at all for Glinda's soldiers to disarm her and her army. When Ozma had collected all their pistols, she made a huge pile of them in front of the palace. She closed her eyes, summoning her magic. The metal began to melt, flowing together to form a liquid silver pool. As Ozma moved her hands, the molten metal formed a miniature replica of the Emerald Palace, perfect down to the last brick. Ozma opened her eyes and looked at her work with satisfaction.

"Take this with you back home," she told Jinjur, "and never return to the Emerald City again. Your actions have gone against everything we hold dear in this country. I will spare your life, and the life of your soldiers, but I will not forgive you. Is that clear?"

"Yes, Your Majesty," Jinjur said, curtsying deeply. She was so humbled she was nearly unrecognizable as the cruel and arrogant girl who'd stood in this same place and issued her challenge to the Scarecrow. He was astonished that Ozma had been able to work this change without violence. Maybe Ozma was right, and Glinda's way wasn't the only one. He had much to think about.

Jinjur and her soldiers filed out of the Emerald City, their heads down. Several girls carried Ozma's statue of the Emerald Palace. Jinjur turned one last time and waved farewell. "Thank you, Highness," she said. "I'm sorry." Ozma nodded regally, and Jinjur turned away.

When the last of the girls had dwindled into the distance, Ozma sighed deeply and ran one hand through her hair. "I'm so tired," she said softly, and suddenly she was just a girl again, young and inexperienced.

"We must get you into the palace, Your Majesty," Glinda said, putting an arm around Ozma's shoulders. "You should rest before your coronation."

"Is it soon?" Ozma asked plaintively.

"The Lion and his people should be here shortly, and I'll send messengers to all the corners of Oz. We'll have your coronation in a week, my dear. I'll plan everything while you rest. You shouldn't have to worry about details at a time like this. Why, you've just liberated Oz!"

"Thank you, Glinda," Ozma said, leaning her head on Glinda's shoulder. "You've been so good to me. Both of you have," she added, taking the Scarecrow's hand. "I couldn't have done this without you." She let go of the two of them and walked into the palace.

"Don't you forget it," Glinda muttered under her breath. She fixed a sickly-sweet smile on her face and stalked after Ozma. The Scarecrow watched them go, his mind churning. How was he supposed to figure out what to do next? Was he on Glinda's side—or Ozma's? Was there a way for him to find a side of his own—to come out of this ahead of them both? He had a lot of thinking to do. Maybe he needed a bigger brain, or more gifts from the Wizard. Maybe he needed a shot of Glinda's magic. Could he trick her into making him more clever?

The palace wasn't in nearly as bad a shape as the Scarecrow had feared. Many of the servants had fled or been killed, but Jinjur had done little damage to the palace itself other than to paint STRAWBAG in huge, dripping red letters across each wall of the Scarecrow's chambers. The servants who remained greeted Ozma with surprise that soon turned to delight.

He tried to ask one about dear Fiona, but didn't get far. She had not seen her among the living, but she had not seen her among the dead either. Before he could investigate further, Glinda swept into the room.

"We have so much work to do!" Glinda exclaimed cheerfully. "Scare, why don't you find some temporary chambers for Ozma. I'll go down to the kitchens and see what we'll need for the coronation banquet." She looked down at her armor. "I'll need chambers of my own, too, of course," she said. "Make sure I have a large wardrobe."

The Scarecrow wasn't used to taking orders in his own palace, but there wasn't any point in arguing something so trivial with the witch. If Glinda could bide her time, so could he. And perhaps he would spot his missing servant along the way.

"Come on, Your Majesty," he said to the sleepy-eyed Ozma. "I know just the rooms for you." Ozma yawned and followed him upstairs.

The Scarecrow put her in a set of unused rooms, luckily untouched by Jinjur's soldiers, with a small balcony that over-looked the gardens. All the remaining servants were in the kitchen with Glinda, so he made up the bed himself and found Ozma a spare nightgown in one of the cupboards. It was still early evening, but the exhausted princess climbed into bed as soon as he turned down the covers. "Don't go yet, Scarecrow," Ozma murmured. "Won't you stay and talk to me until I fall asleep?"

"Of course, Princess," he said, sitting at the edge of her bed and taking her hand. Her skin felt hot and feverish.

"Too much magic," she said. "It tires me out so. I didn't know if I had it in me to defeat those girls!" She smiled weakly at him. And despite himself, he filed away that piece of knowl-edge. Her weakness seemed important somehow. He was struck by what a sweet little thing she was. No wonder Glinda's plan was working so well. A part of him felt for her. She never asked for any of this. She had not chosen this life. She'd have been content in a cottage somewhere with a book. She was the definition of Good. But he couldn't help feeling a dark thrill of elation. She knew nothing about his plans, or about what he and Glinda had in store for her. He'd been clever enough to fool a fairy—and the Queen of Oz. Of course, he'd only be helping her, not harming her. Even Glinda, cunning as she was, only had the good of Oz at heart. But more and more he found that he loved watching his plots unspool. This, he was sure, was what it meant to be truly clever.

"Tell me a story, Scare," she asked. Her innocence and trust was an assault to his senses, and he had to gather himself before beginning.

"Once up on a time, there was a man made of straw. He was told when he was first created that he was only good for one thing: scaring away crows. And even that proved quite opposite. He dreamed of a better life . . . a bigger life, while tied to that stake. One filled with books and thoughts. One day a girl came along and took him down and introduced him to new friends. Friends for life. And they helped him obtain the thing he had most wished for. The man was never alone again. And he was free and he could think. And he lived happily ever after."

"And I took your crown. The thing you most wished for?" she said apologetically. Almost as if she would give it back if he asked nicely.

"The crown was never something I wished for. I only ever wanted to have a brain. A brain is everything. And it is worth more than any crown. It is worth more than any magic," he said truthfully.

If I use it right, it can do more than any wand or any crown or even any pair of magic shoes. If I use it right, I can take back what I lost today. If I use it right, I can take over all of Oz. . . .

"What are you thinking, dear Scarecrow?"

"I was thinking how brave you were today," he replied untruthfully.

She yawned. "Do you really think so? Was I as brave as Dorothy?"

"Dorothy?" he asked, startled.

"You know, the Witchslayer. Dorothy who traveled through Oz with you and defeated the Wizard."

He smiled to think of the little girl he'd once known, not so different from Ozma herself. "You were even braver, Princess." But she was already fast asleep.

SEVENTEEN

The Lion and his beasts arrived in the Emerald City early the next morning. Lulu was dressed in her battle outfit, and the winged monkeys flew overhead in tight formation. Lulu brandished her pistol, firing shots into the air as she approached the palace as if she was issuing a challenge, but there was no one to meet her other than the Scarecrow and Glinda. She peered behind them suspiciously as the other monkeys settled on the ground, folding their wings and looking around them cautiously.

"It's fine, we've defeated Jinjur," the Scarecrow said. "She and all her soldiers are gone."

"We?" Lulu barked, poking him in the chest. "You mean to say you had something to do with this?" She looked at him with new, grudging respect. "Not bad for a ball of straw," she admitted. She stared at Glinda. "Who's this frilly hussy?"

Glinda's smile was frosty. "I am Glinda the Good Witch," she said.

"Glinda's just a legend," Lulu sniffed, but she shook Glinda's hand.

"You're just very young," Glinda said sweetly. "Anyway, we have even better news than Jinjur's defeat," she added, surreptitiously wiping the hand Lulu had touched on her dress. "The True Queen of Oz has returned from her long sojourn in the north, and she will be crowned in a few days' time. Ozma, Princess of Oz, is among us once more!"

Several of the beasts gasped in surprise, and one of the monkeys flew several inches into the air. "Ozma is here?" Lulu said, her eyes wide. "Little baby Ozma?"

"Not such a baby anymore," the Scarecrow told her.

Lulu shook her head. "She can't see me," she wailed, unexpectedly bursting into tears. "She'll never forgive me for what I did, never!" The Scarecrow glanced at Glinda, but she clearly had no idea what Lulu was talking about either.

"I don't know what you mean," the Scarecrow said. The Lion and all of the beasts were leaning in with their ears pricked up. Lulu wiped her eyes, all her bravado gone.

"I stole her," Lulu said dully. "Oh, that's not how *he* put it, but that's what I did. I stole her from her rightful place and raised her up ignorant. And then I left her all alone." Lulu sobbed incoherently. "I—I'd do anything to see her except face the past. I can't forgive myself for what I did either. I'm not r-ready. Maybe soon but now—I just can't. Tell her—" The little monkey choked up. "No. Don't tell her anything at all," she managed. "Don't even tell her we were here. *Capisce?*"

"But you'll miss the coronation," the Scarecrow said, utterly confused.

Lulu shook her head. "Not a problem," she said gruffly, clearing her throat and blowing her nose noisily. "It does my heart good to know she's back where she should be. That's all I need." She glanced back at the beasts. "What are you looking at?" she snapped. Immediately, the Lion busied himself washing behind his ears. Lulu flapped her wings, rising awkwardly off the ground. "I wish I could've seen her," she said sadly. "Let's get out of here, fellas." The rest of the winged monkeys took off after her. None of them said good-bye.

Glinda watched the monkeys fly away, her expression thoughtful.

"Enough of this sitting around!" the Lion said. "Who did you say was in charge now? Is there going to be a feast?"

Glinda blinked. "A feast, yes!" she exclaimed. "A feast to celebrate the return and the coronation of our True Queen. Come inside, all of you, and make yourselves at home."

"Is that the Lion I see! I'd know that mane anywhere!" someone shouted from the courtyard.

"Tin!" the Scarecrow exclaimed. Their old friend was just approaching with a small delegation of Winkies, who milled around him and chattered excitedly. Scare ran up to the Woodman and shook his hand enthusiastically. A moment later, the Lion knocked them both over with the enthusiasm of his greeting. "Tin!" he roared, clapping them both on the back with his enormous paws. "Long time no see!" For a moment, Scare banished all thoughts of Glinda, Ozma, and the events of the day, and delighted in being reunited with his two friends.

The days until Ozma's coronation passed quickly. Glinda kept the princess tucked away in her chambers, and she had little contact with the guests who streamed into the Emerald City, eager to catch sight of their new, rightful queen. The Scarecrow tried to see her several times, but each time he knocked Glinda came to the door and told him the princess was resting. He was suspicious, but he could wait until the coronation to find out what Glinda was up to. Instead, he and the Lion caught up with Tin, who was envious of all the excitement they'd been having.

"Battles!" Tin exclaimed wistfully. "I've never even seen a battle."

"You're not missing anything," the Scarecrow told him. "It was awful, really." He still hadn't stopped thinking about the image of the Royal Army's body trampled into the dirt. No, he could do without another battle, even if the rest of his life was as dull as a Munchkin wedding.

"What about your gift?" the Lion asked, changing the subject.

"My heart, you mean?" Tin thumped his chest. "Right as rain. I'm sure of it. The Wizard knew his stuff. What about you?"

"Oh, I'm very brave now," the Lion said. But he didn't sound so sure. The Scarecrow wondered if something had happened during the battle with Jinjur that caused the Lion to doubt himself, but he put that thought out of his mind. *His* gift was certainly working, and that was all that mattered.

At last it was time for Ozma's coronation. The Scarecrow carefully washed his cloth body and the Woodman polished his tin plating to a blinding glow. Even the Lion brushed his luxurious coat and permitted the Woodman to tie a ribbon in his thick mane. They took their place among the other guests in the throne room of the Emerald Palace. It had been decorated beautifully for the occasion. Richly embroidered tapestries hung on the walls. The huge throne that dominated one end of the room had been studded with so many emeralds that it turned the light in the entire room green. Glittering pink streamers fluttered from the ceiling—Glinda's touch, no doubt. A long red carpet stretched from the throne to the doors at the far end of the room. Everyone was craning their necks and looking around them, trying to get a glimpse of the mysterious princess.

Cornelius raised a trumpet to his lips and blew a dignified march. The throne room doors opened slowly of their own accord, revealing Ozma, with Glinda standing beside her. Everyone in the throne room gasped. Ozma was magnificent. Her long black hair hung in heavy ringlets to her waist. Her deep-green dress, studded with more emeralds, brought out the extraordinary, luminous green of her eyes. Her beautiful wings fluttered behind her, glowing with a soft green light. Even Glinda, decked to the nines in an enormous, tiered pink ball gown, her hair piled on top of her head in intricate knots, paled beside the princess—and from the expression on her face, she both knew it and wasn't too happy about it. Glinda carried a delicate, wrought-gold crown on a green satin pillow. *OZ* was spelled out in beautiful golden script.

Cornelius set down his trumpet. "We welcome Ozma, the One True Queen of Oz!" he shouted. As Ozma took the first step onto the red carpet, the entire room erupted into spontaneous cheers. One sobbing Winkie clutched another, wailing, "Have you ever seen anything so beautiful in your life?" Wolves howled, crocodiles clacked their teeth together, and a fox ran halfway up one wall in excitement before falling back to the ground. The Lion roared in approval, and the Woodman joyfully clanged his chest with one tin fist. Winkies threw fistfuls of glitter, and Scraps the Patchwork girl cartwheeled around the room. Even Polychrome, Daughter of the Rainbow, had come all the way from the Rainbow Falls, dressed in a swirling—and transparent—ball gown of rainbow-flecked mist. The Tin Woodman stared at her svelte figure so intently that the Scarecrow had to knock him on the side of the head.

Step-by-step, Ozma crossed the room, pausing almost every few feet to hug a Munchkin or kiss the top of a furry head. Even the Scarecrow was moved, and found himself grateful he had no tear ducts with which to weep. Only Glinda, he noticed, looked less than rapturous.

At last, Ozma reached the throne, and she turned to face her new subjects. It took a long time for the cheering to die down, but finally the room was silent.

"My dear friends," Ozma began. "I am so happy to be back

among you, in the city where I belong. I promise to serve you well as your queen, and to be just and fair." She paused, for a moment seeming almost uncertain. She might look every inch the queen, but it was still clear that she was just a young girl. "I promise to be the best queen I can," she said finally. Glinda, seeing that Ozma's speech was done, stepped forward with the crown and set it delicately on Ozma's head.

Once again, the room burst into excited shouts and applause. Glitter confetti exploded from the ceiling, and huge mirrored balls descended from the rafters and turned slowly overhead. Trays of canapés and glasses of fizzgiggle floated through the crowd, carried by invisible hands. Ozians rushed the throne dais, hugging their new queen and congratulating her.

The Lion stood up on his hind legs and snatched an entire tray of bacon-wrapped shrimps out of the air, crunching it down in a few gulps. "I love parties!" he said through a mouthful of food. The Scarecrow, for once not irritated by his friend's bad manners, laughed out loud. It was impossible to be angry or upset on an occasion like this. Everyone around him was over-joyed at the prospect of a new queen—and such a pretty one, too! Even he was excited, though he did feel a slight pang of loss as he watched Ozma settle into the throne that had so recently been his.

The celebration went on late into the night. The fizzgiggle never stopped flowing, and by midnight several Winkies were snoring loudly in the corners of the throne room. The Lion was dancing the limbo with an extremely tipsy Pixie. The Woodman kept trying to talk to him about timber management, and finally the Scarecrow excused himself to get some fresh air.

The palace gardens were cool and quiet. Crickets chirped contentedly in the grass. The Scarecrow settled himself against a tree with a sigh, stretching his arms over his head. In the distance, he could see the hedge maze that had nearly had to hide him during the battle with Jinjur. Maybe now he was clever enough to solve it. The thought was so delightful he took two steps in its direction before he was interrupted.

"I thought you'd never leave," said a familiar sweet voice behind him. "We have much to discuss."

EIGHTEEN

"Hi, Glinda," the Scarecrow said. She was still wearing her ball gown, but outside the grandeur of the throne room it looked slightly ridiculous. Her hair had come out of its elaborate updo, and her habitual smile was rigid rather than genuine.

"We need to talk," Glinda said, and there was no mistaking the edge in her voice. Away from public scrutiny, she was a different person. A meaner one, he couldn't help thinking. Suddenly he was tired of the witch and her endless scheming.

"About what? Ozma is in place, just like you wanted. She trusts you, and she'll listen to anything you tell her to do."

Glinda didn't even notice that he hadn't bothered to include himself as part of her plan to control Ozma.

He knew now that she never had intended to. It should have hurt or made him angry but instead it made him think. Never again would he be tricked. Just like never again would he be tied to a post in a field. He could still almost feel the crows landing, one, two, three, four. Never, ever, ever . . .

He was only going to get better and smarter. Everything was a lesson. And every lesson was an opportunity. Even this one.

He didn't see any reason to pretend he hadn't figured out she was only using him and had no intention of sharing power. Was she surprised he'd been clever enough to see through her act? She didn't show it. She might be a liar, but Glinda was right about one thing. War meant casualties, and he could no longer be afraid to be ruthless. He'd have to learn fast—and learn on his own. He couldn't trust anyone other than himself. He'd stay one step ahead of Glinda and anyone else who crossed him. Whatever it took, he'd be ready.

"She doesn't listen to me as well as she should," Glinda said tersely. "That business with pardoning Jinjur . . ." She shook her head. "The princess is too used to getting her own way. I think they spoiled her up there in Gillikin Country. She'll listen to me for now, but this independent streak is troubling."

"There's not much you can do about it now," the Scarecrow pointed out. "You're the one who made her queen."

"We could put you back in power," Glinda mused, tapping her chin with one manicured finger.

"You think I'd be any more willing to take your orders than she would?" He laughed.

"Too much trouble," she said, ignoring him. "They're happy to have a new queen, and they wouldn't stand for another switchup. The situation is too volatile right now. We need a stable ruler, at least for the time being. But there has to be a long-term solution."

THE STRAW KING

"I wish Dorothy was here," the Scarecrow said suddenly. "Even if she didn't know what to do, she was always so happy. Those were better times." For a moment, he almost wished he was the old Scarecrow. Maybe he'd been stupid, but he'd also been happy and carefree.

"Well, obviously," Glinda snapped, and then her eyes widened. "Oh, Scare!" she breathed, really looking at him for the first time. "Of course. It's so clear; I can't believe I didn't think of it." She grabbed his hands, and despite himself, a thrill ran through him. He was back in the game—and whatever he'd felt a moment ago, he couldn't resist the excitement. "You're absolutely *brilliant*."

"I am?" He cleared his throat. He hated that praise from her could still, for a moment, take him higher than the flying monkeys had. "I am," he said more confidently. "Brilliant, yes. I can always come up with a good solution."

"I just have to find a way to bring her here," Glinda said. "It'll take time, but I can do it. You'll have to wait for me—can you manage it? I'll set you up outside the Emerald City somewhere. You can build yourself a nice little palace of your own and relax for a bit until it's time for us to act."

The Scarecrow weighed the plan he'd sparked. Bringing Dorothy back was something he'd wanted since she'd left. And when she got here, the Dorothy he remembered would have no interest in being queen. She'd put the Scarecrow back on the throne where he belonged. Wouldn't she? He opened his mouth to agree when they were interrupted. "Glinda? Scarecrow? I've been looking all over for you!" It was Ozma. The Scarecrow gave a guilty start, but Glinda didn't bat an eyelash.

"You've nearly ruined your surprise, silly girl," Glinda chided.

"Surprise?" Ozma asked eagerly. "What surprise?"

"It wouldn't be a surprise if I told you what it was," Glinda told her. "You'll have to be very patient. It might take a little while for me to fetch your gift. But when you meet her, I think you'll be *very* happy."

"My gift is a person?" Ozma asked. "Do you mean—a friend?"

Glinda smiled a radiant, gentle smile that didn't quite reach her eyes. "Just you wait, my dear. Just you wait and see."

The Scarecrow fought a sinking feeling that was overtaking him. Maybe when Dorothy got here, together with the Lion and the Tin Man, they could find a way to take Glinda down.

Or maybe Glinda would convince Dorothy to do whatever she wanted, and he'd have to think of something else.

"Oh, Glinda, you take such good care of me," Ozma said happily, giving Glinda a hug.

"Of course I do, darling," Glinda said over Ozma's shoulder. She met the Scarecrow's eyes and gave him a sinister wink. "I'll always take care of you, Ozma. Always. Just like I take care of all my friends."

NINETEEN

The Scarecrow watched Glinda with Ozma. He knew that promise, like most of the things she'd said, was a lie. Or the truth presented in a way to get what she wanted.

One of the things that she'd told him turned out to be more true than all the rest. It didn't matter how much information he crammed into his brain, it was about how well his brain worked. And Glinda's brain had just outsmarted his by a mile.

If only he could find a way to make his own run faster, smoother better. Smarter . . .

A crow landed on his shoulder just then. His straw did not rattle.

He did not bother to shoo it away.

They didn't scare him anymore.

He decided to go back to his new quarters and walk the grounds.

He saw her before she saw him. She was wearing a new

uniform in Ozma's colors, and unlike some of her singing brethren, she wore a stern expression as if she were deep in thought. But when she saw him, she broke into a smile.

Fiona curtsied at him in passing, as if he was still the king.

The gesture struck him in its simplicity and beauty and stalled him in his tracks, like a rainbow after a storm.

"I'm not the king anymore," he said with a smile in return.

"You always will be to me," she said with a knowing glance that seemed to relay that she understood more than the average Ozian. She bowed slightly and continued on her way.

Good old Fiona. She, at least, was still loyal. And clever. He watched the little servant make her way back toward the palace. Books weren't going to work quickly enough. He had to move on to something else. Something more sure. Something like looking into someone *else's* brain. A sharp, quick, clever Munchkin brain. A brain like Fiona's.

Fiona still thought he was the king. Maybe she'd be able to help him in a way she never could have imagined. The Scarecrow smiled to himself and started back toward the castle.

He had work to do.

RULER OF

BEASTS

ONE

Oz hasn't been interesting in a long time, the Lion thought, picking his teeth.

There was that whole business with General Jinjur, when he'd helped his old friend the Scarecrow attempt to oust the vicious and bloodthirsty usurper to the throne of Oz. Truth be told, the Lion had almost admired Jinjur. She might have been ruthless, but at least she wasn't boring. He hadn't had so much fun since he'd helped little Dorothy to defeat the Wizard. The battles had been terrible, of course, and he was sorry about the many casualties, but he had found that he enjoyed fighting—especially when he knew he was on the side of right. The Wizard had given him courage, but in battle he truly felt alive—as if he was channeling his real lionish nature. None of this loafing around the palace, watching the Scarecrow read encyclopedias thicker than the Lion's paws.

But the battle with Jinjur was ages ago. Now, the Queen

Ozma ruled Oz, and the Scarecrow had retired to a corncob mansion out in Munchkin Country. The Scarecrow had a good heart, but the Lion wasn't sure if this dear old friend had been a very good king. He'd thought his newfound wisdom would make him a better ruler, but, as the Lion himself knew, it wasn't wits alone that made a successful ruler. Ozma, on the other hand, seemed born to rule—which, technically, she was. She was a fair and just queen, making sure her subjects were happy and peaceful and content.

And bored. The Lion yawned and stretched. He was lounging on his platform at the heart of the Kingdom of the Beasts. Ozma had been queen for a year, and absolutely nothing had happened. No mysterious invaders, no battles, no bloodthirsty girl soldiers. His subjects were peaceful and obeyed his decrees. The birds sang prettily in the branches, beautiful wildflowers bloomed amid the rich carpet of moss that covered the forest floor, bees hummed merrily in the warm summer air, and if something didn't happen soon, he was going to chew off his own paws.

"Cornelius!" the Lion roared. Moments later, his closest adviser appeared at his side, bowing deeply. Cornelius was a rabbit, but unlike most of his kindred, he was an extremely clever one. His pronounced buckteeth gave him a slightly sinister air, but he was always neatly dressed in the latest Ozian fashions; he made sure the most current catalog scrolls—printed in glowing sunfruit ink on leaves from the giant sailflower plant—reached the forest, so he could keep up with trends.

"Your Majesty," the rabbit said, bowing again.

"I'm bored," the Lion said petulantly, rolling over on his back and waving his paws in the air. "I'm *dying* of boredom. Nothing happens anymore. Everyone is so *peaceful*."

"Isn't that a good thing, Your Majesty?" Cornelius asked cautiously.

"NO!" the Lion roared, springing to his feet. The rabbit jumped about a foot in the air and stood eyeing the king nervously. Cornelius was important to the Lion—and useful—but the King of the Beasts had a reputation for snacking on his subjects a little too regularly for even his most trusted advisers to feel entirely safe.

"We could, er, invade a neighboring county," the rabbit suggested hastily. "If His Majesty wishes. I am sure the beasts would be happy to go to war."

The Lion sighed loudly, his breath none too sweet, and settled back on his paws. "No, you're right," he said sulkily. "War isn't the answer. Not this time, anyway. Oh, if only something would *happen*!" He brightened. "Have I told you about the time the field mice had to rescue me from the poppy field?"

"No, Your Majesty," said the patient rabbit, who had actually heard the story at least fifty times.

"Well," the Lion began, "this was back in the early days, before I had my courage, and when little Dorothy was traveling through Oz—you wouldn't have met her, of course, but she was . . ." The Lion trailed off, staring into space. He thought of the trip down the Road of Yellow Brick often. It was before he had courage. But that time with Dorothy, Tin, and Scare at his side remained the standard against which he compared every experience after. He had never felt more terrified. But he had also never felt less alone. He had been a part of something. And now he was alone with his crown. Was it possible that the seeking was better than the having? Or were his old friends just better than his subjects?

"She was?" the rabbit prompted.

Dorothy was everything. She had pushed them all to change from heartless to full of heart. From dumb to smart. From fearful to fearless. It had been forever, but he still hated that she had gone from here to home.

"Dorothy was *interesting*," the Lion finally roared crossly, waving his paws. "Not like this bloody stupid forest and all these wretched animals! What am I going to do with the rest of my life, Cornelius? Being king was fun at first, but now all I do is sit around all day. I can't even go on an adventure, because kings aren't supposed to leave their subjects on their own."

Cornelius's whiskers twitched as his mind raced. "You could have a tournament, sir," he suggested.

The Lion brightened. "A tournament!" he exclaimed, clapping Cornelius on the back with an enormous paw. The rabbit winced. "You're a genius! That's the perfect thing. It'll kill an entire weekend, at least, and afterward we can have a feast. Spread the word at once."

Cornelius hadn't seen the Lion so excited in months. He raced off into the Forest of the Beasts to tell the Lion's subjects, feeling very pleased with himself. He'd succeeded in distracting the Lion—and saving his own skin—for the time being. Let the Lion eat some other hapless forest creature. Cornelius was intent on keeping his post—and the Lion's gratitude.

TWO

The morning of the First Annual Beasts' Boredom Battle was clear and sunny. A cool breeze rustled in the branches. Cornelius had gone to great lengths to turn the Lion's royal clearing into a suitable battleground. The grassy center had been dug up, and the earth beneath packed into a hard, flat surface. The perimeter of the clearing was hung with banners. A group of stoats and weasels played a rousing march on tiny trumpets, and birds fluttered through the air with brightly colored ribbons in their beaks like living streamers. Dozens of animals, ranging from fierce-eyed hares to massive, muscular wolves and bobcats, were assembled in the clearing, ready to fight. The Lion sprawled on his platform, eyes heavy-lidded, feigning indifference to the clamor below him. Only Cornelius could tell from the glint in his eyes that he was following the action eagerly.

Once upon a time, the Lion had feared them. It seemed almost impossible looking at him now. But a broken twig behind him in the forest would have sent him scurrying up a tree back then. Once, he had literally hid in one all night until the tiniest of hares had moved from his spot beneath it. The Lion knew he was larger than the hare, stronger than the hare, but it didn't matter. He couldn't bear to have the hare's beady little eyes boring into his. Somehow, he would always blink first. Now he could gobble anything up before it had a chance to blink. Now they were his subjects. Now they were the ones who jumped at the mere hint of a wave of his tail.

The weasels blew a fanfare on their trumpets, and the first of the competitors stepped forward into the ring: a hare and a badger. The badger bared her sharp little teeth, and the hare boxed at the air with his powerful forepaws. Barely waiting for the signal, the two animals leapt at each other.

This is what he was waiting for. Action. The Lion clapped his paws in delight, and then remembered he was pretending to be bored and sank back on his haunches. The Scarecrow had told him once that a ruler was not supposed to appear to be excited about anything—he'd read it in one of his books. But the Lion wasn't so sure. Wouldn't his excitement encourage his subjects to do more of what he wanted? He wanted—he needed—more of this. He didn't know how to put it into words like the Scarecrow could, but seeing the animals facing off in the makeshift ring was the first time he had felt anything at all in days.

The hare clocked the badger on the side of the head. Snarling, the badger sank her teeth into the hare's side. The assembled animals cheered fiercely as the smell of blood carried across the clearing. Ordinarily, they were more or less peaceful, and took the worst of their disputes to the Lion to be settled. But they were still animals, and deep down there was something inside each of them that would rather bite and claw their way to a solution than talk it out.

The Lion wasn't sure who he was rooting for. The hare was feisty and fast. But the badger was single-minded and would not let go. The hare pummeled the badger furiously with his fists, but she only sank her teeth in deeper. His eyes glazed over with pain, and finally he flopped to the ground in defeat. "I yield," he gasped. The triumphant badger released him. The hare limped off to lick his wounds as the other animals crowded around the badger in congratulations. Cornelius quickly swept the ring to prepare it for the next fight.

The Lion stretched and leapt lightly down from his platform, pacing toward the defeated hare. "Good fight," he said, nodding his head at the competitors.

"Thank you, sir," the hare said, still cleaning blood from his fur. The Lion smiled and licked his lips, opening his jaws wide.

"Too bad you lost," he said, and swallowed the hare whole.

The Lion had surprised even himself. He hadn't intended on eating the hare. But seeing the hare give up had been too much for him. The Lion had run away one too many times in cowardice. Giving up was not to be tolerated.

A momentary hush descended on the clearing as the animals realized what had just happened. "No one will be permitted to drop out of this *delicious* contest," the Lion remarked. "I haven't enjoyed a meal this much in *years*."

But what he really enjoyed was the reaction of his subjects. There was a tremble that went through the onlookers. One that he had caused.

"The winners will be awarded the finest dens and burrows in the Forest of the Beasts. The losers will be eaten!" he announced in a fit of genius that was worthy of the Scarecrow. He clambered back up to his perch, settling down with a satisfied burp. "Who's next?"

As soon as the Lion's subjects realized their lives were on the line, the fights grew even more fierce. "Law of the jungle!" the Lion remarked happily to no one in particular as a fox furiously battled a beaver. (The fox won; the beaver scrambled for the edge of the clearing, but the Lion quickly pounced and devoured him. "What fun!" he roared.) But as the afternoon wore on, the Lion grew full—and bored. The losers, at first resistant, gave up and stopped putting up a fight. The Lion pardoned several of them at random, just to give himself something to do. Relieved, they slunk off into the trees, fleeing the Lion's temporary mercy without a backward glance. As the next competitors, a bobcat and a ferret, stepped into the ring, the Lion roared in exasperation.

He couldn't explain it—somewhere between swallowing the hare and this moment, the thrill had subsided again.

"This isn't interesting at *all*!" he complained. "Just go home, all of you." The beasts froze, staring at him in confusion. "Go home!" he bellowed. "Did you hear me?" None of the animals waited for him to say it again. Seconds later, the clearing was empty except for the Lion and Cornelius.

The Lion sighed. "So much for that," he said. "I thought a tournament would be exciting, but it's nowhere near as fun as a real battle. Maybe I should go to war against the winged monkeys." He brightened. "I've never eaten a monkey. I suppose they might taste interesting?"

"As you like, sir," Cornelius said patiently, but his red eyes blinked more than usual.

"No, you're right," the Lion said. "That's not the thing either. I thought it was so nice, being a ruler, when I first came here. But the forest is *boring*, and so are all these wretched animals. I miss adventure, and cities, and seeing new things. Maybe I'm just not cut out to be King of the Beasts."

But he wondered—if not this, what? He had spent his whole life wanting not to be a coward. He had never really thought how it would really feel to be king. Cornelius tried not to let his surprise show. He'd never heard the Lion talk like this before.

"But Glinda gave you the forest to rule, sir," he said. "Who else could do the job?"

"You could, probably," the Lion said. "Or anyone, really. I wonder what she would think if she could see me now." No sooner had he spoken the words aloud than the clearing filled with a soft pink light. A cloud of tiny pink fireflies swirled through the air in a spinning column that gradually took on the shape of a woman.

"Glinda?" the Lion asked in astonishment as the witch floated forward. She was dressed in her usual pink ball gown, and her hair was piled on top of her head and secured with amethyst-studded combs. She hovered daintily a few inches from the ground, fluttering her long eyelashes at the Lion.

"My dear Lion," she said sweetly. "If I'm not mistaken, were you just questioning my judgment?"

THREE

"Oh no, not at all!" exclaimed the Lion hastily, sitting up straight and gesturing furiously to Cornelius, who leapt forward to pick bits of the tournament losers out of the Lion's mane. "If only I'd known you were coming, I would have . . ." The Lion waved a paw at his filthy, matted fur.

He did not want to seem ungrateful. She had helped him, Scare, Tin, and Dorothy get everything their hearts desired. But just like Scare said once in one of his overly long letters, she hadn't exactly given them any instruction on how to use their new gifts.

"Don't trouble yourself, dear Lion," Glinda said in her honey-eyed voice, although Cornelius was almost certain he saw a flicker of distaste in her eyes. "When I go to visit the Kingdom of the Beasts, I expect beasts!" She giggled, and the Lion relaxed.

"Cornelius, make our guest comfortable," he ordered. How exactly Cornelius was supposed to do this was unclear. He quickly dusted fur and the bones of an animal carcass—the Lion's breakfast—away from an area of the Lion's platform and indicated that Glinda should sit before scampering off to find something for the witch to eat. Glinda looked down at the rough platform and actually frowned. The Lion was too busy cleaning his paws to notice. "Sit, sit!" he exclaimed through a mouthful of fur.

"Travel is so, er, cramping," Glinda replied. "I'm much more comfortable standing, dear Lion, and anyway I won't be here long. I have a message of the utmost importance for you—and a mission, if you're up for it."

"A mission?" The Lion left off his grooming to look up at Glinda quizzically. "What kind of mission?"

"I've just come from the Emerald City, where I've been visiting with the queen," Glinda explained.

"How is she?"

Glinda blinked, and for the barest second the Lion thought he saw a scowl flash across her face. "She's very well, of course," Glinda said, a little coolly. "She's really settled into ruling like a duck to water. Just born to run things."

"She is part of the royal line," the Lion pointed out.

"And she lets you know it!" Glinda giggled, but the smile didn't reach her eyes. "I thought I'd have so much to teach her, but really she just runs circles around the Scarecrow and me!"

"But the Scarecrow's in the countryside," the Lion said. At first, the Scarecrow had sent him letters via Pixie Express, but the Lion didn't always finish them. They were pages and pages long filled with what he was learning. Things that were well beyond the Lion's brain. The Lion couldn't help but think that Scare was trying to read his way back to the throne. "Yes, of course, you know that he felt he had to go when he realized Ozma didn't have any use for him. And in fact, I'm on my way back to my summer palace myself. Ozma certainly doesn't need *me*." This time, there was no mistaking the irritation in her voice. The Lion wondered what had happened back at the palace to set Glinda and Ozma at odds, but he knew better than to ask. Glinda might look kind, but she was powerful—and he'd seen her cruel side. He'd think twice before pushing her. Glinda quickly got her expression under control and her voice returned to its habitual sweetness. "But I didn't come here to talk about boring old politics," she cooed. "I came here because I need you, dear Lion, and only you, to help me with a most important project!"

The Lion sat up straight again. "Me?"

"That's exactly right. In fact, there's no one else in Oz who can possibly help me with what I need done. Can I rely on you, dear Lion? On your courage—and your utmost secrecy?"

"Of course you can rely on my courage!" the Lion retorted indignantly, wondering if she was trying to suggest the Wizard's gift was insufficient. He hadn't lost the initial battle against Jinjur's soldiers because he wasn't brave enough, but because he was outnumbered. Surely she remembered that. Glinda laid a soft, perfectly manicured hand on his paw.

"Oh dear, now I've offended you. I didn't mean to imply you

aren't the bravest lion in Oz, but what I'm asking of you will require more than just brawn. I need you to keep your mission a secret, and to conduct it with stealth." Glinda lowered her voice and gazed deeply into the Lion's eyes. "Can you do that for me? Is it too much to ask?"

The Lion drew himself up to his full height, returning her look. "I am at your service, lady Glinda, noblest witch in Oz," he said huskily, though he hardly knew what he was doing. He didn't even know what his assignment was to be, or who would look after the Kingdom of the Beasts while he was away. But Glinda was so persuasive and so compelling. Not to mention so beautiful. Her blue eyes glittered and she squeezed his paw tightly, covering his forehead with kisses. "I knew I could rely on you, my brave, wonderful Lion!" she exclaimed. Raptly closing his eyes in pleasure, the Lion couldn't see that Glinda was holding her nose as she kissed him.

"Then it's settled!" Glinda said happily. "You can prepare to leave in the morning. I'm sure you'll have to make arrangements for the kingdom while you're away. I can't imagine your mission will take *too* long, but you never know."

The Lion nodded, looking up at Glinda in adoration. "My mission," he agreed, and then he frowned slightly. "What is my mission, exactly?"

Glinda giggled. "Oh, right! It's very simple, really. I want you to protect Ozma. As you know, her army is gone. . . ."

The Royal Army had been a single man. And Jinjur had taken him out in a heartbeat right in front of him and Scare.

"But she has you," the Lion said, puzzled. Glinda was power-ful. And she had an army of her own.

Glinda frowned the tiniest of frowns before her forehead smoothed out again and she beamed at the Lion. "I'm—well, I have things to do elsewhere," she said vaguely. "Very impor-tant things. And Ozma can be a little difficult. I think it's best we spend some time apart. And to be honest, there is another reason. Ozma is so bored in the palace—as bored as you are! I thought you might do us all a favor and keep her company for a while. She's in desperate need of cheering up. I know she'd love to see you, and you'll make her a perfect companion!"

The Lion felt his heart lift, perhaps this was what he and his courage were looking for. A mission. A purpose. Perhaps a fight didn't mean anything unless it had one.

"I will bring the beasts. I will train them up into a proper army," he announced.

Glinda's perfect eyebrows raised and she shook her head.

"Perhaps, in time. But you need to have Ozma get used to you. Trust you before bring in an army."

"But how can I keep her safe? You saw how the last Royal Army of One ended up."

"I will know if there is trouble, don't you fret, Lion."

The Lion nodded, swallowing her logic. But it left an after-taste. Something not quite right. He suddenly remembered the other part of what Glinda was asking.

"Which part am I supposed to keep secret?" the Lion asked, his confusion growing.

"Oh, that! I'm planning a most wonderful gift for Ozma, and I thought you could do me a *tiny* favor while you're staying in the palace. She can't know, or it would spoil the surprise. The Wizard left a ruby necklace behind when he departed Oz, and I need it to finish Ozma's gift."

The Lion was getting more confused with every word out of Glinda's mouth. Maybe he should have asked for brains instead of courage, too. Why couldn't Glinda look for the Wizard's necklace herself? Why was she leaving Ozma alone in the palace, if Ozma was bored and lonely? But it didn't really matter in the end. Glinda knew what she was doing, and she'd chosen him to help her. He wasn't stupid, but intrigue and palace politics weren't his style. He was happy to assist the kind, beautiful witch with whatever she wanted, even if her request didn't totally make sense.

"But how will you get the necklace?" he asked.

Glinda stared at him, her smile faltering. "I'm asking *you* to get it, Lion," she said, her voice strained.

"Me?" he asked, astonished. "But I don't know where it is!"

"No one knows where it is," Glinda snapped, and this time her exasperation was clear. "That's why I'm *asking you to find it*."

The Lion nodded eagerly, anxious to please her. "Of course! Find ruby necklace," he repeated obediently. "Keep Ozma company. That's all you need from me?"

Glinda's irritation vanished and she clapped in delight. "You're just as clever as dear Scare, no matter what people say!" she said merrily.

"What people say?" the Lion asked, but Glinda didn't seem to hear.

"But just to be absolutely sure you know what I'm asking of you, I'll show you the necklace. And perhaps I'll do a little spell, just to make sure you don't have any problems keeping your promise."

"Of course I won't have a problem," the Lion replied, slightly offended. But Glinda ignored him, closing her eyes and drawing a circular shape in the air with one finger. As she sketched, a translucent image of an elaborate ruby necklace materialized in the air. It was so elaborate that it was really more of a breastplate. A heavily worked gold setting housed dozens of rubies, ranging from the size of the Lion's claw to the size of his entire paw. The dazzling red stones pulsed with a hypnotic red light of their own. The Lion leaned forward. He could almost see an image reflected in each of the glowing red stones. Whirling clouds forming a dense gray funnel over a broad, empty prairie with a single clapboard farmhouse sitting all by itself in the middle of nowhere. A girl was standing in the doorway; she was too tiny for the Lion to make out her features, but something about her was incredibly familiar . . .

"Where is that? Is that . . ." the Lion asked. Glinda clapped her hands and the image of the necklace vanished with a pop.

"Never you mind about that," she singsonged. "What matters is that you recognize the necklace if you see it again. Will you?"

"Of course," the Lion said, irritated. He realized suddenly

that maybe Glinda wanted him to see it. Glinda wanted him to know that Dorothy was the gift she was planning for Ozma. And Lion would do just about anything to bring Dorothy back to Oz.

"I'm sorry, dear Lion," she said. "I don't mean to imply you're not perfectly capable of the task. It's just so important to me to make Ozma happy that I get stressed about the details."

Something in her voice didn't entirely ring true, but the Lion let it go. Before he knew it, both of Glinda's hands were resting on his head, bathing him in a throbbing pink light. "And now I bind you to your promise," the witch murmured. *"Nexus necto offendix leo."* The Lion felt a creeping sensation, as if hundreds of tiny fleas were crawling through his fur. He tried to twist his head to nip at them, but he was frozen in place by Glinda's spell. The bugs were burrowing *under* his skin. He could feel them like tiny sparks burning through his coat. He roared in pain and surprise but no sound came out of his open mouth.

"All done!" Glinda exclaimed, passing one hand over his head. He blinked. He was sitting on top of his platform in the Forest of the Beasts, a familiar woman standing in front of him with a blinding smile affixed to her face. He knew her. He was supposed to be doing something. His skin burned briefly, and it all became clear. A vision of a ruby necklace hung glittering in the air before him, its powerful pull on him drawing him closer and closer. But as he reached out a paw to touch it, the image burst in a shower of red sparks. He *had* to find the necklace. He simply had to. It was a compulsion.

Glinda, watching him, smiled and nodded. "Very good. Don't

forget your quest." And then it all came flooding back. He was going to the Emerald City on an important errand for Glinda the Good Witch. He'd help her find a magical necklace so that she could present it to Ozma, the Queen of Oz. He'd been specially chosen for the critical task. His chest puffed outward with pride. It wasn't just anyone who Glinda handpicked for her special missions.

At that very moment, Cornelius returned to the clearing, bearing a tray piled high with fruit. The tray looked as though it had been hastily woven together from leaves and branches— which it had, since the Lion's subjects had very little use for dishes. Glinda delicately selected a few fresh dazzleberries, which exploded into bursts of tiny edible jewels in her hand. The Lion, still full from his tournament, waved the tray away.

"I'm going to leave the forest for a few—for a while, Cornelius," he said importantly. "I trust you will be able to look over things while I'm gone?"

The rabbit's ears twitched in surprise, but he only said, "Of course, Your Majesty."

"Then it's settled." The Lion turned to Glinda. "How will I contact you when I've found the—" Glinda shot a warning look at Cornelius. "Cornelius is my most trusted adviser," the Lion said.

"If *anyone* knows, it's not a secret," Glinda said, and there was no mistaking the coldness in her voice this time. "Don't worry, Lion. I'll know when you find it. And I'll know if you tell anyone other than me." Cornelius busied himself cleaning his whiskers, pretending not to listen.

"Yes, Glinda," the Lion said, trying not to show that she had rattled him. But surely keeping the bored young queen company and finding a necklace couldn't be anything too dangerous. Glinda would never do anything that wasn't in the best interests of Oz, or of Ozma herself. After all, Glinda was the one who had made Ozma the new queen. And more than that—more than everything—Glinda might be bringing his friend home. Maybe it was just wishful thinking, and his thinking, wishful or otherwise, had never been as smart as the Scarecrow's. But how much better Oz would be with Dorothy in it again.

Glinda smiled, and just like that she was a sweet, innocent witch again. Had the momentary flash of cruelty been his imagination after all? Already the air around her was sparkling, and her outlines shimmered and began to fade. In moments he could see through her, as if she were a ghost. "Don't fail me, Lion," she called as she vanished.

"Was that encouragement, sir, or a threat?" Cornelius asked quietly. The Lion didn't bother to answer. What had he just gotten himself into?

FOUR

It was good to be traveling again. He'd made this journey before, and not all that long ago—though that time he'd been leaving the Emerald City, not heading toward it, and he and the Scarecrow had been fleeing Jinjur's soldiers, afraid for their own lives. When he'd traveled with Dorothy, the Scarecrow, and the Tin Woodman, they'd had such an eventful and occasionally dangerous journey that he'd never had time to pay attention to the landscape. But Oz was safe and stable now. The Wicked witches had been killed or exiled, and no possible threat faced him on the road. Despite Glinda's ominous farewell words, he dawdled as much as he dared along the way to the Emerald City, stopping often to nap in a sunny patch of starflowers or drink lavender-scented water from one of the many brooks he passed. It didn't take long for his paws to find the Road of Yellow Brick, and once he did he quickened his pace. Soon enough, the city was a dazzling green smear on the horizon that solidified into towers, turrets, and thatch-roof houses as he drew closer to the gates.

Unlike the Wizard, Ozma left the gates of the Emerald City unguarded, as clear a sign as any that Oz had returned to a state of peace and harmony. The Lion slipped past the heavy wooden doors and found himself on the main road to the palace.

The Emerald City was designed like a wheel, with the Emerald Palace at its heart and straight, even roads radiating outward like spokes until they met the city walls. The main roads were paved with a sparkling crust of green gemstones that were eerily smooth under the Lion's paws. Near the city walls, the buildings were mostly neat green houses. Munchkins cheerfully pulled weeds and watered flowers in well-tended gardens, waving at the Lion as he walked by. The closer he got to the palace, the buildings grew larger and more elaborate. Vendors selling green scarves, green songbirds, green pastries, and green suits and dresses hawked their wares to passersby. Here, the streets were crowded with people. Munchkins ran back and forth, on their way to some urgent task or another. An emerald-studded trolley ran past on a shining green track, so full of people that Munchkins hung out its windows and clung to the outside of the car. The Lion licked his lips, realizing how hungry he was from his journey. There were so many Munchkins in the Emerald City— surely no one would miss just one? But he wanted to make a good impression on Ozma, and eating one of her subjects was probably considered poor form.

The Lion made his way slowly through the teeming streets, until at last he reached the gardens outside the Emerald Palace.

The exterior of the palace was dramatically different from the last time the Lion had seen it. The Scarecrow had kept things simple and functional. But now, under Ozma's rule, it was clear that appearance was more important. The gardens were even more elaborately planted. Tiny jewel-colored hummingbirds flitted between enormous green blossoms, and golden butterflies the size of the Lion's head drifted idly from flower to flower. An army of Munchkin gardeners toiled busily: raking the immaculate green gravel paths, planting seedlings in the tidy beds, and trimming the already flawless lawns. Huge green banners emblazoned with the golden crown of Oz fluttered from tall green poles. Courtiers strolled in the gardens, dressed in elaborate, tiered court gowns and well-cut suits of green velvet. Ozma had clearly been busy since the Scarecrow had left the Emerald City. The Lion wondered what his old friend had thought of her changes. But Ozma was the rightful ruler of Oz, after all. It made sense that she would want her palace to be as beautiful as possible.

"Your Highness!" one of the gardeners exclaimed, catching sight of the Lion. He rushed forward, bowing as he ran. "We were not expecting a royal visit! Does Her Majesty know you're here?"

The Lion was pleased to be recognized, but realized quickly he should have sent word to Ozma that he was coming to the city. "Er, I thought I would surprise her," he said. The gardener looked startled, but recovered quickly.

"How wonderful, sir. I'm afraid we are not prepared to receive you properly, but allow me to escort you to the palace."

"Oh, that's all right," the Lion said. "I don't need anything fancy." He followed the gardener through the huge main gates of the palace, and his stomach rumbled. It *definitely* wouldn't do to eat one of Ozma's staff, but he was terribly hungry, and the Munchkin was so tempting.

Inside, the palace was even grander than the outside. Ozma's touch was everywhere, in the giant tapestries that covered the walls and the soft, thick carpets scattered across the stone floor. More servants bustled back and forth on various errands, carrying trays laden with delicacies, cleaning supplies, or stacks of books and papers. It was almost hard to believe that this was the same palace where he'd once lounged with the Scarecrow, and where they'd fought a bloody battle against General Jinjur. The palace even felt different. He could almost smell the magic humming in the air—Ozma's magic, he realized. It buzzed faintly in his ears like a distant beehive. The Emerald Palace had never felt like this before. For the first time, it had a true ruler.

"If you'll just wait here for a moment, Your Majesty," the gardener said. Before the Lion could reply, he was running off down a hallway. Moments later, another servant appeared. This Munchkin was clearly someone important in the palace: his uniform was a beautifully tailored suit, and he wore an emerald pin on his lapel.

"We are honored to have such an illustrious guest. I am

Reedus Appleall, at your service," he said, bowing. "The queen is just finishing some business, but will be ready to receive you soon, Your Highness." He looked at the Lion's dirty, matted fur with the faintest expression of disapproval. "Perhaps His Majesty would like to refresh himself before seeing the queen?"

"I would love some refreshments," the Lion said happily.

"Very well, sir. This way, please."

The Lion followed Reedus down the familiar corridors of the palace. Ozma's touches were everywhere: every alcove was filled with fresh flowers, the floors were spotless and polished, the walls hung with beautiful Ozian landscapes. He recognized the lush field of poppies where he had once fallen into a most perilous sleep. Rainbow Falls was depicted in all its dazzling, multicolored splendor; real mist drifted from the painting and left a faint, sparkling rainbow dust on his fur. Leaning in to examine an image of distant mountains, he could feel a cool breeze drifting from the tall, snowy peaks. The servants all wore matching uniforms and identical expressions of contentment. "The place looks nice," the Lion remarked.

"Ozma is a wonderful queen," his guide agreed earnestly. He ushered the Lion into a large chamber. Huge picture windows looked out over the palace gardens, and an elaborately carved four-poster bed nearly the size of the Lion's entire platform in the forest dominated the far end of the room. The Lion flopped down on the bed with a sigh of satisfaction, ignoring the expression of horror that flashed across the Munchkin's face at the sight of his muddy paws dirtying the lace bedspread.

"About those refreshments," the Lion growled. Bowing and nodding, the little servant backed into the hallway and disappeared.

Moments later, the room was full of activity. A team of a dozen Pixies flew in, steering a huge tub of steaming water that rolled along atop an invisible bubble of magic and a pile of towels. A Munchkin brought a platter of roasted meat, and another hurried toward the Lion with a brush and comb. The Lion was far more interested in a meal than in hygiene, but he allowed himself to be hustled into the bathtub. He munched happily as the Pixies shampooed his fur and combed the tangles out of his mane and tail. When he was thoroughly clean, more Pixies took away the bathwater while a Munchkin toweled him dry and brushed his fur until it shone. Finally, another Munchkin brought him a mirror. The Lion admired himself for a moment. "I look so respectable no one will recognize me!" he exclaimed.

Reedus reappeared. "Ozma is ready to receive you, Your Highness," he said. The Lion followed him down another series of hallways to the Emerald Palace's throne room. As with everywhere else in the palace, Ozma had redecorated the throne room to within an inch of its life. Elaborate murals depicted the history of Oz, and stained-glass windows refracted the sunlight into hundreds of patches of emerald green. Ozma sat regally in her throne, her golden crown sparkling in the sunlight and her rich green robes spilling to the floor around her. But other than a few servants, the throne room was nearly empty, and she looked tiny and lost all alone in the vast space.

"His Highness the Lion, King of the Beasts," Reedus announced, but Ozma was already rising to her feet.

"Lion!" she exclaimed, picking up the hem of her robe and scampering toward him like a little girl. She flung her arms around his neck. "It's so good to see you!" The Lion was so surprised at her delight that he began to purr.

Ozma leaned back and looked at him closely. "You're looking very well, dear Lion," she said. The Lion refrained from mentioning this was due to the attentions of her minions. "What brings you to the palace?"

The Lion realized he hadn't thought of a cover story for his trip to the palace. He couldn't exactly tell Ozma that Glinda had said she was bored and lonely. Glinda had made it clear he wasn't supposed to mention her at all. Now, with Ozma staring at him quizzically, he could barely think.

"It, uh, seemed time to pay my respects," he said, feeling slightly ridiculous. But Ozma only laughed.

"But you were here for my coronation! You didn't need to come all this way just to see me again!"

Suddenly, the Lion was seized by a fit of inspiration. "To tell you the truth, Your Majesty, being king isn't quite what I thought it would be," he confessed in a low voice. "Being in power is a little lonely. I thought you might have some advice."

Silently, he congratulated himself on his cleverness as Ozma's cheerful smile turned to a look of sympathy. "I know just what you mean," she said quietly. "Have you eaten, dear Lion?"

"No," the Lion said untruthfully. Ozma rang a silver bell next to her throne and the servants leapt to attention. "Please serve dinner for my guest and me in my chambers," she ordered. "We wish to dine privately." She turned to the Lion. "Come, dear Lion. We have much to discuss."

FIVE

Ozma's chambers were beautifully appointed, and the Lion cast an admiring glance at the soft, thick carpets and gorgeous antique furniture. "The palace didn't look half so nice when Scare was king," he remarked, and a troubled look passed across Ozma's face.

"Do you think?" she asked politely, but something was clearly bothering her. Glinda had been vague about why the Scarecrow had left the Emerald City and retired to his mansion, and the Scarecrow had never mentioned the reason himself. Or at least he'd never actually gotten to that part in Scare's letters. He regretted now not finishing them.

"Did something happen between you and Scare?" the Lion asked. Ozma flushed.

"We both thought he would be happier away from the palace," she said quickly, but it was clear she wasn't telling him the whole truth. She shot the Lion an uncertain look, and then sighed. "To be honest, I'm not sure the Scarecrow has the best interests of Oz at heart. I know he's your friend, and I don't mean to speak ill of him. But he and Glinda—well, they spent a lot of time together whispering in corners, if you know what I mean. Glinda has her own ideas about how to run Oz, as I'm sure you know." His first thought was to defend Scare. Scare may have had his head too deeply in his books and he might have missed the throne, but he was a threat to no one, and especially not to Oz. He was surprised by the bitter note in her voice, and for a moment he nearly told her that Glinda herself had sent him. But then he remembered the menace in Glinda's parting words and thought better of it. There was some mystery here to be unraveled, and he was beginning to realize that Glinda hadn't been entirely honest with him about her motives—or about why she'd left the palace.

"I haven't spoken to Glinda since the coronation," he said carefully. "Did you quarrel?"

Ozma looked at her hands. "I thought it best if both of them leave the Emerald City for a while. It took some persuading, but they finally agreed." A note of determination entered her voice, and for the first time since he had seen her he realized what a formidable opponent she must be underneath the sweet, girlish surface. If Glinda had had her own ideas about how to govern Oz, she must have been unpleasantly surprised to realize how stubborn its new queen was.

"I see," the Lion replied. Ozma looked as though she was about to say something else, but at that moment the door opened and a procession of servants bearing trays of food entered the room. The Lion sniffed greedily, immediately distracted from his interrogation of Ozma. The Emerald Palace didn't skimp when it came to meals. The servants' trays were piled high with sweet pastries and pies, tureens of soup and baskets of steaming, freshly baked bread, a roasted piglet with an apple in its mouth, and all kinds of hors d'oeuvres. A steward poured champagne into an emerald goblet for Ozma and a green bowl for the Lion, who didn't waste any time before diving into the feast. Ozma, who picked daintily at her food, could only laugh at the Lion's dubious table manners.

At last, when he was full, he ordered another bowl of champagne and settled back on a pile of green cushions. He and Ozma had been discussing something important before dinner arrived, and he cast about for a way to pick up the thread again. As if reading his mind, Ozma sighed and looked into her glass. She seemed distant and sad, as if the true Ozma was slowly being revealed to him.

"It's good to have a friend nearby again," she said quietly. "The palace staff is wonderful, of course, but I haven't really been able to talk to anyone in ages."

"Ruling is lonely business," the Lion agreed, and she brightened.

"Isn't it? I knew you'd understand. I'm honored to be the Queen of Oz, and it is my birthright, after all. But so few people understand what it's like to have this much power. I'm responsible for the well-being of everyone in Oz, and I worry about failing my subjects or making some terrible mistake that will send the country into ruin."

The Lion had never worried all that much about the welfare of his subjects, but he made a sympathetic noise. He'd had no idea Ozma took ruling so seriously. Little word of the Emerald City reached the Forest of the Beasts. No wonder she was sad, if she fretted this much. He patted her on the arm with a reassuring paw. "Perhaps in that way we are the same. We have to figure it out as we go along," she said with a smile. He felt some comfort that she didn't know everything instinctively. He certainly had spent the last few months wondering how to be a king. But his concern had been for himself and not others. Ozma had heaped the welfare of the whole kingdom atop her delicate shoulders.

"I think we're supposed to serve, not just rule," she continued.

Lion shook his head. "The other beasts used to delight in scaring me. And I don't forgive and forget. I usually just eat those who cross me."

She laughed. "In that we differ. I forgive, but I never forget."

"What you need is to lighten up a little," he suggested. "Take a vacation. Or if you can't get away from the palace, at least take some time off to have fun."

Ozma smiled wearily. "Oh, Lion. Maybe it's that easy in the Kingdom of the Beasts, but for me, it's not so simple. The whole country of Oz depends on me. I can't just take a vacation from being queen."

"Can't you at least go stay in Glinda's summer palace for a while?" he prompted. He was determined to get to the bottom of whatever had come between the witch and the fairy. But Ozma only shook her head. "That time is past now," she said quietly, and he saw that he wouldn't get anything else out of her on the subject of Glinda.

Ozma pushed her plate away, and a servant immediately appeared to clear the remains of their meal. The vulnerability vanished from her expression, and she smiled brightly at the Lion. "How long will you be staying with us, dear Lion?"

The Lion's mind raced as he tried to decide how to answer her question. Glinda hadn't said how long it would take to find this mysterious necklace, and the palace was huge. Ozma laughed again at his consternation. "Of course, you can stay as long as you like!" she exclaimed. "As long as you really can leave the forest to itself, I'll be glad of the company. You mustn't think I'm trying to get rid of you."

"That's very generous, Your Highness," the Lion said.

"But only if you promise to call me Ozma," she added in a mock-serious tone. "We're friends, after all. And we're practically equals. Now, I'm sure you must be tired after your journey. I'll see you in the morning?"

The Lion knew a dismissal when he heard one, but at least Ozma hadn't realized his motives for visiting her weren't entirely selfless. He bowed deeply, stifling a burp, and returned to his chambers, leaving Ozma sitting alone in her enormous room like a lost, lonely doll.

SIX

The Lion quickly found that he did not miss the Forest of the Beasts—or being a king—at all. Despite all the servants and palace staff, Ozma was strangely alone in the Emerald Palace. The Lion was the closest thing she had to a friend, and soon Ozma was spending all her free time with him. Ozma loved to stroll through the palace gardens, and never grew tired of pointing out new plantings of flowers or trees. She braided flowers into the Lion's mane and tail while he napped idly in the soft grass of the palace lawns. Occasionally, if she had a free day, the queen would disguise herself in a shabby old dress and cloak, and she and the Lion would wander through the streets of the Emerald City. The Lion had never spent much time in the city itself, and he grew to love its mysterious back alleyways and odd little shops where Ozma bought exotic herbs and spices, rich fabrics from the farthest corners of Oz, and rare old books in languages the Lion didn't know. He suspected that the shopkeepers often recognized the queen but respected her attempt at hiding her identity, and always pretended not to know her.

But Ozma was often busy with royal duties. Not all of the Emerald City had recovered from Jinjur's brief, catastrophic rule, and Ozma was occupied with overseeing reconstruction of areas that had been destroyed. Ozma always invited him to attend her various meetings and conferences with her, but the Lion was easily bored by the endless talking and planning. As the King of the Beasts, he had never had to do much administration. The Lion waited patiently for a good moment to search for Glinda's necklace, but someone was always around—if not Ozma, one of the many courtiers who advised her.

At last, his chance came. Ozma called an important meeting and everyone from her most trusted counselors to the least important state undersecretary shut themselves up in the banquet hall. He was alone and could start the search Glinda had compelled him to perform.

The occupied parts of the palace seemed like an unlikely place to find it; surely someone would have noticed something as unusual as a ruby necklace. Instead, he began his search in the wine cellars, where huge barrels of wine lay in a thick coat of dust. The Lion idly poked his paw into the cracks between barrels, feeling almost silly. What could Glinda possibly want with some silly old piece of jewelry, anyway, even if he was able to find it? His search dislodged an avalanche of dust and debris, and he sneezed violently.

"Hello?" called an anxious voice from the stairwell. The Lion looked around for a hiding place, but the gaps between the wine casks were too narrow. The wine steward, a short, fat Munchkin with an enormous beard that obscured most of his face, came down the stairs and stopped short at the sight of the Lion.

"Your Highness," he said suspiciously. "What are you doing down here, sir?"

The Lion had to stifle a laugh when he realized the steward thought he was trying to steal a drink. "Just, er, checking to make sure everything looks all right down here," he said. "You know how Her Majesty worries."

The steward's eyes narrowed. "It's my job to make sure the cellars are in order."

"And an excellent job you're doing, too," the Lion said loftily, sweeping past him and bounding up the stairs. "Keep up the good work."

He tried again a few days later after dinner, ducking out of the banquet hall just as dessert was being served. (He didn't care for ambleberry custard, which had a habit of walking away from the person trying to eat it.) But he'd barely gotten away from the busiest part of the palace before he heard Ozma's anxious voice behind him. "Lion! Dear Lion, I was hoping you might have tea with me in my chambers." The loneliness in the queen's voice was unmistakable.

"Of course, Your Highness," he said. He wasn't sorry to turn away from his task. It had seemed so important, so burning, when Glinda had left him. But as the days passed in the palace her request seemed less and less important. It was as if the palace itself—or perhaps the continual hum of Ozma's magic—was insulating him from Glinda's will.

After his second attempt, he more or less gave up searching for Glinda's necklace. He must have imagined the threat in her tone when she'd visited him in the Kingdom of the Beasts. As the days turned into weeks, the Lion happily ate his way through the palace stores and spent time with Ozma whenever he could. He forgot the joys of running through the forest with the wind in his fur and the satisfaction of hunting his own prey. He grew lazier and lazier, soon reluctant even to accompany Ozma on her walks. He could have stayed at Ozma's side in the Emerald Palace indefinitely—and he would have, if Ozma hadn't decided it was time to save Oz.

SEVEN

The Lion had gotten into the habit of sleeping in every morning and ordering a late breakfast in his room, but that morning Ozma summoned him just after dawn. She did not seem to have slept, and her face was worried and exhausted. She sent a servant to fetch them breakfast and then turned to face the Lion. "I've been thinking all night," she began, skipping any formalities. "I think it's for the best you've come to the palace now. My dear Lion, I'm afraid I need your courage—and your counsel. No one else knows yet, but Oz is on the brink of war."

The Lion stared at her. "War? Again? With who?"

She sighed wearily and rubbed her forehead with the heel of one hand, looking far more vulnerable than he had ever seen her. "Do you know of the Land of Ev?"

"Ev? But that's just a legend, isn't it?" The Lion had heard stories of the fabled country beyond the Deadly Desert, but he'd always assumed they were just children's fairy stories. "There's nothing past the Deadly Desert but the Other Place."

"I wish that were true. But Ev is another country just like Oz, though the fairies didn't have any hand in founding it. And just like Oz, it has its own counties and rulers. My ancestors traveled through Ev to reach the place where they created Oz, and brought with them stories of their journey. Ev is a far less kind place than Oz is, peopled with strange, cruel creatures who do not love peace the way we do. Many of them have searched for years for a way through the desert to Oz, and now one of their most evil tyrants has found one."

"Who?" the Lion breathed.

"The Nome King," Ozma said. The Lion had never heard of such a person, but something about the way Ozma said the name sent a chill through him. "He lives in an underground palace, and rules over a people who are the distant kin of fairies. He is evil, through and through; he thrives on the pain and suffering of others, and all but the most powerful of his people live like slaves. He forces them to mine the earth for precious metals and jewels, and in addition to being powerful, he's incredibly rich. He's like the fairies in that he can't die—he's hundreds of years old, maybe even older. For a long time he's been building a network of tunnels under the Deadly Desert, and he's finally reached his goal. He'll be at the Emerald City in a matter of days. His magic is so strong that I can sense him coming. I can even sense his plans. He's not trying to hide; he knows how vulnerable we are here."

"How can we stop him?" the Lion asked, and Ozma shook her head.

"I don't know yet. He's incredibly powerful, and the Emerald City has no army."

"Glinda—" the Lion began, and then stopped as Ozma smiled sadly at him.

"Glinda has an army, yes. But I can't trust her, Lion. Not the way I can trust you. I don't think she would throw in her lot with the Nome King, but she has her own ideas about how to govern Oz, and I can't count on her support. It's down to me—and you, if you'll help me. You fought bravely in the battle against Jinjur, and I need every strong fighter we have on my side. The people of Oz aren't used to war."

"Of course," the Lion said immediately. He had come here to protect Ozma, right? He hadn't promised Glinda he wouldn't help Ozma—only that he'd search for the Wizard's necklace, and keep an eye on Ozma while Glinda was away from the city. And he was already coming to care for the young queen. She was such an intriguing combination of youth and wisdom, strength and vulnerability—and she'd treated him like an equal and a friend. Even Glinda hadn't done that. If he hadn't bound himself to Glinda back in the Forest of the Beasts, he would have abandoned his vows to her altogether. He knew Glinda's spell had compelled him to help her, but it seemed as though the strength of it was weakening the longer he was in the palace. He'd worry about Glinda's desire for the necklace later. If the Emerald City fell to the Nome King, he wouldn't be doing much looking for jewelry anyway.

"Do you have a plan?" the Lion asked. "Of course I'll fight

with you, but strategy is Scare's department, not mine."

Ozma frowned. "I'd rather not bring him into this if I can
help it."

So things really *had* gone south between the three of them.
What had the Scarecrow and Glinda tried to do in the aftermath
of the battle with Jinjur? *Never mind*, the Lion thought. *Palace
intrigue is Scare's thing; I just eat and fight. Let him and Glinda
try to outmaneuver each other.* He wondered briefly what would
happen if he disobeyed Glinda altogether. How powerful was
the spell that bound him? Surely she wouldn't actually hurt him
if he decided not to obey her orders? The situation was far more
complicated than he thought, and it seemed entirely possible that
Glinda wasn't on Ozma's side at all. Suddenly, he realized Ozma
was still talking.

". . . can convince him otherwise, we might be able to avoid
fighting altogether. I was hoping you would agree to be my
bodyguard."

"Yes, of course," the Lion said, and then, "what? Isn't that
Tin's department?"

Ozma laughed. "You have to pay better attention before you
make promises, dear Lion!" Did she *know* about the deal Glinda
had forced him into? He stared at her in panic, but her beautiful face was guileless. "You're here, and Tin isn't. We have to
act now. I think if we can meet the Nome King underground,
before he reaches the Emerald City, I might be able to convince
him that there's nothing for him in Oz. My magic is powerful,
but it's not strong enough to hold him back if something goes

wrong. I could use you as a bodyguard."

"We'll have an escort?"

"If anyone in Oz finds out about this, there will be a terrible panic. If I can prevent—if *we* can prevent the Nome King from ever setting foot in Oz, no one will ever have to know."

"We're going underground, alone, to confront an ancient enemy of Oz who might have an entire army with him?"

"Oh, I'm sure the army isn't with him yet," Ozma said cheerfully. "I would probably have sensed it if they were. He'll just be supervising the final construction of the tunnels. The army won't come through until he's ready to invade Oz. It won't be the least bit dangerous—I'd just feel better if you were there. A lion is a very impressive-looking lieutenant."

Probably have sensed an army? The Lion wondered briefly if the stress of the situation had caused Ozma to lose her mind. But she looked happier than he'd seen her since he arrived at the Emerald Palace, now that he'd agreed to go with her. He couldn't let her down now—not if the future of Oz was at stake.

"If you think it's a good idea, I'm sure it is," he said. Ozma's face lit up again and she threw her arms around his chest.

"I knew you'd help!" she cried.

"When will we leave?"

"Why, right now, don't you think? There's no sense in wasting time."

"Right now? Are you sure?" The Lion's stomach rumbled, even though he'd just eaten. "What about lunch?"

Ozma laughed. "You can bring something to eat along the

way. The Nome King is very close—it won't take us long to find him. Why, we could be back in the Emerald Palace by dinnertime if all goes well. There's an old tunnel system underneath the Emerald Palace that we can use to reach the Nome King's tunnel."

"Why hasn't the Nome King used them himself?"

"The fairies—my ancestors—passed down the knowledge of the tunnels among themselves, but no one else knows about them anymore," Ozma explained. "They're very, very old— older than the Emerald Palace itself. Some people say they were there even before the fairies created Oz, although no one knows for sure. They may have been created by the Nomes themselves, ages ago, even before the Deadly Desert formed and separated us from the Land of Ev."

The Lion's eyes widened. "I didn't know there *was* anything before the Deadly Desert."

Ozma laughed. "Of course there was, silly! Nothing is forever. And the Nomes are an ancient people, nearly as old as the fairies, though luckily for us they've forgotten as much as we have about the prehistory of our lands. The Nome King would have invaded long ago if he knew the tunnels existed. Anyway, we should be able to find a way to get close to where the Nome King is digging. My magic connects to the magic of Oz, and I can feel any disturbances, especially this close to the Emerald City. It's difficult to teleport underground, but if we get close enough, I can do it if we have to."

The Lion got to his feet, eyeing the empty breakfast plates

sadly. Ozma, seeing his look, snapped her fingers and a heavy bundle appeared. "There's your lunch," she said, still laughing, and handed it to the Lion. He tucked the bundle over his shoulder, feeling much better about the adventure now that there was food involved.

"Lead the way!" he said, and followed Ozma out of the room.

EIGHT

It was still early, and the palace halls were nearly empty. Ozma led him down out-of-the-way corridors, anxious to avoid anyone who might ask questions about where the queen was going. She had magically transformed her royal gown into a plain traveling dress and covered herself with a drab gray cloak, but she wore her golden crown, and there was no mistaking her queenly air. She was so fiercely intelligent, so alert, that it would have been difficult for her to ever truly disguise herself, the Lion thought. Her intensity shone from her electric green eyes and was clear in her precise, alert movements. Oz's new queen was formidable indeed.

Ozma led him farther and farther into the depths of the palace, and soon they saw no one at all. This part of the castle was silent and oppressive. They were too deep for any natural light to reach them, and the hallways were lit with sooty, guttering torches that flared into life as they approached and then extinguished themselves again, leaving the hall behind them in thick, velvety darkness. Without light from the outside, the Lion had no sense of the passage of time, or how long they had been walking. Down here, the hallways were carpeted with a thick layer of dust that drifted up into his nostrils and made him sneeze. No one had been down here in a long, long time. Here and there, and then more frequently, the cut stone walls gave way to sheer rock, and the floor pitched steeply downward.

"We're going underground now," Ozma said unnecessarily. Hers were the first words either of them had spoken in a long time, and her voice rang out harshly in the dense silence so that both of them flinched. Ozma took a deep breath and straightened her back. "This is a very old part of Oz," she said more firmly, "but it's not a hostile one. You have nothing to fear here, Lion."

He suspected her words were meant to reassure herself as much as him, but he only nodded. The line of torches ended soon after she spoke. Ozma muttered something under her breath and snapped her fingers, and a tiny ball of cheerful yellow light sprung to life and darted back the way they had come. "Over here!" Ozma called, and it dutifully fluttered back to hover directly over Ozma's head, where it seemed to shrink a little.

"Can you make it go ahead of us so it lights the way a little better?" the Lion asked. Ozma said something to the ball of light and it shivered violently.

"It's afraid of the dark," Ozma said apologetically.

"*I'm* not afraid of the dark," the Lion said. But despite the

Wizard's gift of courage, he wasn't quite as confident as he sounded. The darkness itself closed in like a living thing, its menace creeping into his heart and stealing away his bravery. In the distance, he could hear a faint dripping noise, as if water was slowly dribbling from a great height. He could feel the weight of the stone above them, as if the ceiling was beginning to sink. What would they do if the tunnel crumbled? he thought, beginning to panic. He huddled on the floor, covering his head with his paws as if that would somehow protect him, but he knew the feeble gesture was useless. This was the end. He'd never see the light again, or run through the forest, or feel fresh air riffling through his fur. They'd be trapped down here, down in the darkness forever . . .

"Stop!" Ozma's voice rang out into the darkness, and her ball of light blazed a little brighter. "I am Ozma of Oz, direct descendant of the fairy Lurline and rightful ruler of Oz! I come on a mission of protection!" Her wings fluttered, the golden veins catching the light and scattering it like a shower of fireworks. Suddenly, she was every inch a queen, all trace of the lonely, frightened girl he knew completely erased. As she spoke, the panic that had gripped the Lion eased immediately, and the feeling that the tunnel was collapsing around him slipped away. He took a deep, relieved breath.

"This place is very old," Ozma said again in a normal tone of voice. "It doesn't like strangers."

The Lion had nothing to say to that, but he let Ozma go ahead of him as they continued down the tunnel, and he stopped more than once to listen carefully, making sure no one was following them.

As the tunnel continued to descend, the air grew warmer and warmer. The Lion's fur itched in the heat, and even Ozma looked a little wilted in the wan light from her orb. Moisture ran down the rough stone walls and trickled past their feet. Ozma stopped suddenly, and the Lion nearly ran into her. "What is it?" he asked. Ozma pointed at a yawning patch of darkness in the tunnel wall, and it took the Lion a moment to realize it was another tunnel branching off from theirs. Ozma closed her eyes, holding up both hands to the hot, stifling air for several long, tension-filled seconds before dropping them again and opening her eyes. "This way," she said, continuing down the same tunnel.

"Are you sure?" the Lion asked. Ozma didn't answer. The ball of light bobbed slightly, as if it were shrugging. The Lion kept his doubts to himself and padded along after Ozma.

They began to pass side tunnels with increasing frequency. At each juncture, Ozma stopped and performed the same mysterious ritual, her face upturned and her palms lifted, before deciding which way to go. Some of the tunnels they passed opened up on vast, jewel-encrusted caverns where even the orb's meager light was reflected into dazzling brilliance. Once the Lion peered into a doorway, entranced by a dim green glow. He saw a huge, empty hall. Its floor was an elaborate tiled mosaic that had mostly crumbled away. Its walls were painted with rich murals nearly swallowed up by an eerie moss that was the source

of the sickly green light, but here and there sections of the paintings remained. Unable to resist his curiosity, the Lion wandered
in for a closer look. The murals were so vivid their subjects
seemed almost alive: long-limbed, pale-skinned people with
thick white hair cascading down their backs moved through
endless candlelit libraries, or painted beautiful pictures of cave
crystals and pools, or played instruments the Lion didn't recognize. One of the paintings depicted them seated at a huge table in
the hall itself, piled high with strange-looking foods. At the head
of the table sat a stern, pale man wearing a silver crown. His eyes
were cold and hard and cruel.

At the far end of the hall a huge, pale marble staircase led
up into the darkness as far as the Lion could see. The marble,
like the moss that covered the banquet hall's walls, glowed
with a pale, unearthly light. It was cracked and pitted, and in
places chunks of the staircase were missing altogether, leaving
black, cavernous gaps. As soon as he saw the staircase, the Lion
couldn't look away. Where did it lead? The question throbbed
in his brain until he was unable to think of anything else. He
had to know. Before he knew it, his paw was on the first stair.
The marble was as cold as ice and burned like fire. *Welcome*, it
seemed to whisper. *Come with us . . .*

NINE

"Lion!" Ozma's voice was loud and clear in the huge room. The Lion jumped and lifted his paw away from the marble stairs. Immediately, the voice in his mind lessened its grip and he shook his head furiously, trying to dislodge it. Ozma was at his side in seconds, one hand on his shoulder and her light bobbing behind.

"We are still under the Deadly Desert," she said quietly, "but this was once part of the Nome Kingdom in the Land of Ev. The Nomes' magic lingers here even now, all these centuries later."

With Ozma at his side, the pull of the staircase was gone entirely. The Lion padded back to the murals, studying them carefully. "These are Nomes?"

Ozma nodded, looking over his shoulder. "Some people say they are actually fairies themselves, who went down under the earth long ago and became a distant branch of our people. There are fairies living underground in Oz who look very much like them."

"They don't look very nice," he said simply.

"The Nomes are not a kind people." Ozma stared at the cruel-eyed man in the painting of the banquet hall and shivered. "This place is tainted. Its power nearly trapped you. Come back to the tunnel, and be careful not to leave my side again."

After that, the Lion made sure to stay in the circle of Ozma's light. They passed more and more tunnels, but now Ozma seemed sure of where they were going and only rarely stopped to find the way. Soon, the Lion could hear a faint, distant noise echoing through the tunnel. "What is that?" he asked.

"The king," Ozma said quietly. "Digging." As they drew closer, the noise grew louder: a repetitive clanking, like metal striking stone.

Ozma stopped. "We're close," she said. "If you want to rest, now is a good time. We may not be able to later."

The Lion had been so overwhelmed by the strangeness of their descent that he'd forgotten his hunger for the first time in his life, but at Ozma's words his stomach rumbled loudly. Ozma smiled, some of the strain leaving her pale, drawn face as she laughed at the Lion's discomfort. "Even down here, some things never change," she said teasingly.

They found a dry patch on the tunnel floor and settled down. The Lion tore eagerly into his bundle and found a hunk of dried meat, some fruit, and a jug of water. Ozma nibbled starfruit and sipped water while he happily gnawed the meat. They sat in silence for a while, letting some of the weariness fade from their limbs.

"What happens when we meet the Nome King?"

Ozma stretched, and the air around her shimmered for a second as if her magic was stirring with her. "I'll talk to him and explain to him how important it is that Oz remains free."

The Lion thought that this seemed like a naive view of the situation. "I could fight him," he offered, puffing up his chest. "I certainly will if he tries to attack you." Presumably that was why Ozma had brought him along. If things went south, he could protect her. But as brave as he was, he secretly had his doubts about taking on who knew how many evil fairy-like creatures. His only real fighting experience was the battle with Jinjur, and her soldiers had been mortal girls.

As if Ozma could read his mind, she smiled at him. "You don't need to worry, Lion," she said confidently. "I know you think I'm being silly, but I can be very persuasive when I have to." Her words had that steely hint behind them, and he remembered how she had sounded when she talked about Glinda. If anyone could talk an ancient, evil, homicidal king out of invading their country, Ozma was probably the one.

Ozma's magic light bobbed anxiously. "It's time to go," she said, reaching forward to scratch the Lion behind the ears. "I'm so glad you're with me. You don't know what a difference it makes to have you here. It's so lonely down here in the dark." Her voice sounded wistful now, and she resembled the sad, brave creature he'd left sitting alone in her chambers on his first night in the Emerald City. Ozma might be powerful, but she was still barely more than a child.

The Lion stood up and lashed his tail fiercely. "I won't let anything happen to you, Your Majesty," he said. "Not here and not anywhere else. I'll be glad to protect you until—until the day I die."

"Let's hope it doesn't come to that, but thank you." Ozma continued down the tunnel. The Lion followed.

In just a few moments, the clanking noise they'd heard earlier was so loud it was almost deafening. It echoed down the long, dark tunnel so powerfully that the Lion was tempted to cover his ears with his paws. Ozma stopped in front of a blank wall. Even the ball of light was nervous; it wobbled in tiny circles overhead.

"He's here," she said. "Thank goodness. I wasn't actually sure he would be."

"You came down all this way and you didn't even know if the Nome King would be *here*?" the Lion asked in disbelief.

"It seemed likely he would be," Ozma said serenely. "But you never know." She rested her palms on the rough stone wall and the air around her began to glow. Her huge, beautiful gold-veined wings unfurled from her back like a butterfly's and spread outward in the still, hot air, glowing with a brilliant emerald light. "We won't have long to get through," she gasped, her voice thick with exertion. "When I say the word, you have to follow me right away."

As the incredulous Lion watched, the stone began to glow red-hot around Ozma's palms. The red glow spread outward like molten lava, running in channels to form the outline of a door covered in mysterious runes. A golden doorknob, glowing with the same emerald light as Ozma's wings, protruded from the door. "Now!" Ozma yelled, yanking at the doorknob. The entire door-shaped section of wall swung inward, and Ozma leapt into the darkness on the other side with the Lion and the ball of light at her heels. The Lion was half convinced he'd slam into solid stone, but instead he felt as though he were falling from a great distance. And then, with a bone-jarring thump, he landed on the floor of another tunnel.

"Well, well, well," hissed a sinister, sibilant voice. "What under the earth do we have here?"

TEN

The Lion rolled to his feet, looking around frantically. Ozma lay crumpled next to him, her head lolling at an unnatural angle. She looked unconscious—or dead. The Lion swallowed hard. She had to be fine. She had to be. Panic welled up in his chest. What was he going to do now? Everything was up to him! He remembered the terrible darkness in the tunnels, the way he'd thought it was alive. He didn't want to die down here in this awful place.

But then he remembered Ozma's strong, powerful voice when she'd challenged the darkness, and felt ashamed of himself. He was a Lion—and not just any Lion but a king bearing the Wizard's gift of courage. He would be strong. He looked around again, confidence flooding through him.

They had landed in some kind of cavern. The walls were lined with torches that burned with a blue fire and did little to dispel the darkness. The ceiling was high enough to be lost overhead in blackness. The clanging noise was almost deafening, and the air was even hotter than it had been in the tunnel they had just left.

The man who had spoken was looming over him. The Lion recognized him instantly. He looked exactly like the pale, terrifying king from the banquet hall. His skin was a sickly white. His icy pale eyes glittered evilly in the blue torchlight, and he wore robes as densely black as the darkness that surrounded them. But instead of the long white hair the king in the painting had had, this creature was as hairless as an egg. He seemed both ancient and ageless at the same time—there was something fathomless, cold and cruel and very, very old, in his eyes. An iron crown, wrought in the shape of thorny branches, rested on his bald head. He carried a staff topped with a glowing blue crystal. There was no mistaking him for anyone other than the Nome King.

The Lion drew himself upright, hoping his voice sounded more confident than he felt. "I am the Once-Cowardly Lion of Oz, bearer of the Courage of the Wizard of Oz and King of the Beasts, and I demand you desist your invasion of Oz at once," he shouted over the clanging, hoping fervently that Ozma would wake up any minute.

The Nome King laughed and waved one hand. Around him, the darkness seethed, and suddenly he was surrounded by pale, thin warriors in black armor, their faces hidden by black helmets. The Lion's heart missed a beat, but he held his ground, determined not to show his fear.

"You're a long way from home, little cat," the Nome King hissed. "Do you really think you're in a position to be making demands?" He leaned forward, and the Lion took an involuntary step backward. The crystal on top of the Nome King's staff blazed with blue-white light. At last the Lion saw the source of the terrible metallic noise. At one end of the huge cavern, a vast, many-armed machine of iridescent blue metal the Lion had never seen before was chipping away at the rock. More bald Nomes—these stoop-shouldered and scuttling, wearing leather aprons over their shirtless chests—stoked a furnace at the heart of the machine, dumping load after load of coals into the glowing inferno. They wore thick black glass goggles on tattered leather straps to protect their eyes from the heat. Huge leather gloves clanking with chain mail kept the coals from burning their hands. They were all pale as mushrooms but coated in black dust, their lean, wiry bodies scarred and burned where the leather had not been enough to protect them. Many of them had carved elaborate designs into their bare arms and chests and packed the cuts with coal dust so that their skin seemed covered in dense black lace. Others had shoved chunks of iron through their earlobes, noses, or lips. Moving together, they looked like an army of sinister beetles pushing their burdens back and forth like ants carrying food back to their nests.

"I have been working for a very long time to reach the glorious country of Oz," the Nome King snarled. "Do you think I'll stop now because a snippy little house cat says I should?"

"You'll stop because the Queen of Oz tells you to," said a high, clear voice behind the Lion. The Nome King's sneer transformed momentarily to a look of shock. The Lion whirled around. Ozma stood tall and proud, her wings spread out to their full span and their golden veins glowing. Her dark hair whipped around her head, crackling with electricity. Her green eyes had darkened to black and her enchanted orb blazed with a green light that rivaled the Nome King's crystal. The two rulers stared at each other, neither of them giving an inch.

"If it isn't Lurline's little protégé, the Princess of Oz," the Nome King laughed, recovering quickly from his surprise. "Do you really think your magic is a match for mine, child?"

"I'm the Queen of Oz now," Ozma said coldly. "And you know it is, old man. Abandon this foolish plan and leave my country in peace. There is no reason for war between our peoples."

"Oh, there are plenty of reasons," the Nome King said, waving his arm again. The cavern wall behind him shimmered and dissolved into a window onto another world. The sky was a dark, stormy gray over barren fields where blackened stalks of corn and wheat looked like skeletons. A harsh wind blew dust storms across the desolate landscape, whipping against the crumbling stone walls of a tiny village that looked abandoned. But as the Lion looked more closely, he saw gaunt, desperate faces in the windows of the houses. A starving dog limped through the empty streets, too hungry even to howl. And the wall was lined with—the Lion flinched in horror—heads. Some were human, and some were creatures he didn't recognize at all. Creatures he'd never seen before.

As they watched in horror, a group of strange, terrifying creatures descended on the desolate village. Their bodies were human but their arms and legs were the same length so that they moved on all fours. How can they move so quickly? the Lion wondered, and then he saw that the creatures' feet and hands had been replaced by whirling, spiked wheels. As they drew closer to the village, he could see their clothes—crazed, clashing patchworks of garish colors that stood out harshly against the washed-out landscape. Their eyes were mad and wild. One of them hefted a blazing torch aloft and with a screech of laughter hurled it at the nearest house. The straw roof caught immediately, and soon the entire hovel was ablaze as its inhabitants poured out into the dirt street in terror. More of the wheeled creatures set fire to the village, shrieking with glee and laughing and pointing at its helpless, sobbing inhabitants.

"Behold the Land of Ev," hissed the Nome King. "The Deadly Desert is expanding. The drought is so severe nothing can grow. The Wheelers terrorize my subjects. The magic itself is seeping out of the land. Unless Oz shares its bounty, the country is doomed." He glanced back at his warriors. "Plus, I'm getting really tired of living underground," he said in a more conversational tone. "Bad for the complexion, you know? And the only thing to eat is mushrooms. I'm *really* sick of mushrooms."

Ozma looked stunned. "I did not know it was so bad there," she whispered.

"The people above the earth are starving," the Nome King said. "The riches of Oz are vast. Why would you not agree to share them? From what I hear, the Emerald Palace is plenty big enough for two." His words were reasonable, but there was a dangerous glitter in his pale eyes.

The Lion remembered himself. He was the King of the Beasts and the Protector of Ozma, and he was not to be trifled with. "You didn't ask to share!" the Lion roared furiously. "You're tunneling under the Deadly Desert to invade Oz!"

The Nome King barely flinched at the Lion's fierce roar. He drew himself up to his full height, his eyes blazing. "Did you expect us to beg, Lion? To come crawling through the desert like some poor relation? Oz is no greater a country than Ev, and no more deserving of its riches!"

"But why are you invading?" the Lion protested. "You could have sent a messenger! Anything other than spending years digging under the desert in secret."

"The Wizard was no friend of the Land of Ev," the Nome King said coldly. "I did not know Ozma had replaced him."

The Lion narrowed his eyes. *He's lying,* he thought. Did Ozma guess? If she did, she was hiding it. What did she have up her sleeve? He made a noise of protest, but Ozma held up a hand to silence him.

"My dear, brave Lion," she said gently. "The Nome King is right. If the Wizard is partly responsible for the suffering of the people of Ev, it's our duty to help them. I will do what the king asks, if it means avoiding war."

How could the Wizard be responsible if no one knew for certain that Ev even existed? Ozma wasn't making any sense. But the Nome King's eyes lit up, and his warriors took a step back, apparently deciding they would not be needed to defend him.

"We have been preparing for war for a long time, and my people are angry," he said. "Peace will not be quite as easy as you think, Ozma. Ev is not some charity case that you can dismiss with a few loaves of bread."

"How can we avoid a battle?" Ozma asked, her eyes wide. Lion couldn't believe she was still negotiating, when it looked like she had already lost.

The Nome King was silent for a long moment, and then a slow, nasty smile spread across his face. The Lion shivered. And cursed his courage for leaving him when he needed it most.

"I will make you a bargain," he said. "You will allow me to use my magic to disguise you. If your little companion can recognize you, I will return to Ev."

"And if he fails?"

The Nome King smiled. "If I am to sacrifice everything, then your cost must be a great one, too. If he fails, you will remain enchanted—forever."

Ozma tilted her head, considering. "If you return to Ev, you're not sacrificing anything at all except a war with my people."

"You see what Ev is like now," the Nome King hissed. "This is our last chance to survive. If you defeat me, Princess Ozma, my kingdom is ruined. My people will starve. I would not dream of asking any less of you."

"No!" the Lion roared. "If you are enchanted, Princess, he will claim Oz for himself!"

"Perhaps," the Nome King said idly, picking his nails with a triumphant look in his eyes.

"That's not—" the Lion began desperately, but Ozma cut him off.

"He gets six guesses," she said.

The Nome King laughed. "Are you kidding?"

"Five."

"Three," he said, rolling his eyes.

"I'm not—" the Lion said.

"Agreed," Ozma interrupted, extending her hand to the Nome King. He took it, and their clasped hands blazed with a searing green light. Green lightning cracked across the cavern, and for just a second a cool, refreshing breeze wafted past them. The Nome King yelped in surprise and yanked his hand back.

"What have you done, witch?"

"I'm a fairy, not a witch," Ozma said calmly. "And I've bound you to your word with all the power of Oz."

The Nome King stared at her, his eyes glittering with suspicion, but Ozma returned his gaze with an innocent smile. "May I speak to the Lion before you enchant me, Your Highness?" she asked sweetly.

He scowled. "If you must, but be quick about it. My people are hungry. I am not interested in delays."

Ozma knelt down beside the Lion and hugged him. "Trust me, dear Lion," she whispered into his ear.

"How will I know you?" the Lion asked. "What if I fail?"

"You won't," Ozma said confidently. "You can't."

That was hardly reassuring, but Ozma was already standing up to face the king. "I'm ready," she said.

The Nome King's smile was so sinister that even the Lion's courage faltered. He raised both arms, and his robes opened slightly, revealing an elaborate ruby necklace glittering at his throat. A ruby necklace the Lion recognized immediately. It was the necklace Glinda had shown him in the Forest of the Beasts. He blinked. Was it possible? Did the Nome King have the necklace Glinda was looking for? How had he gotten it? Ozma's eyes narrowed. She'd seen the necklace, too. Did she know what it was?

But there was no time to think about that now. The Nome King flicked his wrist, and the cavern began to fill with a silvery, foul-smelling mist. The Lion covered his face with his paws, but he couldn't help breathing in the noxious fumes. *"Replicatum scatterorium,"* the Nome King hissed, and the weird mist evaporated. Coughing, the Lion looked up. The floor of the cavern was covered with tiny silver figurines that looked exactly like the Queen of Oz, and Ozma was gone.

ELEVEN

The Nome King yawned loudly. One of his warriors hurried to bring him a silver stool. He settled onto it, stretching ostentatiously and yawning again. "Hurry up, house cat," he said, examining his silver nails. "We haven't got all day down here."

The Nome King wasn't just an evil tyrant hell-bent on taking over Oz, the Lion thought irritably. He was also incredibly annoying, and he was clearly pretty powerful. But for whatever reason, Ozma had thought this was a good idea, and now it was up to him to save her and the entire Land of Oz.

The Lion bent down to sniff at the silver figurines. Each miniature Ozma was slightly different. Some of the Ozmas were smiling, and others looked like they were about to cry. A few seemed angry. Some of the tiny Ozmas had tiny accessories: one was holding a miniature scepter, and another was carrying a giant cake. They all had one thing in common, however: each one looked exactly like the queen. The Lion almost groaned aloud. How was he supposed to tell which one was the real Ozma?

"Do I get a hint?" he asked, stalling for time. The Nome King only snorted, not bothering to reply.

The Lion didn't have magic and he knew deep down he wasn't particularly smart. But Ozma had seemed to know what she was doing. Why had she thought he'd be able to solve this puzzle? What did he have to help him? Courage wasn't going to do him much good.

"I'm *waiting*," the Nome King said.

"Oh, calm down," the Lion snapped, and the Nome King looked momentarily surprised. He obviously wasn't used to anyone talking back to him. Was that what set the Lion apart? He paced the cavern floor, examining each of the dozens of tiny Ozmas until he found one that seemed to have an extra bit of difference. Its face was just a teensy bit more realistic than the others, and something about the silver folds of its dress looked familiar. "That one," he said, pointing with his paw. With a pop, the silver figurine exploded into confetti.

The Nome King giggled. "Not even close," he said. "You're really bad at this, aren't you? What was Ozma thinking, putting you in a position of responsibility? In *my* kingdom, only *qualified* people get to be in charge."

"I wish you'd stop talking," the Lion muttered under his breath, trying not to panic. He still had two more guesses. There was still a chance to save Ozma—and Oz. But the Nome King was getting restless. His warriors shifted where they stood, their armor clanking.

"Maybe I should just kill you," he said thoughtfully.

"You can't," the Lion said quickly. "You made a bargain. Ozma sealed it."

"The deal was that if you recognized Ozma I'd let you both go," the Nome King said. "I didn't say anything about not killing you."

"I can't recognize Ozma if I'm dead," the Lion pointed out. "So technically you *did* agree to keep me alive."

"An unfortunate technicality," the Nome King said peevishly, sinking back onto his stool. The Lion was proud of himself. That line of argument had been worthy of the Scarecrow's brain. Maybe he wasn't so stupid after all. Maybe that was the secret to finding the real Ozma: using his brain. What would set enchanted Ozma apart from the rest of the silver figurines? She was the Queen of Oz, obviously. Her magic was green. She was young, but somehow also ageless. The Lion was thinking so hard he could practically feel gears turning in his brain. Was this what it felt like to be the Scarecrow? Thinking was exhausting work. He looked up. The Nome King's soldiers had surrounded him. "You can't kill me," he said again, his heart pounding.

"I suppose *I* can't," the Nome King said. "But if *they* do it . . ." He didn't have to finish.

"That one!" the Lion yelped in a panic, pointing to another statuette. It disappeared in a flash of silver smoke, and the Nome King leapt to his feet, clapping.

"Never mind!" he exclaimed. "This is rather fun! You're doing my work for me, you stupid cat. Watching you suffer is almost making up for how boring this whole afternoon has been." He waved at his soldiers, and they advanced toward the Lion in a terrifying ring.

The Lion's fear turned to anger. He was still the King of the Beasts of Oz, and he did not appreciate being bullied by this creepy king. The Lion reared back on his hind legs, roaring fiercely. To his satisfaction, the soldiers took a step backward. It was impossible to read their expressions behind the black helmets, but he imagined they looked impressed and a little afraid. "That's more like it," he said.

"Oh, whatever," said the Nome King. "You've only got one guess left, anyway, and I'm sure you'll botch that one, too." He sat back down, looking sulky.

The Lion's mind raced. This was it. If he chose wrong, both Oz and its queen were toast. His stomach rumbled loudly. He hadn't eaten since he and Ozma had had their little snack. He was starving. If he screwed up now, he wouldn't even get the benefit of a last meal.

Suddenly, he got a whiff of something delicious. His nostrils flared. The Nome King and his army smelled flat and metallic, like hot iron being quenched in water. This was the smell of something living, flesh and bone and blood and *edible*.

And then in a flash he knew why Ozma had trusted him to choose correctly. Ozma wasn't human, and she wasn't mortal, but she *was* flesh and blood. Under other circumstances, he might have eaten her. Obviously he wouldn't dream of snacking on the Queen of Oz—and his friend—but that didn't mean she wouldn't smell like something delicious, especially if he was hungry. He closed his eyes, letting his hunger overwhelm him. His stomach growled again. He let everything else fall away— the king, the warriors, the cavern, the impossible task at hand. He was back in the Forest of the Beasts, hunting for his prey. He crouched low, lashing his tail, his nose to the ground. There it was again: the faintest scent of breathing, living flesh.

"What do you think you're doing?" shrieked the Nome King, but the Lion ignored him. He was on the prowl in the forest, ears tuned to the slightest rustle, all his senses on full alert, placing his paws carefully and noiselessly. There, in the bushes ahead, was his target. He gathered his strength, his muscles coiling like springs, and pounced.

He landed with a clatter of pebbles and opened his eyes. He'd dislodged a tarnished silver figurine from the floor of the cavern, where it was mostly hidden by a pile of gravel. It was duller than the other statuettes, and the rough silver face looked nothing like Ozma. He knew without question that this was the one.

"You weren't supposed to *hide* her," he said to the Nome King. "That's cheating." He nudged the figurine with his paw. The Nome King leapt to his feet, his white face purple with rage.

"I won't have this!" he shrieked. "I won't tolerate you, you fleabag!" But he was too late. At the Lion's feet, the figurine grew rapidly until it was life-size. The dull silver metal turned iridescent, like oil on the surface of a pond. The multitude of colors swirled together and turned green before dripping away, revealing the queen. She smiled up at the Lion.

"I knew it would work," she said, flinging her arms around his neck and burying her face in his mane. "I *knew*. My brave, wonderful Lion!" But she was almost sobbing, and the Lion guessed that she'd been nowhere near as certain she would survive as she insisted. His heart leapt with sympathy and fondness for the brave, beautiful queen. She'd trusted him with her life, and she'd had enough faith in him to believe he could rescue her. Her crazy gamble had paid off—because of him. He felt tremendously close to the queen in that moment. He knew he'd be as willing to risk his life for her as she had for her kingdom.

The Nome King was sputtering like a teakettle, impotent with fury. Ozma rolled her eyes. "He always was a bad loser," she said, and snapped her fingers. His warriors exploded silently into columns of silver smoke. The clanking noise of his digging machine ground to a halt and its fire went out. The huge cavern immediately cooled to a comfortable temperature. The Nome King stood alone in front of them, speechless with rage and brandishing his fists. Ozma snapped her fingers again and he froze into place, pinned by her magic.

"You have something that belongs to Oz," Ozma said cheerfully, skipping over to him and lifting the ruby necklace over his head. "I'll take this back now, thanks." His eyes blazed with fury but his power wasn't enough to break Ozma's spell. This whole quest had been proof that Ozma's power was far greater than the Lion had realized.

Ozma fastened the necklace around the Lion's neck. Somehow it expanded without his seeing it change, so that by the time she fastened the clasp it was big enough to fit him. The cool stones rested on his chest like a breastplate. He stared down at them, lost in their entrancing sparkle.

"Careful," Ozma warned, snapping him out of his reverie. "That's old, old magic, dear Lion. It'll trap you if you're not careful." She turned to face the Nome King. "Even you can't break the bargain we made," Ozma said, her voice clear and authoritative. "You'll abandon this ridiculous plan of invading Oz, and you'll go back to your own country and stay there. I don't *ever* want to see you again. Is that clear?"

Slowly the Nome King nodded. Ozma released him just enough so that he could speak.

"My bargain was with you, little princess," he hissed. "But it lasts only as long as you are the ruler of Oz. Don't think you've seen the last of me." The air around him began to glow with a silver light that grew brighter and brighter until the Lion was forced to cover his eyes. The light brightened still further and then vanished. When the Lion opened his eyes again, he and Ozma were alone in the abandoned cavern.

"Phew," she sighed in relief. "I wasn't totally sure that was going to work."

TWELVE

"What do you mean, you weren't sure that was going to work?" the Lion demanded. Ozma shrugged.

"All the legends about the Nome King say he's obsessed with riddles and gambling, and he loves turning people into furniture and tchotchkes and that sort of thing. I knew there was no way we could actually talk him out of invading Oz, and we're certainly not strong enough to fight him. I was hoping he'd pull something like this, but I couldn't be sure." The Lion stared at her, speechless. Ozma had bet the farm on a handful of legends about a king no one else knew existed and the might of his stomach?

"It worked, didn't it?" she said, as if she could read his mind.

The Lion had no response to that, so he decided to think about something else. "But what will happen to the people of Ev? If the Nome King was invading Oz to help them—"

"Oh, *that*," Ozma said dismissively. "That was a load of hooey. Ev is incredibly rich. If the people are suffering, it's his fault—his and the Princess Langwidere's. There's nothing I can do about that from here, although once I'm sure Oz is stable, I might look into deposing them both."

"The princess who?"

"Langwidere," Ozma said. "She's horrible beyond belief. She has as many heads as there are days in the month and she exchanges them at will. Pray you never meet her—or the Wheelers." The Lion thought of the strange, patchworked creatures he'd seen in the Nome King's vision and shuddered.

"Anyway, we won!" Ozma exclaimed happily. "And we got the Wizard's necklace back, too!"

Should he tell Ozma that Glinda was just as eager to find the necklace as she was? He decided against it. He'd figure out a way out of his deal with Glinda on his own. There was no way to tell Ozma about Glinda's desire for the necklace without confessing she was the one who'd sent him to the Emerald City in the first place. All this intrigue was making his head hurt, especially after the stress of saving Oz from the clutches of the Nome King and rescuing Ozma from certain doom.

"We shouldn't rest here any longer," Ozma warned. His heart sank. He'd been hoping for a nap. But he knew the queen was right. They were practically in the Land of Ev, after all, and he'd seen all he wanted of the Nome King. "He has to obey the bargain we made, but if I know anything about the Nome King, he'll already be trying to find a way around it," she added. "We should go back to the Emerald Palace before he tries to return this way."

Ozma didn't sound too worried about the possibility that the Nome King might persist in his attempt to invade Oz after all. Was she brave, or just foolhardy? Whatever the case, he had no interest in sticking around either. "Can you teleport us back to the Emerald Palace?" he asked hopefully.

"Through a mile of solid rock?" Ozma laughed. "I'm powerful, Lion, but no one is *that* powerful. Magic doesn't work like that. We could step into the Darklands and travel that way, but I'd worry about losing you." Her gaze turned thoughtful. "Although," she mused, "the Wizard's necklace wants to return to the palace; I can feel it. Maybe that's not such a bad idea after all. The necklace will make sure you get there, even if I can't."

At last, he could ask about the necklace without arousing her suspicions. "What is this necklace?"

"No one really knows. It's much older than the Wizard, of course, and how he came by it—well, I'm just not sure. It's possible it's from the Other Place, and he used its power to get here somehow. But now it's bound up in the Deep Magic of Oz, and it will always try to go home."

"To the Emerald City?"

"Exactly. Its magic is incredibly strong, but no one really knows what it's *for*."

Glinda does, the Lion thought, remembering her eager face as she showed him the vision of the ruby necklace. She knew, and she had a plan for it. Of that he had no doubt.

"Everyone thought the necklace was lost when the Wizard

disappeared," Ozma continued. "It's possible he had it with him when he left Oz in his hot air balloon, and somehow lost it over the Land of Ev. I don't know how else the Nome King could have gotten hold of it. He was probably using it to guide his tunneling to the Emerald City. That would explain how he was able to get so close so quickly."

She fell into a thoughtful silence. The necklace seemed to throb slightly against his chest, as if it knew they were talking about it. But that wasn't possible. It was just a bunch of gold and rubies; even magic objects couldn't eavesdrop on people's conversations. Could they?

Ozma roused herself. "The Darklands is too risky," she said decidedly. "It'll take much longer, of course, but we'll have to go back the way we came."

The Lion almost groaned aloud. He was so tired, and the thought of the return journey was almost unbearable. Still, a risky magical journey through a place he'd never heard of where a ruby necklace was his only link to safety sounded even worse. He stood and stretched. Ozma rested one hand on his back. "Are you ready?"

He nodded agreement, and Ozma raised her other hand. The cavern wall in front of them began to glow again. But this time, the lines of Ozma's magic ran in feeble rivulets down the wall, refusing to form a door. "Being turned into a statue really wore me out," she gasped. "We're going to have to do this the hard way." Without waiting for his reply, she grabbed his mane and dragged him toward the wall. He opened his mouth to protest, but before he could say a word they were plowing into solid stone. And it hurt. Somehow, Ozma was dragging them both through the wall. It was like forcing his way through liquid concrete. Stone filled his ears and mouth, and for a long moment he thought he'd be stuck there, trapped inside the wall forever. But with one last, insistent tug, Ozma pulled him through to the other side. They collapsed on the tunnel floor.

"Sorry about that," Ozma wheezed. "Close call. It's a good thing I didn't have to actually fight the Nome King."

The journey back up through the tunnels to the Emerald Palace seemed to take even longer than the journey down. Both the Lion and Ozma were exhausted, but neither of them wanted to rest in the creepy, dark warren of tunnels. Ozma was so tired that several times she lost the way, and they had to backtrack. But finally the steep upward slant of the tunnel floor evened out, and the side tunnels came to an end. The Lion was so relieved to see the first of the torches that marked the corridor down from the Emerald Palace that he nearly cheered aloud, and Ozma perked up visibly.

"Not sure I've got much more in me," she panted. "I'm glad we're almost home."

It was odd seeing her weakened like this. And even more than that, hearing her admit it. He had never once seen Glinda drained of her power. He himself had never let his guard down in front of his subjects, or even Cornelius. Ozma shared her vulnerability with him freely. He felt honored and at the same time, he wanted to warn her that it wasn't the best idea. Someone else, someone other than himself, could pounce when you show your soft underbelly.

At last, the rough-hewn rock of the tunnel walls gave way to the cut stone of the Emerald Palace's corridors. The Lion almost wept in relief. Ozma pulled up her hood in an attempt to conceal herself if they encountered any of the palace servants, but the halls were empty. "That's strange," she said, frowning. "I couldn't begin to guess what time it is, but at least a few of the servants are up at all hours. I don't know where everyone is." With a snap of her fingers, she exchanged her plain dress for a regal ball gown of emerald-green satin embroidered with a pattern in gold thread that echoed the delicate gold veins of her wings. Invisible hands piled her disordered curls into an elegant updo secured with jeweled golden combs, and dazzling emerald earrings appeared in her ears. Not to be outdone, the Lion quickly licked down his mane. The ruby necklace was hidden in his thick fur.

Ozma gave him an approving nod. "We don't look like we've been mucking around in nasty old tunnels and defeating an evil king!" she declared. "No one will ever be the wiser. The fact that we just saved Oz will remain between the two of us." She winked, and the Lion felt an answering surge of pride. They *had* just saved Oz—if you got right down to it, *he* had just saved Oz, more or less by himself. If Scare and Tin could see him now! He might not have done so impressively in the battle against Jinjur, but there was no doubting the courage he'd shown while facing the Nome King.

"Your Majesty!" Both he and Ozma jumped at the sudden cry. One of the palace servants was hurrying toward them—Jellia, the Lion remembered. She was the queen's handmaid; that was why he'd memorized her name. "Thank goodness you're here! Where on *earth* have you been? We've been looking all over for you—your guest is here!"

Ozma looked puzzled. "My guest?"

"Oh yes, and she's in an absolute *state*, the girls are running themselves ragged—please, Your Majesty, you really must come at once!" Without waiting for them to reply, the maid took off in the other direction. Ozma raised her eyebrows at the Lion, shrugging, and followed, with the Lion close on her heels. "I guess we'll have to wait just a bit before we rest," she said ruefully. "I know I didn't invite anyone to the palace. I wonder who's here."

Jellia led them to Ozma's throne room and threw open the doors, curtsying deeply. "Her Majesty, Queen Ozma of Oz!" she announced breathlessly, staying in her curtsy with her eyes cast down as if unwilling to face whoever awaited them. Ozma swept past her, her bearing regal. Beyond her, the Lion could see a figure silhouetted against the throne room's huge picture windows. At first, he thought she was just incredibly tall. And then he realized she was hovering several inches off the ground.

"My goodness," she said in a syrupy-sweet, all-too-familiar voice, turning to face them. "Look what the cat dragged in." She giggled, and something about the sound was infinitely more terrifying than any of the Nome King's threats. "Welcome back, dearest Ozma. And of course, Your Highness," she added, bowing to the Lion in a gesture that was subtly mocking. "I think you have something of mine. I've come to get it back."

THIRTEEN

"Glinda." Ozma's voice was cold enough to freeze boiling water. "What exactly brings you back to the Emerald City after I suggested you not return?"

Glinda laughed. "*Dearest* Ozma, I'm sure you know. The Lion certainly does."

Ozma shot a startled look at the Lion. His heart sank. He had been stupid not to be completely honest with Ozma. Now it was too late. The queen would realize the extent of his deceit and never forgive him. His time in the palace was clearly over, but more than that, he was sorry to lose someone who had become a real friend. "What does Glinda mean, Lion?" Ozma asked.

"It's nothing," the Lion blurted. "I have no idea."

Ozma's eyes narrowed. "Which one is it? Nothing, or no idea?"

Glinda laughed again. "Now, now, Lion. It won't do to try to break the promise you made me. We're connected now—how else do you think I knew you'd found my necklace?"

Ozma was looking back and forth between the two of them. "What promise?"

"Glinda found me in the Kingdom of the Beasts," the Lion said miserably. "She made me promise to find the Wizard's necklace. I had no idea she was going behind your back."

"Why didn't you *tell* me?" Ozma gasped.

"Glinda put a spell on me," the Lion said. "She commanded me to keep it secret. Anyway, it didn't seem important until we actually found the necklace. But by then we'd defeated the Nome King and I guess it just . . . it just slipped my mind," he finished, well aware of how feeble he sounded. Ozma's expression was a mixture of fury and disappointment.

Glinda cleared her throat. "My *necklace*, please."

"It's not your necklace," the Lion said bravely, lashing his tail as he faced Glinda. "It belongs to Oz. I've—I've changed my mind. I won't give it to you."

"No matter what you get in return?"

He thought of the image of the girl in front of the house. Then he thought of Ozma pulling him through the wall. He wanted Dorothy back, but not at Ozma's expense.

"No matter what," he said firmly, feeling stronger and better as each word landed. At that, Glinda threw back her head and laughed even harder. "Oh, Lion," she chuckled. "Silly, silly Cowardly Lion. You don't understand, do you? I'm not giving you a choice." She flicked her wrists, and bolts of pink lightning shot toward the Lion's chest. At the last second, Ozma made a slashing motion, and a wall of green energy sprung up around the Lion. Glinda's bolts slammed into Ozma's force field and splintered harmlessly, crackling and smoking.

He realized at that moment that Glinda hadn't wanted him to protect Ozma from danger. Glinda was the danger.

"You've enchanted one of my subjects without my consent, barged into my palace, and now you want to steal something that isn't yours from under my nose?" Ozma snarled. "After all your promises to help me? We could have been friends, you know."

Glinda hissed, her terrifyingly rigid smile turning to a scowl. "Are you kidding me, you little ingrate? I *made* you queen, and this is how you repay me? By throwing me out of the Emerald Palace and accusing me of treason? The Scarecrow might have been an incompetent idiot, but at least he knew his place."

"He's not an idiot!" the Lion protested. Both Glinda and Ozma glanced at him as if they had only just remembered he was there before returning to stare at each other, the air between them crackling with energy.

"What have you done with it, Ozma?"

"I'm not going to tell you," Ozma said coldly. The Lion blinked. Glinda didn't know where the necklace actually was— she just knew one of them had it, and of course she'd assumed it was Ozma. If he could get out of the throne room unnoticed, he could hide it somewhere safe until Ozma took care of Glinda.

Once the coast was clear, he'd give it back to Ozma and restore her faith in him. It was a plan worthy of the Scarecrow himself.

The air around Glinda was glowing pink and turquoise. She raised her hands, crackling bolts of energy forming between her fingers.

"Do you really want to do this, Glinda?" Ozma said grimly. "Battle me in my own palace? Declare war on the Queen of Oz?"

"It's only your palace because I put you in it," Glinda snarled, hurling a bolt of energy at Ozma's head. "I can take you out of it just as easily."

Ozma flicked her fingers, and Glinda's magic crashed into the wall behind her, leaving a smoking crater. "I'm giving you one last chance, Glinda," she said. "Leave now, and we can forget about this."

In response, Glinda threw another bolt of magic at Ozma. Ozma dodged it neatly, rolling her eyes. "Fine," she said in exasperation. "You know, I've had a really long day. All I want is to go to bed. But apparently a queen's work is never done."

"There's no rest for the Wicked," Glinda snapped. Ozma threw up another shield just in time as Glinda sent more magic at her. The Lion was torn, unsure of what to do or who to fight for, but feeling ready to pounce. He had never had much use for magic, but watching them fight he wished he had some of his own. "You were supposed to be the good witch," Ozma said, returning Glinda's fire. Glinda ducked and flew out of range.

"You were supposed to be a good investment," she snapped.

"You don't know the first thing about ruling a country. You should have listened to me."

"Since you're such an expert?" Ozma flicked her fingers, and green lightning crackled toward Glinda. Glinda waved one hand, and the energy fizzled into tiny sparks. The Lion took a step toward the door, and then another. Self-preservation had kicked in, finally ruling out over his desire to know who would win this fight. He was almost clear of the throne room.

"I know a lot more than you do, child," Glinda hissed.

"I'm not a child!" Ozma yelled. "I'm the last of the line of Lurline and the rightful ruler of Oz!"

"Oh, Lur*line*," Glinda simpered mockingly. "Nobody even cares about *that* old story. Next you're going to try and sell me on some bogus hooey about tapping into the Deep Magic of Oz in order to be a better queen. Face it, honey: you like that throne, but that doesn't mean you're qualified for it. If you'd listened to me from the beginning, none of this would have happened. You'd still be in power, and I'd be right behind you."

"I *am* still in power," Ozma said. "And I'm enjoying it a lot more without you breathing down my *neck*." She whipped a fireball at Glinda so quickly that the witch didn't have time to get out of the way. It hit her solidly in the chest, and she shrieked in rage as her dress began to blacken and burn. Glinda slapped at her chest with one hand, pink spreading outward again to replace the blackened burned sections.

"Don't you *dare* ruin my dress!" Glinda screamed, hurtling

toward Ozma with her fingers outstretched. The Lion saw his chance. He turned around and bolted for the door—and slammed into an invisible wall.

"Not so fast, dear Lion," Glinda said from directly behind him. "I think I know where my necklace is." An invisible hand gripped his tail, dragging him backward. He tried to sink his claws in the stone floor, but Glinda's magic pulled him toward the center of the room.

"Leave him out of this," Ozma growled. "You've done enough damage to my friends."

"Oh, but the Lion was *my* friend first. Isn't that true, Lion?"

The Lion looked miserably toward Ozma as Glinda reached for his neck. But Ozma's eyes were closed, and she was mumbling to herself. This was it, then. She'd lost the rest of what little strength she'd had left after defeating the Nome King. Glinda was going to win, and there was no use resisting her. Would Glinda banish Ozma from the throne, or continue trying to rule through her? "It's time for a new queen in town," Glinda snarled, answering his unspoken question. He felt the necklace loosen itself from around his neck and float upward as he watched it helplessly. At least his part in this was almost over.

"Encomiendum absolum!" Ozma cried, opening her eyes wide and flinging her arms out. An explosion of green light rocked the throne room. Tiles crumbled from the walls, narrowly missing the three figures that stood frozen in the shock wave from Ozma's spell. Glinda's jaw hung open, one hand still outstretched

toward the Wizard's ruby necklace. *"Verteum clausus!"* A green portal opened next to her, revealing a desolate, barren landscape on the other side.

"No!" Glinda screamed as a huge green hand reached out from Ozma's portal and wrapped its fingers around her. "You can't do this!"

"Oh, but I can," Ozma said, her wings unfurling and her entire body outlined in a haze of green light. "It's a last resort, but you're the one who pushed me to it." Glinda kicked and struggled, but Ozma's spell dragged her slowly, inexorably, toward the portal. At the very last second, Glinda lunged through the air, snatching the ruby necklace where it drifted in the air.

"You just wait, little queen," she hissed. "I'm going to use this necklace to make a very special present for a very special person. You'll regret the day you did this to me, mark my words."

"Whatever you say, Glinda," Ozma said tiredly. The green hand heaved Glinda through the portal and the doorway snapped shut on her furious screams. Ozma collapsed to the floor as the entire throne room shuddered.

"We have to get out of here!" the Lion exclaimed as more tiles crashed to the ground. Freed from the grip of Glinda's spell, he raced over to Ozma. The queen weakly dragged herself onto his back, and he bounded out of the throne room just as the rest of the ceiling fell in.

"Your Majesty!" cried Jellia, hurrying toward them at the head of a small army of servants. "Are you all right? What do you need?"

"I need you to put me to bed," Ozma said distinctly. "And then I need you to let me sleep for the next forty thousand years." She tumbled from the Lion's back, unconscious, and landed on the floor with a thud.

FOURTEEN

Ozma didn't sleep for forty thousand years, but she did sleep for several days. Long enough for the Lion to sleep off his own exhaustion—after a restorative trip to the kitchens, first—wake up again, and then eat his way through an impressive quantity of the palace's stores. Finally, Jellia told him the queen was awake and receiving visitors. The Lion bounded joyfully up to her chambers, barreling through her open door and pouncing on the bed, where Ozma lay propped up against a raft of silk pillows. She laughed and scratched him behind the ears as he licked her face with his rough pink tongue.

"Oof, Lion—you really ought to brush your teeth."

"Sorry," the Lion apologized, backing away and settling down at the foot of her bed. "How are you feeling?"

"Like a wrung-out washcloth," the queen admitted. Her skin was pale, and there were dark hollows under her green eyes. But she was smiling, and she managed to look almost perky despite her evident exhaustion.

"You look well," the Lion said, not entirely truthfully.

"I'll be better soon," she agreed. "Battling the Nome King and Glinda in one day was a lot. I'm powerful, but I'm not a superhero."

The Lion sobered instantly at the thought of Glinda. "I owe you an apology," he said, hanging his head. "I should have told you from the very beginning that Glinda sent me here."

"Yes, you should have," Ozma said sternly, her face severe. "Who knows how much of that disaster we could have avoided if you'd been honest with me from the moment you arrived in the Emerald City." Her face softened a little. "But I know you didn't mean any harm, and Glinda can be—well, let's say I know how persuasive she is, and how convincing. I'm sure you had no idea you might be betraying me."

In fact, the Lion had suspected he was doing something furtive—he just hadn't cared until he'd realized how much he liked Ozma. But her cheerful willingness to see the best in everyone was working in his favor, and he wasn't going to argue.

"Where is Glinda now?"

"Banished," Ozma said succinctly. "She'll have a heck of a time getting out of the prison world I put her in. I suppose she'll figure out a way eventually—nothing in Oz stays the same forever, as you know—but I'll have plenty of time to figure out what I'm going to do about her when she frees herself." Ozma sighed. "I don't like fighting with people," she said a little sadly. "I just wish Oz could stay calm and peaceful and everyone could get along."

"She got the Wizard's necklace," the Lion said.

Ozma shrugged. "It won't do her any good in there. It's a powerful weapon, but there's no one for her to fight."

"She said she was going to make a present for someone." He didn't say anything about Dorothy. He just couldn't.

Ozma shook her head. "I have no idea what she meant by that. She's trapped, and it'll take a lot more than a fancy ruby necklace to get her out of there."

The Lion nodded, but he wasn't convinced. Neither, he was sure, was Ozma. She was too canny to dismiss Glinda's threat so easily. More likely she didn't trust him to the extent that she once had—or at least she wasn't going to trust him with any serious information. He'd already proven that Glinda could control him. Ozma wouldn't let him fail her twice. But the green eyes that gazed up at him were as guileless as ever, and she quickly changed the subject. "Did you get enough to eat while I was resting?"

"Oh yes," the Lion replied, eager for a safer subject. He'd had enough of politics. Let Ozma worry about Glinda's sinister plans—he suddenly remembered that he had a forest of his own to rule. "I suppose I should return to the Forest of the Beasts," he said, hoping Ozma would protest. She didn't.

"I think that's a good idea."

"I don't want to overstay my welcome."

"No," Ozma agreed, batting her eyelashes at him to soften the harshness of her reply. His heart sank a little. Thanks to Glinda, his cushy stay at the palace was over. It had been good while it lasted.

Ozma gave him a kiss on the forehead, and he allowed himself one last, wistful glance around her chambers. He could have stayed here like a prince if he'd played his cards better. But at least he was returning to being a king.

"You said once that we were the same. Both of us figuring out how to rule," he offered. It wasn't a plea. But he was still holding out for a reprieve.

"I thought so, too, at first. But we are more different than we are the same. You are not Wicked, dear Lion. But sometimes you put what you want over what is good for Oz. I don't know how much you care about good over bad, Lion. I think that you just like the thrill. You love the fight more than you love what you are fighting for. Be careful, there."

Her words stung more than Glinda's spell had. He blinked hard at Ozma. "How should I get back to the Kingdom of the Beasts?" he asked, hoping Ozma would offer a magical ride back to his home. She looked surprised.

"The same way you got here, I would imagine. Thank you again for coming to visit me, and for all your help. I'm afraid I must rest now. Please do come see me again someday."

He was dismissed. He slunk back into the corridor, his ears burning. It was true that he hadn't been entirely honest with Ozma, but he'd still risked his life to help her battle the Nome King. He'd saved her in the caverns—not only that, he'd saved Oz. He was the one who'd found the necklace and carried it to safety, and he was the one who'd faced the worst of Glinda's wrath. He could have been killed at any point. And what did he get in repayment? A summary dismissal, without even the offer of a last meal with Ozma before he left the Emerald City? The queen had a lot of nerve sending him away like a bad kitty who'd peed on her best quilt. Was it his imagination, or did even the servants give him pitying glances as he slunk past them down the hall?

Resentment burned within him—resentment and something else. It was almost as though seeing Glinda had somehow reactivated the spell she'd put on him. He could feel those same fiery sparks crawling through his coat—only this time they were invigorating. Glinda had power, Glinda had a plan, and Glinda had trusted him with an important mission, too. Ozma had treated the witch the same way she'd just treated him—throwing her out like a houseguest who'd stayed past her welcome. Maybe he and Glinda had more in common than he thought. Maybe that was why Glinda had chosen him. Not just because of his courage. Because she saw something in him that Ozma didn't. That Ozma couldn't. She saw how powerful he could be if the right person believed in him.

He didn't bother stopping in the chambers Ozma had given him while he'd stayed in the palace. He didn't say good-bye to anyone else, or acknowledge any of the servants' greetings as he passed them. He kept his head down on the way out of the palace, seething as his ire grew.

The street outside was as bustling as it had been the day he'd arrived at the Emerald Palace what seemed like months ago, though really it had only been a few weeks. He raised his nose to sniff at the city air, full of the scents of spices and cooking and exotic wares.

He thought of Ozma's words. She was wrong about him. Wasn't she? *I don't know how much you care about good over bad, Lion. I think that you just like the thrill.* The words pierced his pride. But that did not mean that there wasn't some truth in them. She had forgiven him, but she would not let him in again. She was not, after everything, his friend. Not like Scare or Tin or Dorothy. They were his friends. They were the ones he would do anything for.

Had Glinda been right after all? Was Ozma too temperamental and unstable to rule? Ozma had said Glinda would find a way to escape her prison someday. Maybe it would be soon. He'd find his way back to the Emerald Palace somehow, and next time he wouldn't be sent home quite so easily.

The Lion felt like fighting again. He felt like gobbling up the world. He set his paws on the Road of Yellow Brick and turned his face toward the Kingdom of the Beasts. For now, he'd wait in the forest. But the wind was shifting. This time, when Glinda returned, he'd be ready for her.

Follow Amy Gumm's mission to take down Dorothy:

ONE

I first discovered I was trash three days before my ninth birthday—one year after my father lost his job and moved to Secaucus to live with a woman named Crystal and four years before my mother had the car accident, started taking pills, and began exclusively wearing bedroom slippers instead of normal shoes.

I was informed of my trashiness on the playground by Madison Pendleton, a girl in a pink Target sweat suit who thought she was all that because her house had one and a half bathrooms.

"Salvation Amy's trailer trash," she told the other girls on the monkey bars while I was dangling upside down by my knees and minding my own business, my pigtails scraping the sand. "That means she doesn't have any money and all her clothes are dirty. You shouldn't go to her birthday party or you'll be dirty, too."

When my birthday party rolled around that weekend, it turned out everyone had listened to Madison. My mom and I were sitting at the picnic table in the Dusty Acres Mobile Community

Recreation Area wearing our sad little party hats, our sheet cake gathering dust. It was just the two of us, same as always. After an hour of hoping someone would finally show up, Mom sighed, poured me another big cup of Sprite, and gave me a hug.

She told me that, whatever anyone at school said, a trailer was where I lived, not who I was. She told me that it was the best home in the world because it could go anywhere.

Even as a little kid, I was smart enough to point out that our house was on blocks, not wheels. Its mobility was severely oversold. Mom didn't have much of a comeback for that.

It took her until around Christmas of that year when we were watching *The Wizard of Oz* on the big flat-screen television— the only physical thing that was a leftover from our old life with Dad—to come up with a better answer for me. "See?" she said, pointing at the screen. "You don't need wheels on your house to get somewhere better. All you need is something to give you that extra push."

I don't think she believed it even then, but at least in those days she still cared enough to lie. And even though I never believed in a place like Oz, I did believe in her.

That was a long time ago. A lot had changed since then. My mom was hardly the same person at all anymore. Then again, neither was I.

I didn't bother trying to make Madison like me anymore, and I wasn't going to cry over cake. I wasn't going to cry, period. These days, my mom was too lost in her own little world to bother cheering me up. I was on my own, and crying wasn't worth the effort.

Tears or no tears, though, Madison Pendleton still found ways of making my life miserable. The day of the tornado—although I didn't know the tornado was coming yet—she was slouching against her locker after fifth period, rubbing her enormous pregnant belly and whispering with her best friend, Amber Boudreaux.

I'd figured out a long time ago that it was best to just ignore her when I could, but Madison was the type of person it was pretty impossible to ignore even under normal circumstances. Now that she was eight and a half months pregnant it was really impossible.

Today, Madison was wearing a tiny T-shirt that barely covered her midriff. It read Who's Your Mommy across her boobs in pink cursive glitter. I did my best not to stare as I slunk by her on my way to Spanish, but somehow I felt my eyes gliding upward, past her belly to her chest and then to her face. Sometimes you just can't help it.

She was already staring at me. Our gazes met for a tiny instant. I froze.

Madison glared. "What are you looking at, Trailer Trash?"

"Oh, I'm sorry. Was I staring? I was just wondering if *you* were the Teen Mom I saw on the cover of *Star* this week."

It wasn't like I tried to go after Madison, but sometimes my sarcasm took on a life of its own. The words just came out.

Madison gave me a blank look. She snorted.

"I didn't know you could afford a copy of *Star*." She turned to Amber Boudreaux and stopped rubbing her stomach just long enough to give it a tender pat. "Salvation Amy's jealous. She's had a crush on Dustin forever. She wishes this were her baby."

I didn't have a crush on Dustin, I definitely didn't want a baby, and I absolutely did not want Dustin's baby. But that didn't stop my cheeks from going red.

Amber popped her gum and smirked an evil smirk. "You know, I saw her talking to Dustin in third period," she said. "She was being all flirty." Amber puckered her lips and pushed her chest forward. "Oh, Dustin, I'll help you with your algebra."

I knew I was blushing, but I wasn't sure if it was from embarrassment or anger. It was true that I'd let Dustin copy my math homework earlier that day. But as cute as Dustin was, I wasn't stupid enough to think I'd ever have a shot with him. I was Salvation Amy, the flat-chested trailer-trash girl whose clothes were always a little too big and a lot too thrift store. Who hadn't had a real friend since third grade.

I wasn't the type of girl Dustin would go for, with or without the existence of Madison Pendleton. He had been "borrowing" my algebra almost every day for the entire year. But Dustin would never look at me like that. Even at forty-pounds pregnant, Madison sparkled like the words on her oversize chest. There was glitter embedded in her eye shadow, in her lip gloss, in her nail polish, hanging from her ears in shoulder-grazing hoops, dangling from her wrists in blingy bracelets. If the lights went out in the hallway, she could light it up like a human disco ball.

Like human bling. Meanwhile, the only color I had to offer was in my hair, which I'd dyed pink just a few days ago.

I was all sharp edges and angles—words that came out too fast and at the wrong times. And I slouched. If Dustin was into shiny things like Madison, he would never be interested in me.

I don't know if I was exactly interested in Dustin, either, but we did have one thing in common: we both wanted out of Flat Hill, Kansas.

For a while, it had almost looked like Dustin was going to make it, too. All you need is a little push sometimes. Sometimes it's a tornado; sometimes it's the kind of right arm that gets you a football scholarship. He had been set to go. Until eight and a half months ago, that is.

I didn't know what was worse: to have your shot and screw it up, or to never have had a shot in the first place.

"I wasn't . . . ," I protested. Before I could finish, Madison was all up in my face.

"Listen, Dumb Gumm," she said. I felt a drop of her spit hit my cheek and resisted the urge to wipe it away. I didn't want to give her the satisfaction. "Dustin's mine. We're getting married as soon as the baby comes and I can fit into my aunt Robin's wedding dress. So you'd better stay away from him—not that he'd ever be interested in someone like you anyway."

By this point, everyone in the hallway had stopped looking into their lockers, and they were looking at us instead. Madison was used to eyes on her—but this was new to me.

"Listen," I mumbled back at her, wanting this to be over. "It was just homework." I felt my temper rising. I'd just been trying to help him. Not because I had a crush on him. Just because he deserved a break.

"She thinks Dustin needs her help," Amber chimed in. "Taffy told me she heard Amy offered to *tutor* him after school. Just a little one-on-one academic counseling." She cackled loudly. She said "tutor" like I'd done a lap dance for Dustin in front of the whole fourth period.

I hadn't offered anyway. He had asked. Not that it mattered. Madison was already steaming.

"Oh, she did, did she? Well why don't I give this bitch a little tutoring of my own?"

I turned to walk away, but Madison grabbed me by the wrist and jerked me back around to face her. She was so close to me that her nose was almost touching mine. Her breath smelled like Sour Patch Kids and kiwi-strawberry lip gloss.

"Who the hell do you think you are, trying to steal my boyfriend? Not to mention my baby's dad?"

"He asked me," I said quietly so that only Madison could hear.

"What?"

I knew I should shut up. But it wasn't fair. All I'd tried to do was something good.

"I didn't talk to him. He asked me for help," I said, louder this time.

"And what could he find so interesting about you?" she snapped back, as if Dustin and I belonged to entirely different species.

It was a good question. The kind that gets you where it hurts. But an answer popped into my head, right on time, not two seconds after Madison wobbled away down the hall. I knew it was mean, but it flew out of my mouth before I had a chance to even think about it.

"Maybe he just wanted to talk to someone his own size."

Madison's mouth opened and closed without anything coming out. I took a step back, ready to walk away with my tiny victory. And then she rolled onto her heels, wound up, and—before I could duck—punched me square in the jaw. I felt my head throbbing as I stumbled back and landed on my butt.

It was my turn to be surprised, looking up at her in dazed, fuzzy-headed confusion. Had that just happened? Madison had always been a complete bitch, but—aside from the occasional shoulder check in the girls' locker room—she wasn't usually the violent type. Until now.

Maybe it was the pregnancy hormones.

"Take it back," she demanded as I began to get to my feet.

Out of the corner of my eye, I saw Amber a second too late. Always one to take a cue from her best friend, she yanked me by the hair and pushed me back down to the ground.

The chant of "Fight! Fight! Fight!" boomed in my ears. I checked for blood, relieved to find my skull intact. Madison stepped forward and towered over me, ready for the next round. Behind her, I could see that a huge crowd had gathered around us.

"Take it back. I'm not fat," Madison insisted. But her lip

quivered a tiny bit at the f-word. "I may be pregnant, but I'm still a size two."

"Kick her!" Amber hissed.

I scooted away from her rhinestone-studded sandal and stood up just as the assistant principal, Mr. Strachan, appeared, flanked by a pair of security guards. The crowd began to disperse, grumbling that the show was over.

Madison quickly dropped her punching arm and went back to rubbing her belly and cooing. She scrunched her face up into a pained grimace, like she was fighting back tears. I rolled my eyes. I wondered if she would actually manage to produce tears.

Mr. Strachan looked from me to Madison and back again through his wire rims.

"Mr. Strachan," Madison said shakily. "She just came at me! At us!" She patted her belly protectively, making it clear that she was speaking for two these days.

He folded his arms across his chest and lowered his glare to where I still crouched. Madison had him at "us." "Really, Amy? Fighting with a pregnant girl? You've always had a hard time keeping your mouth shut when it's good for you, but this is low, even for you."

"She threw the first punch!" I yelled. It didn't matter. Mr. Strachan was already pulling me to my feet to haul me off to the principal's office.

"I thought you could be the bigger person at a time like this. I guess I overestimated you. As usual."

As I walked away, I looked over my shoulder. Madison lifted

her hand from her belly to give me a smug little wave. Like she knew I wouldn't be coming back.

When I'd left for school that morning, Mom had been sitting on the couch for three days straight. In those three days, my mother had taken zero showers, had said almost nothing, and—as far as I knew—had consumed only half a carton of cigarettes and a few handfuls of Bugles. Oh, and whatever pills she was on. I'm not even sure when she got up to pee. She'd just been sitting there watching TV.

It used to be that I always tried to figure out what was wrong with her when she got like this. Was it the weather? Was she thinking about my father? Was it just the pills? Or was there something else that had turned her into a human slug?

By now, though, I was used to it enough to know that it wasn't any of that. She just got like this sometimes. It was her version of waking up on the wrong side of the bed, and when it happened, you just had to let her ride it out. Whenever it happened, I wondered if this time she'd be *stuck* like this.

So when I pushed the door to our trailer open an hour after my meeting with the principal, carrying all the books from my locker in a black Hefty bag—I'd been suspended for the rest of the week—I was surprised to see that the couch was empty except for one of those blankets with the sleeves that Mom had ordered off TV with money we didn't have.

In the bathroom, I could hear her rustling around: the faucet running, the clatter of drugstore makeup on a tiny counter. I

guess she'd ridden it out again after all. Not that that was always
a good thing.

"Mom?" I asked.

"Shit!" she yelped, followed by the sound of something falling into the sink. She didn't come out of the bathroom, and she
didn't ask what I was doing home so early.

I dropped my backpack and my Hefty bag on the floor, slid
off my sneakers, and looked over at the screen. Al Roker was
pointing to my hometown on one of those big fake maps. He was
frowning.

I didn't think I'd ever seen America's Weatherman frown
before. Wasn't he supposed to be reassuring? Wasn't it, like, his
job to make us feel like everything, including the weather, would
be better soon? If not tomorrow then at some point during the
extended ten-day forecast?

"Hey," Mom said. "Did you hear? There's a tornado coming!"

I wasn't too worried about it. They were always predicting
disaster around here, but although nearby towns had been hit a
few times, Dusty Acres had always been spared. It was like we
had cliché to shield us—Tornado Sweeps Through Trailer Park,
Leaves Only an Overturned Barbecue. That's something that
happens in a movie, not in real life.

My mom emerged from the bathroom, fussing with her
hair. I was glad to see her vertical again, freshly scrubbed with
her face all done up, but I had to wince at the length of her
skirt. It was shorter than anything I owned. It was shorter than

anything Madison Pendleton owned. That could only mean one thing.

"Where are you going?" I asked, even though I knew the answer. "For three days, you're one step away from a coma and now you're heading to the bar?"

It was no surprise. In my mother's world, there were only two pieces of scenery: the couch and the bar. If she wasn't on one, she was in the other.

She let out an accusatory sigh. "Don't start. I thought you'd be happy that I'm back on my feet again. Would you rather I just lie on the couch? Well, you might be content to mope around the house all day, but *some* of us have a life." She fluffed up her already teased hair and began looking for her purse.

There were so many things wrong with everything she'd just said that I couldn't even begin to process all the ways it was infuriating. Instead, I decided to try the sensible argument. "You're the one who just told me there's a tornado on the way. It's dangerous. You could get hit by a tree or something. Won't Tawny understand?"

"It's a *tornado* party, Miss Smarty-Pants," Mom said, as if that explained things. Her bloodshot eyes lit up as she spotted her purse lying on the floor next to the refrigerator and slung it over her shoulder.

I knew there was no point arguing when she got this way. "You need to sign this," I demanded, holding out the slip of paper Strachan had given me. It was to show that she understood what I'd supposedly done today, and what the consequences were.

"I got suspended," I told her.

It took her a few seconds to react, but when she did, her face registered not surprise or anger, but pure annoyance. "Suspended? What did you do?" Mom pushed past me again to get to her keys. Like I was just a thing that was in the way of something she wanted.

If we lived in a regular house, with one and a half bathrooms, I wondered, would she still hate me this much? Was resentment something that grew better in small spaces, like those flowers that Mom used to force to bloom inside in little vases?

"I got in a fight," I said evenly. Mom kept staring. "With a pregnant girl."

At that, Mom let out a long, whistling sigh and looked up at the ceiling.

"That's just great," Mom said, her voice dripping with something other than motherly concern.

I could have explained it to her. I could have told her exactly what happened; that it wasn't my fault. That I hadn't even hit anyone.

But the thing is, at that moment, I kind of liked having her think I'd done something wrong. If I was the kind of girl who got in fights with pregnant girls, it meant it was on her. And her stellar lack of parenting skills.

"Who was it?" Mom demanded, her plastic purse slamming into the counter.

"Madison Pendleton."

She narrowed her eyes but not at me. She was remembering

Madison. "Of course. That little pink bitch who ruined your birthday party."

Mom paused and bit her lip. "You don't see it, do you? She's already getting hers. You don't need to help it along."

"What are you talking about? I'm the one who was suspended."

Mom flung her hand out and gripped the air, mimicking a pregnant belly. "I give her a year. Two tops before she's got a trailer of her own around the corner. That boy she's with won't stay. And she'll be left with a little bundle of karma."

I shook my head. "She's walking around like she's God's gift. Like she and Dustin are still going to be prom king and queen."

"Ha!" Mom hooted. "Now. But the second that kid comes, her life is over." There was a pause I could drive a truck through.

For a split second, I thought of how things used to be. My *before* Mom. The one who'd dried my tears and challenged me to a cake-eating contest at that fateful birthday party. "More cake for us," she'd said. That was when I was nine. After Dad left, but before the accident and the pills. It was the last time she'd even bothered remembering my birthday.

I didn't know what to do when she acted like this. When we were almost having a normal conversation. When she almost seemed like she cared. When I almost saw some glimmer of who she used to be. I knew better but I leaned into the kitchenette counter anyway.

"One second, you have everything, your whole life ahead of you," she said, fluffing her hair in the reflection from the stove.

"And then, boom. They just suck it all out of you like little vampires till there's nothing left of you."

It was clear she wasn't talking about Madison anymore. She was talking about me. I was her little vampire.

Anger pricked in my chest. Leave it to my mother to turn any situation into another excuse to feel sorry for herself. To blame me.

"Thanks, Mom," I said. "You're right. I'm the one who ruined your life. Not you. Not Dad. The fact that I've been taking care of you every day since I was thirteen—that was just my evil scheme to ruin everything for you."

"Don't be so sensitive, Amy," she huffed. "It's not all about you."

"All about me? How could it be, when it's always about you?"

Mom glared at me, and then there was a honk from outside. "I don't have to stand here and listen to this. Tawny's waiting." She stormed to the door.

"You're just going to leave me in the middle of a tornado?"

It wasn't that I cared about the weather. I wasn't expecting it to be a big deal. But I wanted her to care; I wanted her to be running around gathering up batteries for flashlights and making sure we had enough water to last through the week. I wanted her to take care of me. Because that's what mothers do.

Just because I'd learned how to take care of myself didn't mean I didn't still feel panic setting in every time she left me like this—all alone, with no clue when she'd be back, or if she'd ever be back at all. Even without a tornado on the way, it was always an open question.

"It's better out there than in here," she snapped.

Before I could think of a good enough retort, she was gone.

I opened the door as she slid into the front seat of Tawny's Camaro; I watched as Mom adjusted the mirror to look at herself and saw her catch a glimpse of me instead, just before the car vroomed away.

Before I could have the satisfaction of slamming the door myself, the wind did it for me. So maybe this tornado was coming after all.

I thought of Dustin and his wasted scholarship, and about my father, who'd left me behind just to get out of here. I thought of what this place did to people. Tornado or no tornado, I wasn't Dorothy, and a stupid little storm wasn't going to change anything for me.

I walked to my dresser, pushed up flush against the kitchen stove, and opened the top drawer, feeling around for the red-and-white gym sock that was fat with cash—the stash of money I'd been saving for an emergency for years: $347. Once the storm cleared, that could get me bus tickets. That could get me a lot farther than Topeka, which was the farthest I had ever gone. I could let my mother fend for herself. She didn't want me. School didn't want me. What was I waiting for?

My hand hit the back of the drawer. All I found were socks.

I pulled the drawer out and rifled through it. Nothing.

The money was gone. Everything I'd spent my life saving up for. Gone.

It was no mystery who'd taken it. It was less of a mystery what she'd spent it on. With no cash, no car, and no one to wave a magic wand, I was stuck where I was.

It didn't matter anyway. Leaving was just a fantasy.

In the living room, Al Roker was back on TV. His frown was gone, sort of, but even though his face was now plastered with a giant grin, his jaw was quivering and he looked like he might start crying at any second. He kept chattering away, going on and on about isotopes and pressure systems and hiding in the basement.

Too bad they don't have basements in trailer parks, I thought.

And then I thought: Bring it on. There's no place like any-where but here.